PENGUIN

DAR

SHIRLEY JACKSON (1916–1965) re͟ ͟ ͟ ͟ ͟ ͟͟ ͟ critical acclaim for her short story "The Lottery," which was first published in *The New Yorker* in 1948. Her works available from Penguin Classics include *We Have Always Lived in the Castle*, *The Haunting of Hill House*, *Come Along With Me*, *Hangsaman*, *The Bird's Nest*, and *The Sundial*, as well as *Life Among the Savages* and *Raising Demons* available from Penguin Books.

OTTESSA MOSHFEGH is a fiction writer from New England. Her first book, *McGlue*, a novella, won the Fence Modern Prize in Prose and the Believer Book Award. Her short stories have been published in *The Paris Review*, *The New Yorker*, and *Granta*, and have earned her a Pushcart Prize, an O. Henry Award, the Plimpton Prize for Fiction, and a grant from the National Endowment for the Arts. Her short story collection, *Homesick for Another World*, was published in January 2017. *Eileen*, her first novel, was shortlisted for the National Book Critics Circle Award, won the PEN/Hemingway Award for debut fiction, and was shortlisted for the Man Booker Prize.

SHIRLEY JACKSON

Dark Tales

Foreword by
OTTESSA MOSHFEGH

PENGUIN BOOKS

PENGUIN BOOKS

An imprint of Penguin Random House LLC
375 Hudson Street
New York, New York 10014
penguin.com

First published in Penguin Books (UK) 2016
Published in Penguin Books (USA) 2017

The stories in this volume were selected from earlier collections
of Shirley Jackson's writings as follows:

"Louisa, Please Come Home," "The Beautiful Stranger," "The Bus," "A Visit," and "The Summer
People" appeared in *Come Along With Me*, edited by Stanley Edgar Hyman (The Viking Press, 1968).
"Louisa, Please Come Home" (as "Louisa, Please") was first published in
The Ladies' Home Journal; "The Bus" in *The Saturday Evening Post*; "The Visit"
(as "The Lovely House") in *New World Writing*; and "The Summer People" in *Charm*.
Copyright © 1960 by Shirley Jackson
Copyright © 1950, 1965, 1968 by Stanley Edgar Hyman

"The Possibility of Evil," "The Honeymoon of Mrs. Smith," "The Story We Used to Tell,"
"Jack the Ripper," "All She Said Was Yes," "What a Thought," "The Good Wife,"
and "Home" appeared in *Just an Ordinary Day*, edited by Laurence Jackson Hyman
and Sarah Hyman DeWitt (Bantam Books, 1996).
"The Possibility of Evil" was first published in *The Saturday Evening Post*;
"All She Said Was Yes" in *Vogue*; and "Home" in *The Ladies' Home Journal*.
Copyright © 1996 by Laurence Jackson Hyman, J. S. Holly,
Sarah Hyman DeWitt, and Barry Hyman

"Paranoia," "The Sorcerer's Apprentice," "Family Treasures," and "The Man in the Woods"
appeared in *Let Me Tell You*, edited by Laurence Jackson Hyman
and Sarah Hyman DeWitt (Random House, 2015)
"Paranoia" and "The Man in the Woods" were first published in *The New Yorker*
and "The Sorcerer's Apprentice" in *McSweeney's*.
Copyright © 2015 by Laurence Jackson Hyman, J. S. Holly,
Sarah Hyman DeWitt, and Barry Hyman

LIBRARY OF CONGRESS CATALOGING-IN-PUBLICATION DATA
Names: Jackson, Shirley, 1916-1965, author. | Moshfegh, Ottessa, writer of foreword.
Title: Dark tales / Shirley Jackson ; foreword by Ottessa Moshfegh.
Description: New York : Penguin Books, 2017. | Series: Penguin classics
Identifiers: LCCN 2017022205 (print) | LCCN 2017032531 (ebook) | ISBN
9780525503798 (ebook) | ISBN 9780143132004 (softcover)
Subjects: | BISAC: FICTION / Horror. | FICTION / Romance / Gothic. | GSAFD:
Horror fiction. | Gothic fiction.
Classification: LCC PS3519.A392 (ebook) | LCC PS3519.A392 A6 2017 (print) |
DDC 813/.54—dc23
LC record available at https://lccn.loc.gov/2017022205

Printed in the United States of America
13 15 14

Set in Dante MT Std

Contents

Foreword

On three separate occasions, I stood within feet of people I knew intimately—one a best friend since adolescence, one a former lover, and one a member of my family—and I did not recognize them. Rosie who lives in Massachusetts suddenly appeared at a reading I was giving in California, and I thought, "Why is that girl staring at me like that?" A man I had lived with once in Brooklyn sat across from me in a coffee shop in LA, and all I could think was, "He's strangely attractive." A green-eyed woman in a silk scarf approached me at the Port Authority Bus Terminal and said my name, smiling. I looked at her and thought, "My mother is at least two inches taller than that woman," then turned and kept searching for her face in the crowd. There is a peculiar malfunction in the brain, I think, when something deeply familiar appears in a strange context. And in fiction, this malfunction can turn into a ride through a new dimension of possibility. A character's misperceptions can actually transform her world: paranoia is no longer a state of mind. The conspiracy is real: the girl at my reading isn't Rosie at all, but a doppelgänger sent to make me lose my mind in a public forum; the man in the coffee shop and I fall in love again, and all the while I'm afraid to let on that I think I know him from before—he looks just like Jeremy, talks just like him, but says his name is Andrew. Maybe I'm crazy, and some evil spirit has taken the place of my mother—swapped bodies with her on the Greyhound bus, perhaps. Here she comes, this strange lady in a scarf, to taunt and beguile me, and to steal my soul.

After reading *Dark Tales*, I think of these occasions of failed recognition as Shirley Jackson moments. In each story in this collection, the everyday world becomes tinted with an odd sheen of terror. My faith in the consistency of day-to-day life wanes as I read. Though Jackson often starts off rather benignly—her characters are never panicked from the get-go, but snake their way into states of dismay—she has a mystifying knack for illustrating the horrifying uncertainties around the basic laws of reality. Am I alone in doubting that things aren't always what they seem? Upon awakening, I often ask myself, "Who am I? Where am I? What am I doing here?" and from time to time, I've felt that the answers were merely memorized responses, and that my reality might be an arbitrary dash of the imagination—believable, sure, but not entirely trustworthy. This specific vulnerability—of the conscious, willful mind—is precisely what Jackson titillates and exacerbates in her stories. Identity, in particular, becomes flimsy and uncertain in her hands. In "The Beautiful Stranger," for example, a man returns from a business trip, but is not quite sly enough to convince his wife that he's the same person he was before he left. Similarly, in "Louisa, Please Come Home," a runaway returns to her family after years living under an assumed name, but her parents have been so disabused by the fantasy of her return that they don't recognize her. "What is your name, dear?" her mother asks her. It's not quite a case of mistaken identity, but the cruel perversion of perception and memory under duress. Don't be hypnotized by the sanctity of the superficial rhythm of humdrum life, Jackson warns, for under the surface of things, people change, sometimes irrevocably, and yet they may appear unaltered.

At other times, Jackson seems to be writing about the illusory trick of fiction itself. In "The Bus," a woman's complaint to her bus driver prompts him to leave her stranded at night on an empty road. Her misadventures in search of safety and sanity take the reader on a surreal exploration of what might be just a slip of dark reverie, a bad dream as she's dozing off in her seat—she did take a sleeping pill before she boarded the bus, after all. Or, we wonder, is she actually trapped on a circuitous passage around the hell of her own grumpy psyche? Is the story real, or a parable for her frailty as an aging curmudgeon riding toward death? It's often unclear in these stories whether the eerie peaks and turns are happening in the mind or in actuality. Either way, the experience of existential insecurity is very exciting as a reader. And it seems, too, that Jackson's characters are in on the game—one's mind always operates in the hypothetical. Fiction and fact are only delineated in the present moment. In "What a Thought," a housewife sits reading a boring book and fantasizes bashing in her husband's head with a glass ashtray. Shocked by her own violent vision, she reels into reasons to not kill him, as though to convince herself not to do it: "What would I do without him? she wondered. How would I live, who would ever marry me, where would I go?" And the next moment, Jackson delivers this bit of fascinating science from the would-be murderer's point of view:

> They say if you soak a cigarette in water overnight the water will be almost pure nicotine by morning, and deadly poisonous. You can put it in coffee and it won't taste.
>
> "Shall I make *you* some coffee?"

Jackson's narrators are not freaks or psychopaths, but actually very sane people—self-possessed, observant, and highly logical. In "Family Treasures," for instance, an orphaned young woman in a college dormitory systematically pilfers cherished objects from her housemates, then uses her status as a heartbroken stray to manipulate the search for the thief in every misdirection. There's a lavishness of reason in that story—I don't think it's any coincidence: clarity is truly terrifying—but there is also a perversion of sense through the narrator's self-talk and doubt and analysis. The mind runs, and its course is often rife with pitfalls. In "Paranoia," a man leaving his office for the day debates with himself about what method of transportation he ought to take to get home in time to have dinner with his wife for her birthday. The mundane anxiety over his commute mounts. As his mind swirls, his senses betray him, and he comes to believe that he is being followed by a stranger in a light hat all around the city. He evades the man in fumbling swoops via bus, taxi, subway, and on foot through the bustling streets of Manhattan, a menace on every corner. But is it the same man in a light hat that he keeps running into? It seems impossible. The protagonist has clearly lost his mind. But by the end of the story, his delusion has superseded his suspicion and becomes the truth in the fiction: the man gets home and his wife is in on the conspiracy to capture him—why? We don't know. She pretends to go to the next room to make him a drink and calls someone on the phone—the man in the light hat, we suppose. "I've got him," she says. It's terrifying.

And so Jackson asks: Dear reader, have you, too, lost your mind? Can you ever be sure you had one to lose in the first place? Have you ever mistaken the mew of a cat in heat for someone being murdered? Have you ever thought you saw your own self waiting at the crosswalk as you drive past in your car? Do you trust your own perceptions? And how far will you walk down a road at night before the wind at your back feels like the hands of a madman pushing you forward? Will you run? How fast? And whose door will you knock on? Everything looks perfectly normal as you rush up the front steps, and maybe you've just been spooked, maybe you're just being silly. In Jackson's world, the safe house is a trap. Enter it, and you might get lost in the dark.

                                              OTTESSA MOSHFEGH

Dark Tales

The Possibility of Evil

Miss Adela Strangeworth stepped daintily along Main Street on her way to the grocery. The sun was shining, the air was fresh and clear after the night's heavy rain, and everything in Miss Strangeworth's little town looked washed and bright. Miss Strangeworth took deep breaths, and thought that there was nothing in the world like a fragrant summer day.

She knew everyone in town, of course; she was fond of telling strangers—tourists who sometimes passed through the town and stopped to admire Miss Strangeworth's roses—that she had never spent more than a day outside this town in all her long life. She was seventy-one, Miss Strangeworth told the tourists, with a pretty little dimple showing by her lip, and she sometimes found herself thinking that the town belonged to her. "My grandfather built the first house on Pleasant Street," she would say, opening her blue eyes wide with the wonder of it. "This house, right here. My family has lived here for better than a hundred years. My grandmother planted these roses, and my mother tended them, just as I do. I've watched my town grow; I can remember when Mr. Lewis, Senior, opened the grocery store, and the year the river flooded out the shanties on the low road, and the excitement when some young folks wanted to move the park over to the space in front of where the new post office is today. They wanted to put up a statue of Ethan Allen"—Miss Strangeworth would frown a little and sound stern—"but it should have been a statue of my grandfather. There wouldn't have been a town here at all if it hadn't been for my grandfather and the lumber mill."

Miss Strangeworth never gave away any of her roses, although the tourists often asked her. The roses belonged on Pleasant Street, and it bothered Miss Strangeworth to think of people wanting to carry them away, to take them into strange towns and down strange streets. When the new minister came, and the ladies were gathering flowers to decorate the church, Miss Strangeworth sent over a great basket of gladioli; when she picked the roses at all, she set them in bowls and vases around the inside of the house her grandfather had built.

Walking down Main Street on a summer morning, Miss Strangeworth had to stop every minute or so to say good morning to someone or to ask after someone's health. When she came into the grocery, half a dozen people turned away from the shelves and the counters to wave at her or call out good morning.

"And good morning to you, too, Mr. Lewis," Miss Strangeworth said at last. The Lewis family had been in the town almost as long as the Strangeworths; but the day young Lewis left high school and went to work in the grocery, Miss Strangeworth had stopped calling him Tommy and started calling him Mr. Lewis, and he had stopped calling her Addie and started calling her Miss Strangeworth. They had been in high school together, and had gone to picnics together, and to high school dances and basketball games; but now Mr. Lewis was behind the counter in the grocery, and Miss Strangeworth was living alone in the Strangeworth House on Pleasant Street.

"Good morning," Mr. Lewis said, and added politely, "lovely day."

"It is a very nice day," Miss Strangeworth said as though she had only just decided that it would do after all. "I would like a chop, please, Mr. Lewis, a small, lean veal chop. Are those strawberries from Arthur Parker's garden? They're early this year."

"He brought them in this morning," Mr. Lewis said.

"I shall have a box," Miss Strangeworth said. Mr. Lewis looked worried, she thought, and for a minute she hesitated, but then she decided that he surely could not be worried over the strawberries. He looked very tired indeed. He was usually so chipper, Miss Strangeworth thought, and almost commented, but it was far too personal a subject to be introduced to Mr. Lewis, the grocer, so she only said, "And a can of cat food and, I think, a tomato."

Silently, Mr. Lewis assembled her order on the counter and waited. Miss Strangeworth looked at him curiously and then said, "It's Tuesday, Mr. Lewis. You forgot to remind me."

"Did I? Sorry."

"Imagine your forgetting that I always buy my tea on Tuesday," Miss Strangeworth said gently. "A quarter-pound of tea, please, Mr. Lewis."

"Is that all, Miss Strangeworth?"

"Yes, thank you, Mr. Lewis. Such a lovely day, isn't it?"

"Lovely," Mr. Lewis said.

Miss Strangeworth moved slightly to make room for Mrs. Harper at the counter. "Morning, Adela," Mrs. Harper said, and Miss Strangeworth said, "Good morning, Martha."

"Lovely day," Mrs. Harper said, and Miss Strangeworth said, "Yes, lovely," and Mr. Lewis, under Mrs. Harper's glance, nodded.

"Ran out of sugar for my cake frosting," Mrs. Harper explained. Her hand shook slightly as she opened her pocketbook. Miss Strangeworth wondered, glancing at her quickly, if she had been taking proper care of herself. Martha Harper was not as young as she used to be, Miss Strangeworth thought. She probably could use a good, strong tonic.

"Martha," she said, "you don't look well."

"I'm perfectly all right," Mrs. Harper said shortly. She handed her money to Mr. Lewis, took her change and her sugar, and went out without speaking again. Looking after her, Miss Strangeworth shook her head slightly. Martha definitely did *not* look well.

Carrying her little bag of groceries, Miss Strangeworth came out of the store into the bright sunlight and stopped to smile down on the Crane baby. Don and Helen Crane were really the two most infatuated young parents she had ever known, she thought indulgently, looking at the delicately embroidered baby cap and the lace-edged carriage cover.

"That little girl is going to grow up expecting luxury all her life," she said to Helen Crane.

Helen laughed. "That's the way we want her to feel," she said. "Like a princess."

"A princess can be a lot of trouble sometimes," Miss Strangeworth said dryly. "How old is her highness now?"

"Six months next Tuesday," Helen Crane said, looking down with rapt wonder at her child. "I've been worrying, though, about her. Don't you think she ought to move around more? Try to sit up, for instance?"

"For plain and fancy worrying," Miss Strangeworth said, amused, "give me a new mother every time."

"She just seems—slow," Helen Crane said.

"Nonsense. All babies are different. Some of them develop much more quickly than others."

"That's what my mother says." Helen Crane laughed, looking a little bit ashamed.

"I suppose you've got young Don all upset about the fact that his daughter is already six months old and hasn't yet begun to learn to dance?"

"I haven't mentioned it to him. I suppose she's just so precious that I worry about her all the time."

"Well, apologize to her right now," Miss Strangeworth said. "*She* is probably worrying about why you keep jumping around all the time." Smiling to herself and shaking her old head, she went on down the sunny street, stopping once to ask little Billy Moore why he wasn't out riding in his daddy's shiny new car, and talking for a few minutes outside the library with Miss Chandler, the librarian, about the new novels to be ordered, and paid for by the annual library appropriation. Miss Chandler seemed absentminded and very much as though she was thinking about something else. Miss Strangeworth noticed that Miss Chandler had not taken much trouble with her hair that morning, and sighed. Miss Strangeworth hated sloppiness.

Many people seemed disturbed recently, Miss Strangeworth thought. Only yesterday the Stewarts' fifteen-year-old Linda had run crying down her own front walk and all the way to school, not caring who saw her. People around town thought she might have had a fight with the Harris boy, but they showed up together at the soda shop after school as usual, both of them looking grim and bleak. Trouble at home, people concluded, and sighed over the problems of trying to raise kids right these days.

From halfway down the block Miss Strangeworth could catch the heavy accent of her roses, and she moved a little more quickly. The perfume of roses meant home, and home meant the Strangeworth House on Pleasant Street. Miss Strangeworth stopped at her own front gate, as she always did, and looked with deep pleasure at her house, with the red and pink and white roses massed along the narrow lawn, and the rambler going up along the porch; and the neat, the unbelievably trim lines of the house itself, with its slimness and its washed white look. Every window sparkled, every curtain hung stiff and straight, and even the stones of the front walk were swept and clear. People around town wondered how old Miss Strangeworth managed to keep the house looking the way it did, and there was a legend about a tourist once mistaking it for the local museum and going all through the place without finding out about his mistake. But the town was proud of Miss Strangeworth and her roses and her house. They had all grown together. Miss Strangeworth went up her front steps, unlocked her front door with her key, and went into the kitchen to put away her groceries. She debated having a cup of tea and then decided that it was too close to midday dinnertime; she would not have the appetite for her little chop if she had tea now. Instead she went into the light, lovely sitting room, which still glowed from the hands of her mother and her grandmother, who had covered the chairs with bright chintz and hung the curtains. All the furniture was spare and shining, and the round hooked rugs on the floor had been the work of Miss Strangeworth's grandmother and her mother. Miss Strangeworth had put a bowl of her red roses on the low table before the window, and the room was full of their scent.

Miss Strangeworth went to the narrow desk in the corner, and unlocked it with her key. She never knew when she might feel like writing letters, so she kept her notepaper inside, and the desk locked. Miss Strangeworth's usual stationery was heavy and cream-colored, with "Strangeworth House" engraved across the top, but, when she felt like writing her other letters, Miss Strangeworth used a pad of various-colored paper, bought from the local newspaper shop. It was almost a town joke, that colored paper, layered in pink and green and blue and yellow; everyone in town bought it and used it for odd, informal notes and shopping lists. It was usual to remark, upon receiving a note written on a blue page, that so-and-so would be needing a new pad soon—here she was, down to the blue already. Everyone used the matching envelopes for tucking away recipes, or keeping odd little things in, or even to hold cookies in the school lunch boxes. Mr. Lewis sometimes gave them to the children for carrying home penny candy.

Although Miss Strangeworth's desk held a trimmed quill pen, which had belonged to her grandfather, and a gold-frost fountain pen, which had belonged to her father, Miss Strangeworth always used a dull stub of pencil when she wrote her letters, and she printed them in a childish block print. After thinking for a minute, although she had been phrasing the letter in the back of her mind all the way home, she wrote on a pink sheet: *Didn't you ever see an idiot child before? Some people just shouldn't have children, should they?*

She was pleased with the letter. She was fond of doing things exactly right. When she made a mistake, as she sometimes did, or when the letters were not spaced nicely on the page, she had to take the discarded page to the kitchen stove and burn it at once. Miss Strangeworth never delayed when things had to be done.

After thinking for a minute, she decided that she would like to write another letter, perhaps to go to Mrs. Harper, to follow up the ones she had already mailed. She selected a green sheet this time and wrote quickly: *Have you found out yet what they were all laughing about after you left the bridge club on Thursday? Or is the wife really always the last one to know?*

Miss Strangeworth never concerned herself with facts; her letters all dealt with the more negotiable stuff of suspicion. Mr. Lewis would never have imagined for a minute that his grandson might be lifting petty cash from the store register if he had not had one of Miss Strangeworth's letters. Miss Chandler, the librarian, and

Linda Stewart's parents would have gone unsuspectingly ahead with their lives, never aware of possible evil lurking nearby, if Miss Strangeworth had not sent letters to open their eyes. Miss Strangeworth would have been genuinely shocked if there *had* been anything between Linda Stewart and the Harris boy, but, as long as evil existed unchecked in the world, it was Miss Strangeworth's duty to keep her town alert to it. It was far more sensible for Miss Chandler to wonder what Mr. Shelley's first wife had really died of than to take a chance on not knowing. There were so many wicked people in the world and only one Strangeworth left in town. Besides, Miss Strangeworth liked writing her letters.

She addressed an envelope to Don Crane after a moment's thought, wondering curiously if he would show the letter to his wife, and using a pink envelope to match the pink paper. Then she addressed a second envelope, green, to Mrs. Harper. Then an idea came to her and she selected a blue sheet and wrote: *You never know about doctors. Remember they're only human and need money like the rest of us. Suppose the knife slipped accidentally. Would Doctor Burns get his fee and a little extra from that nephew of yours?*

She addressed the blue envelope to old Mrs. Foster, who was having an operation next month. She had thought of writing one more letter, to the head of the school board, asking how a chemistry teacher like Billy Moore's father could afford a new convertible, but all at once she was tired of writing letters. The three she had done would do for one day. She could write more tomorrow; it was not as though they all had to be done at once.

She had been writing her letters—sometimes two or three every day for a week, sometimes no more than one in a month—for the past year. She never got any answers, of course, because she never signed her name. If she had been asked, she would have said that her name, Adela Strangeworth, a name honored in the town for so many years, did not belong on such trash. The town where she lived had to be kept clean and sweet, but people everywhere were lustful and evil and degraded, and needed to be watched; the world was so large, and there was only one Strangeworth left in it. Miss Strangeworth sighed, locked her desk, and put the letters into her big, black leather pocketbook, to be mailed when she took her evening walk.

She broiled her little chop nicely, and had a sliced tomato and good cup of tea ready when she sat down to her midday dinner at the table in her dining room, which could be opened to seat twenty-two, with a second table, if necessary, in the hall. Sitting in the warm sunlight that came through the tall windows of the dining room, seeing her roses massed outside, handling the heavy, old silverware and the fine, translucent china, Miss Strangeworth was pleased; she would not have cared to be doing anything else. People must live graciously, after all, she thought, and sipped her tea. Afterward, when her plate and cup and saucer were washed and dried and put back onto the shelves where they belonged, and her silverware was back in the mahogany silver chest, Miss Strangeworth went up the graceful staircase and into her bedroom, which was the front room overlooking the roses, and had been her mother's and her grandmother's. Their Crown Derby dresser set and furs had been kept here, their fans and silver-backed brushes and their own bowls of roses; Miss Strangeworth kept a bowl of white roses on the bed table.

She drew the shades, took the rose-satin spread from the bed, slipped out of her dress and her shoes, and lay down tiredly. She knew that no doorbell or phone would ring; no one in town would dare to disturb Miss Strangeworth during her afternoon nap. She slept, deep in the rich smell of roses.

After her nap she worked in her garden for a little while, sparing herself because of the heat; then she went in to her supper. She ate asparagus from her own garden, with sweet-butter sauce, and a soft-boiled egg, and, while she had her supper, she listened to a late-evening news broadcast and then to a program of classical music on her small radio. After her dishes were done and her kitchen set in order, she took up her hat—Miss Strangeworth's hats were proverbial in the town; people believed that she had inherited them from her mother and her grandmother—and, locking the front door of her house behind her, set off on her evening walk, pocketbook under her arm. She nodded to Linda Stewart's father, who was washing his car in the pleasantly cool evening. She thought that he looked troubled.

There was only one place in town where she could mail her letters, and that was the new post office, shiny with red brick and silver letters. Although Miss Strangeworth had never given the matter any particular thought, she had always made a point of mailing her letters very secretly; it would, of course, not have been wise to let anyone see her mail them. Consequently, she timed her walk so she could reach the post office just as darkness was starting to dim the outlines of the trees and the shapes of people's faces, although no one could ever mistake Miss Strangeworth, with her dainty walk and her rustling skirts.

There was always a group of young people around the post office, the very youngest roller-skating upon its driveway, which went all the way around the building and was the only smooth road in town; and the slightly older ones already knowing how to gather in small groups and chatter and laugh and make great, excited plans for going across the street to the soda shop in a minute or two. Miss Strangeworth had never had any self-consciousness before the children. She did not feel that any of them were staring at her unduly or longing to laugh at her; it would have been most reprehensible for their parents to permit their children to mock Miss Strangeworth of Pleasant Street. Most of the children stood back respectfully as Miss Strangeworth passed, silenced briefly in her presence, and some of the older children greeted her, saying soberly, "Hello, Miss Strangeworth."

Miss Strangeworth smiled at them and quickly went on. It had been a long time since she had known the name of every child in town. The mail slot was in the door of the post office. The children stood away as Miss Strangeworth approached it, seemingly surprised that anyone should want to use the post office after it had been officially closed up for the night and turned over to the children. Miss Strangeworth stood by the door, opening her black pocketbook to take out the letters, and heard a voice which she knew at once to be Linda Stewart's. Poor little Linda was crying again, and Miss Strangeworth listened carefully. This was, after all, her town, and these were her people; if one of them was in trouble, she ought to know about it.

"I can't tell you, Dave," Linda was saying—so she *was* talking to the Harris boy, as Miss Strangeworth had supposed—"I just *can't*. It's just *nasty*."

"But why won't your father let me come around anymore? What on earth did I do?"

"I can't tell you. I just wouldn't tell you for *anything*. You've got to have a dirty dirty mind for things like that."

"But something's happened. You've been crying and crying, and your father is all upset. Why can't *I* know about it, too? Aren't I like one of the family?"

"Not anymore, Dave, not anymore. You're not to come near our house again; my father said so. He said he'd horsewhip you. That's all I can tell you: You're not to come near our house anymore."

"But I didn't *do* anything."

"Just the same, my father said . . ."

Miss Strangeworth sighed and turned away. There was so much evil in people. Even in a charming little town like this one, there was still so much evil in people.

She slipped her letters into the slot, and two of them fell inside. The third caught on the edge and fell outside, onto the ground at Miss Strangeworth's feet. She did not notice it because she was wondering whether a letter to the Harris boy's father might not be of some service in wiping out this potential badness. Wearily Miss Strangeworth turned to go home to her quiet bed in her lovely house, and never heard the Harris boy calling to her to say that she had dropped something.

"Old lady Strangeworth's getting deaf," he said, looking after her and holding in his hand the letter he had picked up.

"Well, who cares?" Linda said. "Who cares anymore, anyway?"

"It's for Don Crane," the Harris boy said, "this letter. She dropped a letter addressed to Don Crane. Might as well take it on over. We pass his house anyway." He laughed. "Maybe it's got a check or something in it and he'd be just as glad to get it tonight instead of tomorrow."

"Catch old lady Strangeworth sending anybody a check," Linda said. "Throw it in the post office. Why do anyone a favor?" She sniffed. "Doesn't seem to me anybody around here cares about us," she said. "Why should we care about them?"

"I'll take it over, anyway," the Harris boy said. "Maybe it's good news for them. Maybe they need something happy tonight, too. Like us."

Sadly, holding hands, they wandered off down the dark street, the Harris boy carrying Miss Strangeworth's pink envelope in his hand.

Miss Strangeworth awakened the next morning with a feeling of intense happiness and, for a minute, wondered why, and then remembered that this morning three people would open her letters. Harsh, perhaps, at first, but wickedness was never easily banished, and a clean heart was a scoured heart. She washed her soft, old face and brushed her teeth, still sound in spite of her seventy-one years, and dressed herself carefully in her sweet, soft clothes and buttoned shoes. Then, going downstairs, reflecting that perhaps a little waffle would be agreeable for breakfast in the sunny dining room, she found the mail on the hall floor, and bent to pick it up. A bill, the morning paper, a letter in a green envelope that looked oddly familiar. Miss Strangeworth stood perfectly still for a minute, looking down at the green envelope with the penciled printing, and thought: It looks like one of my letters. Was one of my letters sent back? No, because no one would know where to send it. How did this get here?

Miss Strangeworth was a Strangeworth of Pleasant Street. Her hand did not shake as she opened the envelope and unfolded the sheet of green paper inside. She began to cry silently for the wickedness of the world when she read the words: *Look out at what used to be your roses.*

Louisa, Please Come Home

"Louisa," my mother's voice came over the radio; it frightened me badly for a minute. "Louisa," she said, "please come home. It's been three long long years since we saw you last; Louisa, I promise you that everything will be all right. We all miss you so. We want you back again. Louisa, please come home."

Once a year. On the anniversary of the day I ran away. Each time I heard it I was frightened again, because between one year and the next I would forget what my mother's voice sounded like, so soft and yet strange with that pleading note. I listened every year. I read the stories in the newspapers—"Louisa Tether vanished one year ago"—or two years ago, or three; I used to wait for the twentieth of June as though it were my birthday. I kept all the clippings at first, but secretly; with my picture on all the front pages I would have looked kind of strange if anyone had seen me cutting it out. Chandler, where I was hiding, was close enough to my old home so that the papers made a big fuss about all of it, but of course the reason I picked Chandler in the first place was because it was a big enough city for me to hide in.

I didn't just up and leave on the spur of the moment, you know. I always knew that I was going to run away sooner or later, and I had made plans ahead of time, for whenever I decided to go. Everything had to go right the first time, because they don't usually give you a second chance on that kind of thing and anyway if it had gone wrong I would have looked like an awful fool, and my sister Carol was never one for letting people forget it when they made fools of themselves. I admit I planned it for the day before Carol's wedding on purpose, and for a long time afterward I used to try and imagine Carol's face when she finally realized that my running away was going to leave her one bridesmaid short. The papers said that the wedding went ahead as scheduled, though, and Carol told one newspaper reporter that her sister Louisa would have wanted it that way; "She would never have meant to spoil my wedding," Carol said, knowing perfectly well that that would be exactly what I'd meant. I'm pretty sure that the first thing Carol did when they knew I was missing was go and count the wedding presents to see what I'd taken with me.

Anyway, Carol's wedding may have been fouled up, but *my* plans went fine—better, as a matter of fact, than I had ever expected. Everyone was hurrying around the house putting up flowers and asking each other if the wedding gown had been delivered, and opening up cases of champagne and wondering what they were going to do if it rained and they couldn't use the garden, and I just closed the front door behind me and started off. There was only one bad minute when Paul saw me; Paul has always lived next door and Carol hates him worse than she does me. My mother always used to say that every time I did something to make the family ashamed of me Paul was sure to be in it somewhere. For a long time they thought he had something to do with my running away, even though he told over and over again how hard I tried to duck away from him that afternoon when he met me going down the driveway. The papers kept calling him "a close friend of the family," which must have overjoyed my mother, and saying that he was being questioned about possible clues to my whereabouts. Of course he never even knew that I was running away; I told him just what I told my mother before I left—that I was going to get away from all the confusion and excitement for a while; I was going downtown and would probably have a sandwich somewhere for supper and go to a movie. He bothered me for a minute there, because of course he wanted to come too. I hadn't meant to take the bus right there on the corner but with Paul tagging after me and wanting me to wait while he got the car so we could drive out and have dinner at the Inn, I had to get away fast on the first thing that came along, so I just ran for the bus and left Paul standing there; that was the only part of my plan I had to change.

I took the bus all the way downtown, although my first plan had been to walk. It turned out much better, actually, since it didn't matter at all if anyone saw me on the bus going downtown in my own home town, and I managed to get an earlier train out. I bought a round-trip ticket; that was important, because it would make them think I was coming back; that was always the way they thought about things. If you did something you had to have a reason for it, because my mother and my father and Carol never did anything unless *they* had a reason for it, so if I bought a round-trip ticket the only possible reason would be that I was coming back. Besides, if they thought I was coming back they would not be frightened so quickly and I might have more time to hide before they came looking for me. As it happened, Carol found out I was gone that same night when she couldn't sleep and came into my room for some aspirin, so at the time I had less of a head start than I thought.

I knew that they would find out about my buying the ticket; I was not silly enough to suppose that I could steal off and not leave any traces. All my plans were based on the fact that the people who get caught are the ones who attract attention by doing something strange or noticeable, and what I intended all along was to fade into some background where they would never see me. I knew they would find out about the round-trip ticket, because it was an odd thing to do in a town where you've lived all your life, but it was the last unusual thing I did. I thought when I bought it that knowing about that round-trip ticket would be some consolation to my mother and father. They would know that no matter how long I stayed away at least I always had a ticket home. I did keep the return-trip ticket quite a while, as a matter of fact. I used to carry it in my wallet as a kind of lucky charm.

I followed everything in the papers. Mrs. Peacock and I used to read them at the breakfast table over our second cup of coffee before I went off to work.

"What do you think about this girl disappeared over in Rockville?" Mrs. Peacock would say to me, and I'd shake my head sorrowfully and say that a girl must be really crazy to leave a handsome, luxurious home like that, or that I had kind of a notion that maybe she didn't leave at all—maybe the family had her locked up somewhere because she was a homicidal maniac. Mrs. Peacock always loved anything about homicidal maniacs.

Once I picked up the paper and looked hard at the picture. "Do you think she looks something like me?" I asked Mrs. Peacock, and Mrs. Peacock leaned back and looked at me and then at the picture and then at me again and finally she shook her head and said, "No. If you wore your hair longer, and curlier, and your face was maybe a little fuller, there might be a little resemblance, but then if you looked like a homicidal maniac I wouldn't ever of let you in my house."

"I think she kind of looks like me," I said.

"You get along to work and stop being vain," Mrs. Peacock told me.

Of course when I got on the train with my round-trip ticket I had no idea how soon they'd be following me, and I suppose it was just as well, because it might have made me nervous and I might have done something wrong and spoiled everything. I knew that as soon as they gave up the notion that I was coming back to Rockville with my round-trip ticket they would think of Crain, which is the largest city that train went to, so I only stayed in Crain part of one day. I went to a big department store where they were having a store-wide sale; I figured that would land me in a crowd of shoppers and I was right; for a while there was a good chance that I'd never get any farther away from home than the ground floor of that department store in Crain. I had to fight my way through the crowd until I found the counter where they were having a sale of raincoats, and then I had to push and elbow down the counter and finally grab the raincoat I wanted right out of the hands of some old monster who couldn't have used it anyway because she was much too fat. You would have thought she had already paid for it, the way she howled. I was smart enough to have the exact change, all six dollars and eighty-nine cents, right in my hand, and I gave it to the salesgirl, grabbed the raincoat and the bag she wanted to put it in, and fought my way out again before I got crushed to death.

That raincoat was worth every cent of the six dollars and eighty-nine cents; I wore it right through until winter that year and not even a button ever came off it. I finally lost it the next spring when I left it somewhere and never got it back. It was tan, and the minute I put it on in the ladies' room of the store I began thinking of it as my "old" raincoat; that was good. I had never before owned a raincoat like that and my mother would have fainted dead away. One thing I did that I thought was kind of clever. I had left home wearing a light short coat; almost a jacket, and when I put on the raincoat of course I took off my light coat. Then all I had to do was empty the pockets of the light coat into the raincoat and carry the light coat casually over to a counter where they were having a sale of jackets and drop it on the counter as though I'd taken it off a little way to look at it and had decided against it. As far as I ever knew no one paid the slightest attention to me, and before I left the counter I saw a woman pick up my jacket and look it over; I could have told her she was getting a bargain for three ninety-eight.

It made me feel good to know that I had gotten rid of the light coat. My mother picked it out for me and even though I liked it and it was expensive it was also recognizable and I had to change it somehow. I was sure that if I put it in a bag and dropped it into a river or into a garbage truck of something like that sooner or later it would be found and even if no one saw me doing it, it would almost certainly be found, and then they would know I had changed my clothes in Crain.

That light coat never turned up. The last they ever found of me was someone in Rockville who caught a glimpse of me in the train station in Crain, and she recognized me by the light coat. They never found out where I went after that; it was partly luck and partly my clever planning. Two or three days later the papers were still reporting that I was in Crain; people thought they saw me on the streets and one girl who went into a store to buy a dress was picked up by the police and held until she could get someone to identify her. They were really looking, but they were looking for

Louisa Tether, and I had stopped being Louisa Tether the minute I got rid of that light coat my mother bought me.

One thing I was relying on: there must be thousands of girls in the country on any given day who are nineteen years old, fair-haired, five feet four inches tall, and weighing one hundred and twenty-six pounds. And if there are thousands of girls like that, there must be, among those thousands, a good number who are wearing shapeless tan raincoats; I started counting tan raincoats in Crain after I left the department store and I passed four in one block, so I felt well hidden. After that I made myself even more invisible by doing just what I told my mother I was going to—I stopped in and had a sandwich in a little coffee shop, and then I went to a movie. I wasn't in any hurry at all, and rather than try to find a place to sleep that night I thought I would sleep on the train.

It's funny how no one pays any attention to you at all. There were hundreds of people who saw me that day, and even a sailor who tried to pick me up in the movie, and yet no one really *saw* me. If I had tried to check into a hotel the desk clerk might have noticed me, or if I had tried to get dinner in some fancy restaurant in that cheap raincoat I would have been conspicuous, but I was doing what any other girl looking like me and dressed like me might be doing that day. The only person who might be apt to remember me would be the man selling tickets in the railroad station, because girls looking like me in old raincoats didn't buy train tickets, usually, at eleven at night, but I had thought of that, too, of course; I bought a ticket to Amityville, sixty miles away, and what made Amityville a perfectly reasonable disguise is that at Amityville there is a college, not a little fancy place like the one I had left so recently with nobody's blessing, but a big sprawling friendly affair, where my raincoat would look perfectly at home. I told myself I was a student coming back to the college after a weekend at home. We got to Amityville after midnight, but it still didn't look odd when I left the train and went into the station, because while I was in the station, having a cup of coffee and killing time, seven other girls—I counted—wearing raincoats like mine came in or went out, not seeming to think it the least bit odd to be getting on or off trains at that hour of the night. Some of them had suitcases, and I wished that I had had some way of getting a suitcase in Crain, but it would have made me noticeable in the movie, and college girls going home for weekends often don't bother; they have pajamas and an extra pair of stockings at home, and they drop a toothbrush into one of the pockets of those invaluable raincoats. So I didn't worry about the suitcase then, although I knew I would need one soon. While I was having my coffee I made my own mind change from the idea that I was a college girl coming back after a weekend at home to the idea that I was a college girl who was on her way home for a few days; all the time I tried to think as much as possible like what I was pretending to be, and after all, I *had* been a college girl for a while. I was thinking that even now the letter was in the mail, traveling as fast as the U.S. Government could make it go, right to my father to tell him why I wasn't a college student any more; I suppose that was what finally decided me to run away, the thought of what my father would think and say and do when he got that letter from the college.

That was in the paper, too. They decided that the college business was the reason for my running away, but if that had been all, I don't think I would have left. No, I had been wanting to leave for so long, ever since I can remember, making plans till I was sure they were foolproof, and that's the way they turned out to be.

Sitting there in the station at Amityville, I tried to think myself into a good reason why I was leaving college to go home on a Monday night late, when I would hardly be going home for the weekend. As I say, I always tried to think as hard as I could the way that suited whatever I wanted to be, and I liked to have a good reason for what I was doing. Nobody ever asked me, but it was good to know that I could answer them if they did. I finally decided that my sister was getting married the next day and I was going home at the beginning of the week to be one of her bridesmaids. I thought that was funny. I didn't want to be going home for any sad or frightening reason, like my mother being sick, or my father being hurt in a car accident, because I would have to look sad, and that might attract attention. So I was going home for my sister's wedding. I wandered around the station as though I had nothing to do, and just happened to pass the door when another girl was going out; she had on a raincoat just like mine and anyone who happened to notice would have thought that it was me who went out. Before I bought my ticket I went into the ladies' room and got another twenty dollars out of my shoe. I had nearly three hundred dollars left of the money I had taken from my father's desk and I had most of it in my shoes because I honestly couldn't think of another safe place to carry it. All I kept in my pocketbook was just enough for whatever I had to spend next. It's uncomfortable walking around all day on a wad of bills in your shoe, but they were good solid shoes, the kind of comfortable old shoes you wear whenever you don't really care how you look, and I had put new shoelaces in them before I left home so I could tie them good and tight. You can see, I planned pretty carefully, and no little detail got left out. If they had let me plan my sister's wedding there would have been a lot less of that running around and screaming and hysterics.

I bought a ticket to Chandler, which is the biggest city in this part of the state, and the place I'd been heading for all along. It was a good place to hide because people from Rockville tended to bypass it unless they had some special reason for going there—if they couldn't find the doctors or orthodontists or psychoanalysts or dress material they wanted in Rockville or Crain, they went directly to one of the really big cities, like the state capital; Chandler was big enough to hide in, but not big enough to look like a metropolis to people from Rockville. The ticket seller in the Amityville station must have seen a good many college girls buying tickets for Chandler at all hours of the day or night because he took my money and shoved the ticket at me without even looking up.

Funny. They must have come looking for me in Chandler at some time or other, because it's not likely they would have neglected any possible place I might be, but maybe Rockville people never seriously believed that anyone would go to Chandler from choice, because I never felt for a minute that anyone was looking for me there. My picture was in the Chandler papers, of course, but as far as I ever knew no one ever looked at me twice, and I got up every morning and went to work and went shopping in the stores and went to movies with Mrs. Peacock and went out to the beach all that summer without ever being afraid of being recognized. I behaved just like everyone else, and dressed just like everyone else, and even *thought* just like everyone else, and the only person I ever saw from Rockville in three years was a friend of my mother's, and I knew *she* only came to Chandler to get her poodle bred at the kennels there. She didn't look as if she was in a state to recognize anybody but another poodle-fancier, anyway, and all I had to do was step into a doorway as she went by, and she never looked at me.

Two other college girls got on the train to Chandler when I did; maybe both of them were going home for their sisters' weddings. Neither of them was wearing a tan raincoat, but one of them had on an old blue jacket that gave the same general effect. I fell asleep as soon as the train started, and once I woke up and for a minute I wondered where I was and then I realized that I was doing it, I was actually carrying out my careful plan and had gotten better than halfway with it, and I almost laughed, there in the train with everyone asleep around me. Then I went back to sleep and didn't wake up until we got into Chandler about seven in the morning.

So there I was. I had left home just after lunch the day before, and now at seven in the morning of my sister's wedding day I was so far away, in every sense, that I *knew* they would never find me. I had all day to get myself settled in Chandler, so I started off by having breakfast in a restaurant near the station, and then went off to find a place to live, and a job. The first thing I did was buy a suitcase, and it's funny how people don't really notice you if you're buying a suitcase near a railroad station. Suitcases look *natural* near railroad stations, and I picked out one of those stores that sell a little bit of everything, and bought a cheap suitcase and a pair of stockings and some handkerchiefs and a little traveling clock, and I put everything into the suitcase and carried that. Nothing is hard to do unless you get upset or excited about it.

Later on, when Mrs. Peacock and I used to read in the papers about my disappearing, I asked her once if she thought that Louisa Tether had gotten as far as Chandler and she didn't.

"They're saying now she was kidnapped," Mrs. Peacock told me, "and that's what *I* think happened. Kidnapped, and murdered, and they do *terrible* things to young girls they kidnap."

"But the papers say there wasn't any ransom note."

"That's what they *say*." Mrs. Peacock shook her head at me. "How do we know what the family is keeping secret? Or if she was kidnapped by a homicidal maniac, why should *he* send a ransom note? Young girls like you don't know a lot of the things that go on, *I* can tell you."

"I feel kind of sorry for the girl," I said.

"You can't ever tell," Mrs. Peacock said. "Maybe she went with him willingly."

I didn't know, that first morning in Chandler, that Mrs. Peacock was going to turn up that first day, the luckiest thing that ever happened to me. I decided while I was having breakfast that I was going to be a nineteen-year-old girl from upstate with a nice family and a good background who had been saving money to come to Chandler and take a secretarial course in the business school there. I was going to have to find some kind of a job to keep on earning money while I went to school; courses at the business school wouldn't start until fall, so I would have the summer to work and save money and decide if I really wanted to take secretarial training. If I decided not to stay in Chandler I could easily go somewhere else after the fuss about my running away had died down. The raincoat looked wrong for the kind of conscientious young girl I was going to be, so I took it off and carried it over my arm. I think I did a pretty good job on my clothes, altogether. Before I left home I decided that I would have to wear a suit, as quiet and unobtrusive as I could find, and I picked out a gray suit, with a white blouse, so with just one or two small changes like a different blouse or some kind of a pin on the lapel, I could look like whoever I decided to be. Now the suit looked absolutely right for a young girl planning to take a secretarial course, and I looked like a thousand other people when I walked down the street carrying my suitcase and my raincoat over my arm; people get off trains every minute looking just like that. I bought a morning paper and stopped in a drugstore for a cup of coffee and a look to see the rooms for rent. It was all so usual—suitcase, coat, rooms for rent—that when I asked the soda clerk how to get to Primrose Street he never even looked at me. He certainly didn't care whether I ever got to Primrose Street or not, but he told me very politely where it was and what bus to take. I didn't really need to take the bus for economy, but it would have looked funny for a girl who was saving money to arrive in a taxi.

"I'll never forget how you looked that first morning," Mrs. Peacock told me once, much later. "I knew right away you were the kind of girl I like to rent rooms to—quiet, and well-mannered. But you looked almighty scared of the big city."

"I wasn't scared," I said. "I was worried about finding a nice room. My mother told me so many things to be careful about I was afraid I'd never find anything to suit her."

"*Anybody's* mother could come into my house at any time and know that her daughter was in good hands," Mrs. Peacock said, a little huffy.

But it was true. When I walked into Mrs. Peacock's rooming house on Primrose Street, and met Mrs. Peacock, I knew that I couldn't have done this part better if I'd been able to plan it. The house was old, and comfortable, and my room was nice, and Mrs. Peacock and I hit it off right away. She was very pleased with me when she heard that my mother had told me to be sure the room I found was clean and that the neighborhood was good, with no chance of rowdies following a girl if she came home after dark, and she was even more pleased when she heard that I wanted to save money and take a secretarial course so I could get a really good job and earn enough to be able to send a little home every week; Mrs. Peacock believed that children owed it to their parents to pay back some of what had been spent on them while they were growing up. By the time I had been in the house an hour Mrs. Peacock knew all about my imaginary family upstate: my mother, who was a widow, and my sister, who had just gotten married and still lived at my mother's home with her husband, and my young brother, Paul, who worried my mother a good deal because he didn't seem to want to settle down. My name was Lois Taylor, I told her. By that time, I think I could have told her my real name and she would never have connected it with the girl in the paper, because by then she was feeling that she almost knew my family, and she wanted me to be sure and tell my mother when I wrote home that Mrs. Peacock would make herself personally responsible for me while I was in the city and take as good care of me as my own mother would. On top of everything else, she told me that a stationery store in the neighborhood was looking for a girl assistant, and there I was. Before I had been away from home for twenty-four hours I was an entirely new person. I was a girl named Lois Taylor who lived on Primrose Street and worked down at the stationery store.

I read in the papers one day about how a famous fortune-teller wrote to my father offering to find me and said that astral signs had convinced him that I would be found near flowers. That gave me a jolt, because of Primrose Street, but my father and Mrs. Peacock and the rest of the world thought that it meant that my body was buried somewhere. They dug up a vacant lot near the railroad station where I was last seen, and Mrs. Peacock was very disappointed when nothing turned up. Mrs. Peacock and I could not decide whether I had run away with a gangster to be a gun moll, or whether my body had been cut up and sent somewhere in a trunk. After a while they stopped looking for me, except for an occasional false clue that would turn up in a small story on the back pages of the paper, and Mrs. Peacock and I got interested in the stories about a daring daylight bank robbery in Chicago. When the anniversary of my running away came around, and I realized that I had really been gone for a year, I treated myself to a new hat and dinner downtown, and came home just in time for the evening news broadcast and my mother's voice over the radio.

"Louisa," she was saying, "please come home."

"That poor poor woman," Mrs. Peacock said. "Imagine how she must feel. They say she's never given up hope of finding her little girl alive someday."

"Do you like my new hat?" I asked her.

I had given up all idea of the secretarial course because the stationery store had decided to expand and include a lending library and a gift shop, and I was now the manager of the gift shop and if things kept on well would someday be running the whole thing; Mrs. Peacock and I talked it over, just as if she had been my mother, and we decided that I would be foolish to leave a good job to start over somewhere else. The money that I had been saving was in the bank, and Mrs. Peacock and I thought that one of these days we might pool our savings and buy a little car, or go on a trip somewhere, or even a cruise.

What I am saying is that I was free, and getting along fine, with never a thought that I knew about ever going back. It was just plain rotten bad luck that I had to meet Paul. I had gotten so I hardly ever thought about any of them any more, and never wondered what they were doing unless I happened to see some item in the papers, but there must have been something in the back of my mind remembering them all the time because I never even stopped to think; I just stood there on the street with my mouth open, and said "Paul!" He turned around and then of course I realized what I had done, but it was too late. He stared at me for a minute, and then frowned, and then looked puzzled; I could see him first trying to remember, and then trying to believe what he remembered; at last he said, "Is it possible?"

He said I had to go back. He said if I didn't go back he would tell them where to come and get me. He also patted me on the head and told me that there was still a reward waiting there in the bank for anyone who turned up with conclusive news of me, and he said that after he had collected the reward I was perfectly welcome to run away again, as far and as often as I liked.

Maybe I did want to go home. Maybe all that time I had been secretly waiting for a chance to get back; maybe that's why I recognized Paul on the street, in a coincidence that wouldn't have happened once in a million years—he had never even *been* to Chandler before, and was only there for a few minutes between trains; he had stepped out of the station for a minute, and found me. If I had not been passing at that minute, if he had stayed in the station where he belonged, I would never have gone back. I told Mrs. Peacock I was going home to visit my family upstate. I thought that was funny.

Paul sent a telegram to my mother and father, saying that he had found me, and we took a plane back; Paul said he was still afraid that I'd try to get away again and the safest place for me was high up in the air where he knew I couldn't get off and run.

I began to get nervous, looking out the taxi window on the way from the Rockville airport; I would have sworn that for three years I hadn't given a thought to that town, to those streets and stores and houses I used to know so well, but here I found that I remembered it all, as though I hadn't ever seen Chandler and *its* houses and streets; it was almost as though I had never been away at all. When the taxi finally turned the corner into my own street, and I saw the big old white house again, I almost cried.

"Of course I wanted to come back," I said, and Paul laughed. I thought of the return-trip ticket I had kept as a lucky charm for so long, and how I had thrown it away one day when I was emptying my pocketbook; I wondered when I threw it away whether I would ever want to go back and regret throwing away my ticket. "Everything looks just the same," I said. "I caught the bus right there on the corner; I came down the driveway that day and met you."

"If I had managed to stop you that day," Paul said, "you would probably never have tried again."

Then the taxi stopped in front of the house and my knees were shaking when I got out. I grabbed Paul's arm and said, "Paul . . . wait a minute," and he gave me a look I used to know very well, a look that said "If you back out on me now I'll see that you never forget it," and put his arm around me because I was shivering and we went up the walk to the front door.

I wondered if they were watching us from the window. It was hard for me to imagine how my mother and father would behave in a situation like this, because they always made such a point of being quiet and dignified and proper; I thought that Mrs. Peacock would have been halfway down the walk to meet us, but here the front door ahead was still tight shut. I wondered if we would have to ring the doorbell; I had never had to ring this doorbell before. I was still wondering when Carol opened the door for us. "Carol!" I said. I was shocked because she looked so old, and then I thought that of course it had been three years since I had seen her and she probably thought that *I* looked older, too. "Carol," I said, "Oh, Carol!" I was honestly glad to see her.

She looked at me hard and then stepped back and my mother and father were standing there, waiting for me to come in. If I had not stopped to think I would have run to them, but I hesitated, not quite sure what to do, or whether they were angry with me, or hurt, or only just happy that I was back, and of course once I stopped to think about it all I could find to do was just stand there and say "Mother?" kind of uncertainly.

She came over to me and put her hands on my shoulders and looked into my face for a long time. There were tears running down her cheeks and I thought that before, when it didn't matter, I had been ready enough to cry, but now, when crying would make me look better, all I wanted to do was giggle. She looked old, and sad, and I felt simply foolish. Then she turned to Paul and said, "Oh, *Paul*—how can you do this to me again?"

Paul was frightened; I could see it. "Mrs. Tether—" he said.

"What is your name, dear?" my mother asked me.

"Louisa Tether," I said stupidly.

"No, dear," she said, very gently, "your *real* name?"

Now I could cry, but now I did not think it was going to help matters any. "Louisa Tether," I said. "That's my name."

"Why don't you people leave us alone?" Carol said; she was white, and shaking, and almost screaming because she was so angry. "We've spent years and years trying to find my lost sister and all people like you see in it is a chance to cheat us out of the reward—doesn't it mean *anything* to you that *you* may think you have a chance for some easy money, but *we* just get hurt and heart-broken all over again? Why don't you leave us *alone*?"

"Carol," my father said, "you're frightening the poor child. Young lady," he said to me, "I honestly believe that you did not realize the cruelty of what you tried to do. You look like a nice girl; try to imagine your own mother—"

I tried to imagine my own mother; I looked straight at her.

"—if someone took advantage of her like this. I am sure you were not told that twice before, this young man—" I stopped looking at my mother and looked at Paul—"has brought us young girls who pretended to be our lost daughter; each time he protested that he had been genuinely deceived and had no thought of profit, and each time we hoped desperately that it would be the right girl. The first time we were taken in for several days. The girl *looked* like our Louisa, she *acted* like our Louisa, she knew all kinds of small family jokes and happenings it seemed impossible that anyone *but* Louisa could know, and yet she was an imposter. And the girl's mother—my wife—has suffered more each time her hopes have been raised." He put his arm around my mother—his wife—and with Carol they stood all together looking at me.

"Look," Paul said wildly, "give her a *chance*—she *knows* she's Louisa. At least give her a chance to *prove* it."

"How?" Carol asked. "I'm sure if I asked her something like— well—like what was the color of the dress she was supposed to wear at my wedding—"

"It was pink," I said. "I wanted blue but you said it had to be pink."

"I'm sure she'd know the answer," Carol went on as though I hadn't said anything. "The other girls you brought here, Paul—*they* both knew."

It wasn't going to be any good. I ought to have known it. Maybe they were so used to looking for me by now that they would rather keep on looking than have me home; maybe once my mother had looked in my face and seen there nothing of Louisa, but only the long careful concentration I had put into being Lois Taylor, there was never any chance of my looking like Louisa again.

I felt kind of sorry for Paul; he had never understood them as well as I did and he clearly felt there was still some chance of talking them into opening their arms and crying out "Louisa! Our long-lost daughter!" and then turning around and handing him the reward; after that, we could all live happily ever after. While Paul was still trying to argue with my father I walked over a little way and looked into the living room again; I figured I wasn't going to have much time to look around and I wanted one last glimpse to take away with me; sister Carol kept a good eye on me all the time, too. I wondered what the two girls before me had tried to steal, and I wanted to tell her that if I ever planned to steal anything from that house I was three years too late; I could have taken whatever I wanted when I left the first time. There was nothing there I could take now, any more than there had been before. I realized that all I wanted was to stay—I wanted to stay so much that I felt like hanging onto the stair rail and screaming, but even though a temper tantrum might bring them some fleeting recollection of their dear lost Louisa I hardly thought it would persuade them to invite me to stay. I could just picture myself being dragged kicking and screaming out of my own house.

"Such a lovely old house," I said politely to my sister Carol, who was hovering around me.

"Our family has lived here for generations," she said, just as politely.

"Such beautiful furniture," I said.

"My mother is fond of antiques."

"Fingerprints," Paul was shouting. We were going to get a lawyer, I gathered, or at least Paul thought we were going to get a lawyer and I wondered how he was going to feel when he found out that we weren't. I couldn't imagine any lawyer in the world who could get my mother and my father and my sister Carol to take me back when they had made up their minds that I was not Louisa; could the law make my mother look into my face and recognize me?

I thought that there ought to be some way I could make Paul see that there was nothing we could do, and I came over and stood next to him. "Paul," I said, "can't you see that you're only making Mr. Tether angry?"

"Correct, young woman," my father said, and nodded at me to show that he thought I was being a sensible creature. "He's not doing himself any good by threatening me."

"Paul," I said, "these people don't want us here."

Paul started to say something and then for the first time in his life thought better of it and stamped off toward the door. When I turned to follow him—thinking that we'd never gotten past the front hall in my great homecoming—my father—excuse me, Mr. Tether—came up behind me and took my hand. "My daughter was younger than you are," he said to me very kindly, "but I'm sure you have a family somewhere who love you and want you to be happy. Go back to them, young lady. Let me advise you as though I were really your father—stay away from that fellow, he's wicked and he's worthless. Go back home where you belong."

"We know what it's like for a family to worry and wonder about a daughter," my mother said. "Go back to the people who love you."

That meant Mrs. Peacock, I guess.

"Just to make sure you get there," my father said, "let us help toward your fare." I tried to take my hand away, but he put a folded bill into it and I had to take it. "I hope someday," he said, "that someone will do as much for our Louisa."

"Good-by, my dear," my mother said, and she reached up and patted my cheek. "Very good luck to you."

"I hope your daughter comes back someday," I told them. "Good-by."

The bill was a twenty, and I gave it to Paul. It seemed little enough for all the trouble he had taken and, after all, I could go back to my job in the stationery store. My mother still talks to me on the radio, once a year, on the anniversary of the day I ran away.

"Louisa," she says, "Please come home. We all want our dear girl back, and we need you and miss you so much. Your mother and father love you and will never forget you. Louisa, please come home."

Paranoia

Mr. Halloran Beresford, pleasantly tired after a good day in the office, still almost clean-shaven after eight hours, his pants still neatly pressed, pleased with himself particularly for remembering, stepped out of the candy shop with a great box under his arm and started briskly for the corner. There were twenty small-size gray suits like Mr. Beresford's on every New York block, fifty men still clean-shaven and pressed after a day in an air-cooled office, a hundred small men, perhaps, pleased with themselves for remembering their wives' birthdays. Mr. Beresford was going to take his wife out to dinner, he decided, going to see if he could get last-minute tickets to a show, taking his wife candy. It had been an exceptionally good day, altogether, and Mr. Beresford walked along swiftly, humming musically to himself.

He stopped on the corner, wondering whether he would save more time by taking a bus or by trying to catch a taxi in the crowd. It was a long trip downtown, and Mr. Beresford ordinarily enjoyed the quiet half-hour on top of a Fifth Avenue bus, perhaps reading his paper. He disliked the subway intensely, and found the public display and violent exercise necessary to catch a taxi usually more than he was equal to. However, tonight he had spent a lot of time waiting in line in the candy store to get his wife's favorite chocolates, and if he was going to get home before dinner was on the table he really had to hurry a little.

Mr. Beresford went a few steps into the street, waved at a taxi, said "Taxi!" in a voice that went helplessly into a falsetto, and slunk back, abashed, to the sidewalk while the taxi went by uncomprehending. A man in a light hat stopped next to Mr. Beresford on the sidewalk, and for a minute, in the middle of the crowd, he stared at Mr. Beresford and Mr. Beresford stared at him as people sometimes do without caring particularly what they see. What Mr. Beresford saw was a thin face under the light hat, a small mustache, a coat collar turned up. Funny-looking guy, Mr. Beresford thought, lightly touching his own clean-shaven lip. Perhaps the man thought Mr. Beresford's almost unconscious gesture was offensive; at any rate he frowned and looked Mr. Beresford up and down before he turned away. Ugly customer, Mr. Beresford thought.

The Fifth Avenue bus Mr. Beresford usually took came slipping up to the corner, and Mr. Beresford, pleased not to worry about a taxi, started for the stop. He had reached out his hand to take the rail inside the bus door when he was roughly elbowed aside and the ugly customer in the light hat shoved on ahead of him. Mr. Beresford muttered and started to follow, but the bus door closed on the packed crowd inside, and the last thing Mr. Beresford saw as the bus went off down the street was the man in the light hat grinning at him from inside the door.

"*There's* a dirty trick," Mr. Beresford told himself, settling his shoulders irritably in his coat. Still under the influence of his annoyance, he ran a few steps out into the street and waved again at a taxi, not trusting his voice, and was almost run down by a delivery truck. As Mr. Beresford skidded back to the sidewalk, the truck driver leaned out and yelled something unrecognizable at Mr. Beresford, and when Mr. Beresford saw the people around him on the corner laughing he decided to start walking downtown; in two blocks he would reach another bus stop, a good corner for taxis, and a subway station; much as Mr. Beresford disliked the subway, he might still have to take it, to get home in any sort of time. Walking downtown, his candy box under his arm, his gray suit almost unaffected by the crush on the corner, Mr. Beresford decided to swallow his annoyance and remember that it was his wife's birthday; he began to hum again as he walked.

He watched the people as he walked along, his perspective sharpened by being a man who had just succeeded in forgetting an annoyance; surely the girl in the very high-heeled shoes, coming toward him with a frown on her face, was not so able to put herself above petty trifles, or maybe she was frowning because of the shoes; the old lady and man looking at the shop windows were quarreling. The funny-looking guy in the light hat coming quickly through the crowd looked as though he hated someone . . . the funny-looking guy in the light hat; Mr. Beresford turned clean around in the walking line of people and watched the man in the light hat turn abruptly and start walking downtown, about ten feet in back of Mr. Beresford. What do you know about that?, Mr. Beresford marveled, and began to walk a little more quickly. Probably got off the bus for some reason; wrong bus, maybe. Then why would he start walking uptown instead of catching another bus where he was? Mr. Beresford shrugged and passed two girls walking together and talking both at once.

Halfway from the corner he wanted, Mr. Beresford realized with a sort of sick shock that the man in the light hat was at his elbow, walking steadily along next to him. Mr. Beresford turned his head the other way and slowed his step. The other man slowed down as well, without looking at Mr. Beresford.

Nonsense, Mr. Beresford thought, without troubling to work it out any further than that. He settled his candy box firmly under his arm and cut abruptly across the uptown line of people and into a shop; a souvenir and notions shop, he realized as he came through the door. There were a few people inside—a woman and a little girl, a sailor—and Mr. Beresford retired to the far end of the counter and began to fuss with an elaborate cigarette box on which was written SOUVENIR OF NEW YORK CITY, with the Trylon and the Perisphere painted beneath.

"Isn't this cute?" the mother said to the little girl, and they both began to laugh enormously over the match holder made in the form of a toilet; the matches were to go in the bowl, and on the cover, Mr. Beresford could see, were the Trylon and the Perisphere, with SOUVENIR OF NEW YORK CITY written above.

The man in the light hat came into the shop, and Mr. Beresford turned his back and busied himself picking up one thing after another from the counter; with half his mind he was trying to find something that did not say SOUVENIR OF NEW YORK CITY, and with the other half of his mind he was wondering about the man in the light hat. The question of what the man in the light hat wanted was immediately subordinate to the question of *whom* he wanted; if his light-hatted designs were against Mr. Beresford they must be nefarious, else why had he not announced them before now? The thought of accosting the man and demanding his purpose crossed Mr. Beresford's mind fleetingly, and was succeeded, as always in an equivocal situation, by Mr. Beresford's vivid recollection of his own small size and innate cautiousness. Best, Mr. Beresford decided, to avoid this man. Thinking this, Mr. Beresford walked steadily toward the doorway of the shop, intending to pass the man in the light hat and go out and catch his bus home.

He had not quite reached the man in the light hat when the shop's clerk came around the end of the counter and met Mr. Beresford with a genial smile and a vehement "See anything you like, mister?"

"Not tonight, thanks," Mr. Beresford said, moving left to avoid the clerk, but the clerk moved likewise and said, "Got some nice things you didn't look at."

"No, thanks," Mr. Beresford said, trying to make his tenor voice firm.

"Take a look," the clerk insisted. This was unusually persistent even for such a clerk; Mr. Beresford looked up and saw the man in the light hat on his right, bearing down on him. Over the shoulders of the two men he could see that the shop was empty. The street looked very far away, the people passing in either direction looked smaller and smaller; Mr. Beresford realized that he was being forced to step backward as the two men advanced on him.

"Easy does it," the man in the light hat said to the clerk. They continued to move forward slowly.

"See here, now," Mr. Beresford said, with the ineffectuality of the ordinary man caught in such a crisis; he still clutched his box of candy under his arm. "See *here*," he said, feeling the solid weight of the wall behind him.

"Ready," the man in the light hat said. The two men tensed, and Mr. Beresford, with a wild yell, broke between them and ran for the door. He heard a sound more like a snarl than anything else behind him and the feet coming after him. I'm safe on the street, Mr. Beresford thought as he went through the door into the line of people; as long as there are lots of people, they can't do anything to me. He looked back, walking downtown between a fat woman with many packages and a girl and a boy leaning on each other's shoulders, and he saw the clerk standing in the doorway of the shop looking after him; the man in the light hat was not in sight. Mr. Beresford shifted the box of candy so that his right arm was free, and thought, Perfectly silly. It's still broad daylight. How they ever hoped to get away with it . . .

The man in the light hat was on the corner ahead, waiting. Mr. Beresford hesitated in his walk and then thought, It's preposterous, all these people watching. He walked boldly down the street; the man in the light hat was not even watching him, but was leaning calmly against a building lighting a cigarette. Mr. Beresford reached the corner, darted quickly into the street, and yelled boisterously "Taxi!" in a great voice he had never suspected he possessed until now. A taxi stopped as though not daring to disregard that great shout, and Mr. Beresford moved gratefully toward it. His hand was on the door handle when another hand closed over his, and Mr. Beresford was aware of the light hat brushing his cheek.

"Come on if you're coming," the taxi driver said; the door was open, and Mr. Beresford, resisting the push that urged him into the taxi, slipped his hand out from under the other hand and ran back to the sidewalk. A crosstown bus had stopped on the corner, and Mr. Beresford, no longer thinking, hurried onto it, dropped a nickel into the coin register, and went to the back of the bus and sat down. The man in the light hat sat a little ahead, between Mr. Beresford and the door. Mr. Beresford put his box of candy on his lap and tried to think. Obviously the man in the light hat was not carrying a grudge all this time about Mr. Beresford's almost unconscious gesture toward his mustache, unless he was peculiarly sensitive. In any case, there was also the clerk in the souvenir shop; Mr. Beresford realized suddenly that the clerk in the souvenir shop was a very odd circumstance indeed. Mr. Beresford set the clerk aside to think about later and went back to the man in the light hat. If it was not the insult to the mustache, what was it? And then another thought caught Mr. Beresford breathless: How long, then, had the man in the light hat been following him? He thought back along the day: He had left his office with a group of people, all talking cheerfully, all reminding Mr. Beresford that it was his wife's birthday; they had escorted Mr. Beresford to the candy shop and left him there. He had been in his office all day except for lunch with three fellows in the office; Mr. Beresford's mind leaped suddenly from the lunch to his first sight of the man in the light hat at the bus stop; it seemed that the man in the light hat had been trying to push him *onto* the bus and into the crowd, instead of pushing in ahead. In that case, once he was on the bus . . . Mr. Beresford looked around. In the bus he was riding on now there were only five people left. One was the driver, one Mr. Beresford, one the man in the light hat, sitting slightly ahead of Mr. Beresford. The two others were an old lady with a shopping bag and a man who looked as though he might be a foreigner. Foreigner, Mr. Beresford thought, while he looked at the man. Foreigner, foreign plot, spies. Better not rely on any foreigner, Mr. Beresford thought.

The bus was going swiftly along between high dark buildings. Mr. Beresford, looking out the window, decided that they were in a factory district, remembered that they had been going east, and decided to wait until they got to one of the lighted, busy sections before he tried to get off. Peering off into the growing darkness, Mr. Beresford noticed an odd thing. There had been someone standing on the corner beside a sign saying BUS STOP and the bus had not stopped, even though the dim figure waved its arms. Surprised, Mr. Beresford glanced up at the street sign, noticing that it said E. 31 ST. At the same moment he reached for the cord to signal the driver that he wanted to get off. As he stood up and went down the aisle, the foreign-looking man rose also and went to the door beside the driver. "Getting off," the foreign man said, and the bus slowed. Mr. Beresford pressed forward, and somehow the old lady's shopping bag got in his way and spilled, sending small items, a set of blocks, a package of paper clips, spilling in all directions.

"Sorry," Mr. Beresford said desperately as the bus doors opened. He began to move forward again, and the old lady caught his arm and said, "Don't bother if you're in a hurry. I can get them, dear." Mr. Beresford tried to shake her off, and she said, "If this is your stop, don't worry. It's perfectly all right."

A coil of pink ribbon was caught around Mr. Beresford's shoe; the old lady said, "It was clumsy of me, leaving my bag right in the aisle."

As Mr. Beresford broke away from her, the doors closed and the bus started. Resigned, Mr. Beresford got down on one knee in the swaying bus and began to pick up paper clips, blocks, a box of letter paper that had opened and spilled sheets and envelopes all over the floor. "I'm so sorry," the old lady said sweetly. "It was all my fault, too."

Over his shoulder, Mr. Beresford saw the man in the light hat sitting comfortably. He was smoking, and his head was thrown back and his eyes were shut. Mr. Beresford gathered together the old lady's possessions as well as he could, then made his way forward to stand by the driver. "Getting off," Mr. Beresford said.

"Can't stop in the middle of the block," the driver said, not turning his head.

"The next stop, then," Mr. Beresford said.

The bus moved rapidly on. Mr. Beresford, bending down to see the streets out the front window, saw a sign saying BUS STOP.

"Here," he said.

"What?" the driver said, going past.

"Listen," Mr. Beresford said. "I want to get off."

"It's okay with me," the driver said. "Next stop."

"You just passed one," Mr. Beresford said.

"No one waiting there," the driver said. "Anyway, you didn't tell me in time." Mr. Beresford waited. After a minute he saw another bus stop and said, "Okay."

The bus did not stop, but went past the sign without slowing down.

"Report me," the driver said.

"Listen, now," Mr. Beresford said, and the driver turned one eye up at him; he seemed to be amused.

"Report me," the driver said. "My number's right here on this card."

"If you don't stop at the next stop," Mr. Beresford said, "I shall smash the glass in the door and shout for help."

"What with?" the driver said. "That box of candy?"

"How do you know it's—" Mr. Beresford said before he realized that if he got into a conversation he would miss the next bus stop. It had not occurred to him that he could get off anywhere except at a bus stop; he saw lights ahead, and at the same time the bus slowed down and Mr. Beresford, looking quickly back, saw the man in the light hat stretch and get up.

The bus pulled to a stop in front of a bus sign; there was a group of stores.

"OKAY," the bus driver said to Mr. Beresford, "you were so anxious to get off." The man in the light hat got off at the rear door. Mr. Beresford, standing by the open front door, hesitated and said, "I guess I'll stay on for a while."

"Last stop," the bus driver said. "Everybody off." He looked sardonically up at Mr. Beresford. "Report me if you want to," he said. "My number's right on that card there." Mr. Beresford got off and went directly up to the man in the light hat, standing on the sidewalk. "This is perfectly ridiculous," he said emphatically. "I don't understand any of it, and I want you to know that the first policeman I see—"

He stopped when he realized that the man in the light hat was looking not at him but, bored and fixedly, over his shoulder. Mr. Beresford turned and saw a policeman standing on the corner.

"Just you wait," he said to the man in the light hat, and started for the policeman. Halfway to the policeman he began to wonder again: What did he have to report? A bus driver who would not stop when directed to, a clerk in a souvenir shop who cornered customers, a mysterious man in a light hat—and why? Mr. Beresford realized that there was nothing he could tell the policeman; he looked over his shoulder and saw the man in the light hat watching him, then Mr. Beresford bolted suddenly down a subway entrance. He had a nickel in his hand by the time he reached the bottom of the steps, and he went right through the turnstile; to the left was downtown, and he ran that way.

He was figuring as he ran: He'll think if I'm very stupid I'd head downtown, if I'm smarter than that I'd go uptown, if I'm really smart I'd go downtown. Does he think I'm middling smart or very smart?

The man in the light hat reached the downtown platform only a few seconds after Mr. Beresford and sauntered down the platform, his hands in his pockets. Mr. Beresford sat down on the bench listlessly. It's no good, he thought, no good at all; he knows just how smart I am.

The train came blasting into the station; Mr. Beresford ran into one car and saw the light hat disappear into the next car. Just as the doors were closing, Mr. Beresford dived, caught the door, and would have been out except for a girl who seized his arm and shouted, "Harry! Where in God's name are you going?"

The door was held halfway open by Mr. Beresford's body, his arm left inside with the girl, who seemed to be holding it with all her strength. "Isn't this a fine thing," she said to the people in the car. "He sure doesn't want to see his old friends."

A few people laughed; most of them were watching.

"Hang on to him, sister," someone said.

The girl laughed and tugged on Mr. Beresford's arm. "He's gonna get away," she said laughingly to the people in the car, and a big man stepped up to her with a grin and said, "If you gotta have him that bad, we'll bring him in for you."

Mr. Beresford felt the grasp on his arm turn suddenly into an irresistible force that drew him in through the doors, and they closed behind him. Everyone in the car was laughing at him by now, and the big man said, "That ain't no way to treat a lady, chum."

Mr. Beresford looked around for the girl, but she had melted into the crowd somewhere and the train was moving. After a minute the people in the car stopped looking at him, and Mr. Beresford smoothed his coat and found that his box of candy was still intact.

The subway train was going downtown. Mr. Beresford, who was now racking his brains for detective tricks, for mystery-story dodges, thought of one that seemed foolproof. He stayed docilely on the train, as it went downtown, and got a seat at Twenty-third Street. At Fourteenth he got off, the light hat following, and went up the stairs and into the street. As he had expected, the large department store ahead of him advertised OPEN TILL 9 TONIGHT, and the doors swung wide, back and forth, with people going constantly in and out. Mr. Beresford went in. The store bewildered him at first—counters stretching away in all directions, the lights much brighter than anywhere else, the voices clamoring. Mr. Beresford moved slowly along beside a counter; it was stockings first, thin and tan and black and gauzy, and then it was handbags, piles on sale, neat solitary ones in the cases, and then it was medical supplies, with huge almost-human figures wearing obscene trusses, standing right there on the counter, and people coming embarrassedly to buy. Mr. Beresford turned the corner and came to a counter of odds and ends. Scarves too cheap to be at the scarf counter, postcards, a bin marked ANY ITEM 25¢, dark glasses. Uncomfortably, Mr. Beresford bought a pair of dark glasses and put them on.

He went out of the store at an entrance far away from the one he had used to come in; he could have chosen any of eight or nine entrances, but this seemed complicated enough. There was no sign of the light hat, no one tried to hinder Mr. Beresford as he stepped up to the taxi stand, and, although he debated taking the second or third car, he finally took the one in front and gave his home address.

He reached his apartment building without mishap, and stole cautiously out of the taxi and into the lobby. There was no light hat, no odd person watching for Mr. Beresford. In the elevator, alone, with no one to see which floor button he pressed, Mr. Beresford took a long breath and began to wonder if he had dreamed his wild trip home. He rang his apartment bell and waited; then his wife came to the door, and Mr. Beresford, suddenly tired out, went into his home.

"You're *terribly* late, darling," his wife said affectionately, and then, "But what's the matter?"

He looked at her; she was wearing her blue dress, and that meant she knew it was her birthday and expected him to take her out; he handed her the box of candy limply and she took it, hardly noticing it in her anxiety over him. "What on *earth* has happened?" she asked. "Darling, come in here and sit down. You look terrible."

He let her lead him into the living room, into his own chair, where it was comfortable, and he lay back.

"Is there something wrong?" she was asking anxiously, fussing over him, loosening his tie, smoothing his hair. "Are you sick? Were you in an accident? What *has* happened?"

He realized that he seemed more tired than he really was, and was glorying in all this attention. He sighed deeply and said, "Nothing. Nothing wrong. Tell you in a minute."

"Wait," she said. "I'll get you a drink."

He put his head back against the soft chair as she went out. Never knew that door had a key, his mind registered dimly as he heard it turn. Then he was on his feet with his head against the door listening to her at the telephone in the hall.

She dialed and waited. Then: "Listen," she said, "listen, he came here after all. I've got him."

The Honeymoon of Mrs. Smith

When she came into the grocery she obviously interrupted a conversation about herself and her husband. The grocer leaning across the counter to speak confidentially to a customer straightened up abruptly and signaled at her with his eyes, so that the customer, in a fairly obvious attempt at dissimulation, looked stubbornly in the opposite direction for almost a minute before turning quickly to take one swift, eager look.

"Good morning," she said.

"What'll it be for you this morning?" he asked, his eyes moving to the right and left to insure that all present observed him speaking boldly to Mrs. Smith.

"I don't need very much," she said. "I may be going away over the weekend."

A long sigh swept through the store; she had a clear sense of people moving closer, as though the dozen other customers, the grocer, the butcher, the clerks, were pressing against her, listening avidly.

"A small loaf of bread," she said clearly. "A pint of milk. The smallest possible can of peas."

"Not laying in much for the weekend," the grocer said with satisfaction.

"I may be going away," she said, and again there was that long breath of satisfaction. She thought: how silly of all of us—I'm not sure any more than *they* are, we all of us only suspect, and of course there won't be any way of knowing for sure . . . but still it would be a shame to have all that food in the kitchen, and let it go to waste, just rotting there while . . .

"Coffee?" the grocer said. "Tea?"

"I'm going to get a pound of coffee," she said, smiling at him. "After all, I like coffee. I can probably drink up a pound before . . ."

The anticipatory pause made her say quickly, "And I'll want a quarter-pound of butter, and I guess two lamb chops."

The butcher, although he had been trying to pretend indifference, turned immediately to get the lamb chops, and he came the width of the store and set the small package on the counter before the grocer had finished adding up her order.

One good thing, she was thinking about all this—I never have to *wait* anywhere. It's as though everyone knew I was in a hurry to get small things done. And I suppose no one really wants me around for very long, not after they've had their good look at me and gotten something to talk about.

When her groceries were all in a bag and the grocer was ready to hand it to her across the counter, he hesitated, as he had done several times before, as though he tried to gather courage to say something to her; she was aware of this, and knew fairly well what he wanted to say—listen, Mrs. Smith, it would start, we don't want to make any trouble or anything, and of course it isn't as though anyone around here was *sure*, but I guess you must know by now that it all looks mighty suspicious, and we just figured—with an inclusive glance around, for support from the butcher and the clerks—we all got talking, and we figured—well, we figured someone ought to say something to you about it. I guess people must have made this mistake before about you? Or your husband? Because of course no one likes to come right out and *say* a thing like that, when they could so easily be wrong. And of course the more everyone talks about this kind of thing, the harder it is to know whether you're right or not . . .

The man in the liquor store had said substantially that to her, fumbling and letting his voice die away under her cool, inquiring stare. The man in the drugstore had begun to say it, and then, blushing, had concluded, "Well, it's not *my* business, anyway." The woman in the lending library, the landlady, had given her the nervous, appraising look, wondering if she knew, if anyone had told her, wondering if they dared, and had ended by treating her with extreme gentleness and a sweet forbearance, as they would have treated some uncomplaining, incurable invalid. She was different in their eyes, she was marked; if the dreadful fact were not true (and they all hoped it was), she was in a position of such incredible, extreme embarrassment that their solicitude was even more deserved. If the dreadful fact *were* true (and they all hoped it was), they had none of them, the landlady, the grocer, the clerks, the druggist, lived in vain, gone through their days without the supreme excitement of being close to and yet secure from an unbearable situation. If the dreadful fact *were* true (and they all hoped it was), Mrs. Smith was, for them, a salvation and a heroine, a fragile, lovely creature whose preservation was in hands other than theirs.

Some of this Mrs. Smith realized dimly as she walked back to her apartment with the bag of groceries. She, at least, was almost not in doubt; she had known almost certainly that the dreadful fact was true for three weeks and six days, since she had met it face to face on a bench facing the ocean.

"I hope you won't think I'm rude," Mr. Smith had said at that moment, "if I open a conversation by saying that it's a lovely day."

She thought he was incredibly daring, she thought he was unbelievably vulgar, but she did not think he was rude; it was a word ridiculous when applied to him.

"No," she had said, recognizing him, "I don't think you're rude."

If she had ever tried to phrase it to herself—it would hardly be possible to describe it to anyone else—she might have said, in the faintly clerical idiom she had learned so thoroughly, that she had been chosen for this, or that it was like being carried unresisting on the surface of a river which took her on inevitably into the sea. Or she might have said that, just as in her whole life before she had not questioned the decisions of her father but had done quietly as she was told, so it was a relief to know that there was now someone again to decide for her, and that her life, inevitable as it had been before, was now clear as well. Or she might have said—with a blush for a possible double meaning, that they, like all other married couples, were two halves of what was essentially one natural act.

"A man gets very lonesome, I think," he had told her at dinner that night, in a restaurant near the sea, where even the napkins smelled of fish and the bare wood of the table had an indefinable salty grain, "a man alone needs to find himself some kind of company." And then, as though the words had perhaps not been complimentary enough, he added hastily, "Except not everyone is lucky enough to meet a charming young lady like yourself." She had smiled and simpered, by then fully aware of these preliminaries to her destiny.

Three weeks and six days later, turning to go in through the door of the shabby apartment house, she wondered briefly about the weekend ahead; she had been naturally reluctant to buy too much food, but then, if it turned out that she *should* be there, there would be no way to buy more food on Sunday; a restaurant, she thought, we will have to go to a restaurant—although they had not been together to a restaurant since that first dinner together since, even though they did not actually have to economize, they both felt soberly that the fairly large mutual bank account they now had ought not to be squandered unnecessarily, but should be kept as nearly intact as possible; they had not discussed this, but Mrs. Smith's instinctive tactful respect for her husband's methods led her to fall in with him silently in his routine of economy.

The three flights of stairs were narrow and high, and Mrs. Smith, with the immediate recognition of symbols she had inherited, had always had, potentially, and was now using almost exclusively, saw the eternal steps going up and up as an irrevocable design for her life; she had really no choice but to go up, wearily if she chose; if she turned and went down again, retracing laboriously the small progress she had made, she would merely have to go up another way, beginning, as she now almost realized, beginning again a search which could only, for her, have but one ending. "It happens to everybody," she told herself consolingly as she climbed.

Pride would not allow her to make any concessions to her position, so she did not try particularly to walk silently on the second-floor landing; for a minute, going on up the next flight, she thought she had got safely past, but then, almost as she reached her own door, the door on the second landing opened and Mrs. Jones called, piercingly and as though she had run from some back recess of her apartment to the door when she heard footsteps.

"Mrs. Smith, is that you?"

"Hello," Mrs. Smith called back down the stairs.

"Wait a minute, I'm coming up." The lock on Mrs. Jones's door snapped, and the door closed. Mrs. Jones came hurriedly, still a little out of breath, down the landing and up the stairs to the third floor. "Thought I'd missed you," she said on the stairs, and, "Good heavens, you look tired."

It was part of the attitude that treated Mrs. Smith as a precious vessel. Her slightest deviation from the normal, in the course of more than a week, was noted and passed from gossip to gossip, a faint paling of her cheeks became the subject of nervous speculation, any change in her voice, a dullness of her eye, a disarrangement in her dress—these were what her neighbors lived on. Mrs. Smith had thought early in the week that a loud crash from her apartment would be the sweetest thing she could do for Mrs. Jones, but by now it no longer seemed important: Mrs. Jones could live as well on the most minute crumbs.

"Thought you'd never get home," Mrs. Jones said. She followed Mrs. Smith into the bare little room which, with a small bedroom, a dirty kitchen, and a bath, was the honeymoon home of Mr. and Mrs. Smith. Mrs. Jones took the package of groceries into the kitchen while Mrs. Smith hung up her coat in the closet; she had not bothered to unpack many things and the closet looked empty; there were two or three dresses and a light overcoat and extra suit of Mr. Smith's; this was so obviously only a temporary home for them both, a stopping-place. Mrs. Smith did not regard her three dresses with regret, nor did she particularly admire the suits of Mr. Smith, although they were still a little unfamiliar to her, hung up next to her own clothes (as his underwear in the dresser, lying quietly beside her own); neither Mr. nor Mrs. Smith were of the abandoned sort who indulge recklessly in trousseaus or other loving detail for a preliminary purification.

"Well," said Mrs. Jones, coming out of the kitchen, "*you* certainly aren't planning to do much cooking this weekend."

Privacy was not one of the blessings of Mrs. Smith's position. "I thought I might be going away," she said.

Again there was that soft, anticipatory moment; Mrs. Jones looked quickly, and then away, and then, sitting herself down firmly upon the meager couch, obviously decided to come to the point.

"Now, look, Mrs. Smith," she began, and then interrupted herself. "Look, why this 'Mrs.' all the time? You call me Polly, and from now on I'll call you Helen. All right?" She smiled, and Mrs. Smith, smiling back, thought, how do they find out your first name? "Well, now, look here, Helen," Mrs. Jones went on, determined to establish her new familiarity immediately, "I think it's time someone sat down and talked sensibly to you. I mean, you must know by now pretty well what people are saying."

Here we are, Helen Smith was thinking, two women of the singular type woman, one standing uneasily and embarrassed in front of a window, wearing a brown dress and brown hair and brown shoes and differing in no essential respect from the other, sitting solidly and earnestly, wearing a green and pink flowered housedress and bedroom slippers—differing, actually in no essential, although we would both deny indignantly that we were the same person, seeking the same destiny. And we are about to enter into a conversation upon a fantastic subject.

"I've noticed," Mrs. Smith said carefully, "that there's a lot of unusual interest in us. I've never been on a honeymoon before, of course, so I can't really tell whether it's only that." She laughed weakly, but Mrs. Jones was not to be put off by sentiment.

"I think you must know better than that," she said. "You're not *that* wrapped up in your husband."

"Well . . . no," Mrs. Smith had to say.

"And furthermore," Mrs. Jones went on, looking cynically at Mrs. Smith, "you're not any blushing eighteen-year-old girl, you know, and Mr. Smith isn't any young man. You're both people of a reasonably mature age." Mrs. Jones seemed to feel that she had made a point here, and she said it again. "You are both people who have outlived their youth," she said, "and naturally no one expects that you're going to go around billing and cooing. And *furthermore* you yourself are old enough to show some intelligence about this terrible business."

"I don't know what kind of intelligence I ought to show," Mrs. Smith said meekly.

"Well, good heavens!" Mrs. Jones spread her hands helplessly. "Don't you realize your position? *Everyone* knows it. Look." She settled back, prepared to demonstrate reasonably. "You came here a week ago, newly married, and moved into this apartment with your husband. The very first day you were here, people thought there was something funny. In the first place, you two didn't act like you were the types for each other at all. You know what I mean—you so sort of refined and ladylike, and him . . ."

Rude, Mrs. Smith thought, wanting to laugh; he said he was rude. Mrs. Jones shrugged. "In the second place," she said, "you didn't look like you belonged in this house, or in this neighborhood, because you always had plenty of money, which, believe me, the rest of us don't, and you always acted sort of as though you ought to be in a better kind of situation. And in the *third* place," Mrs. Jones said, hurrying on to her climax, "it wasn't two days before people began to think they recognized your husband from the pictures in the paper."

"I see what you mean," Mrs. Smith said. "But a picture in the paper—"

"That's just what started us really thinking," Mrs. Jones said. She enumerated on her fingers. "New bride. Cheap apartment. You made a will in his favor? Insurance?"

"Yes, but that is only natural—" said Mrs. Smith.

"Natural? And him looking just like the man in the paper who mur—" She stopped abruptly. "I don't want to frighten you," she said. "But you should know all about him."

"I appreciate your concern," Mrs. Smith said in her turn, coming away from the window, to stand in front of Mrs. Jones so that Mrs. Jones had to look up from her seat on the couch. "I know all these things. But how many newly married couples are there who make wills in each other's favor? Or take out insurance? And how many women over thirty get married to men over forty? And maybe sometimes the men look like pictures in the paper? And with all this talk and gossip about us all around the neighborhood, you notice no one's been even sure enough to say anything?"

"I wanted to call the police two, three days ago," Mrs. Jones said sullenly. "Ed wouldn't let me."

"He probably said," Mrs. Smith said, "that it was none of your business."

"But everybody's *wondering*," Mrs. Jones said. "And of course no one can know for sure."

"You won't know for sure until . . ." Mrs. Smith tried not to smile. Mrs. Jones sighed. "I wish you wouldn't talk like that," she said.

"Well," said Mrs. Smith reasonably, "what exactly is it you want me to do?"

"You could get some kind of information," Mrs. Jones said. "Something that would let you know for sure."

"I keep telling you," Mrs. Smith said, "there's only one way I can ever know for sure."

"Don't *talk* like that," Mrs. Jones said.

"I could run away from my husband," Mrs. Smith said. Mrs. Jones was surprised. "You can't run away from your *husband*," she said. "Not if it isn't true, you couldn't do that."

"I have really no grounds for divorce," Mrs. Smith said. "It is a very difficult subject to mention to him."

"Naturally, you wouldn't have discussed it," Mrs. Jones said.

"Naturally," Mrs. Smith said. "I could hardly search his clothes— there is nothing, I happen to know, in the pockets of the suit hanging in the closet and searching his overcoat pockets and his dresser drawers would hardly turn up anything convincing."

"Why not?"

"Well, I mean," said Mrs. Smith in explanation, "even if I discovered, say, a knife—what difference would it make?"

"But he doesn't do it with—" Mrs. Jones began, and stopped abruptly again.

"I know," Mrs. Smith said. "As I recall the details—and I haven't read much about them, after all—he generally does it—"

"In the bathtub," Mrs. Jones said, and shivered. "I don't know but what a knife would be better," she said.

"It's not our choice," Mrs. Smith said wryly. "You see how silly we sound? Here we are, talking as though we were children telling ghost stories. We'll end up convincing each other of some horrible notion."

Mrs. Jones hesitated for a minute over her own reactions, and finally decided to be mildly offended. "I really only came up," she explained with dignity, "to let you know what people were saying. If you stop to *think* about it for a minute, you ought to be able to understand why someone might want to help you. After all, it's not me."

"That's why I think you ought not to worry," Mrs. Smith said gently. Mrs. Jones rose, but as she reached the door she was unable to keep herself from turning and saying urgently, "Look, I just want you to know that if you ever *ever* need any help—of *any* kind—just open your mouth and scream, see? Because my Ed will be up as fast as he can come. All you have to do is scream, or stamp on the floor, or, if you can, race downstairs to our place. We'll be waiting for you." She opened the door, said with a voice that she tried to make humorous, "Don't take any baths," and went out. Her voice trailed up from the stairs, "And remember—all you have to do is scream. We'll be waiting."

Mrs. Smith closed the door rather quickly and, before she started to think, went out to the kitchen to see to her groceries, but Mrs. Jones had put the things away. Mrs. Smith found the pound of coffee, and measured water into the coffeepot, thinking of her promise to the grocer that she would finish the pound of coffee herself. Mr. Smith drank coffee sparingly; it made him nervous.

Mrs. Smith, as she moved about the bleak little kitchen, thought, as she had often before, that she would not like to spend her whole life with things like this. It had not been so in her father's life, where a peaceful, well-ordered existence went placidly on among objects which, if not lovely, had at least the pleasures of familiarity, and the near-beauty of order, and Mrs. Smith, who had then been Helen Bertram, had been able to spend long days working in the garden, or mending her father's socks, or baking the nut cake she had learned from her mother, and pausing only occasionally to wonder what was going to happen to her in her life.

It had been clear to her after her father's death that this patterned existence was no longer meaningful, and had been a product of her father's life rather than hers. So that when Mr. Smith had said to her, "I don't suppose you'd ever consider marrying a fellow like me?" Helen Bertram had nodded, seeing then the repeated design which made the complete pattern.

She had worn her best dark-blue dress to be married in, and Mr. Smith had worn a dark-blue suit so that they looked unnervingly alike when they went down the street together. They had gone directly to the lawyer's, for the wills, and then to the insurance company. On the way, Mr. Smith had insisted on stopping and buying for the new Mrs. Smith a small felt dog which amused her; there had been a man selling these on the street corner, and all around his small stand were tiny wound-up dogs which ran in circles, squeaking in shrill imitation of a bark. Mrs. Smith brought the box with the dog in it into the insurance company and set it on the desk, and while they were waiting for the doctor she had opened the box and found that there was no key to wind the dog; Mr. Smith, saying irritably, "Those fellows always try to cheat you," had hurried back to the street corner and found the stand, the salesman, and the performing dogs gone.

"Nothing makes me more furious," he told Mrs. Smith, "than to be cheated by someone like that."

The small dog stood now on the shelf in the kitchen and Mrs. Smith, glancing at it, thought, I could not endure spending the rest of my life with that tawdry sort of thing. She sometimes thought poignantly of her father's house, realizing that such things were gone from her forever, but, as she told herself again now, "I had my eyes open." It will have to be soon, she thought immediately after, people are beginning to wonder too openly. Everyone is waiting; it will spoil everything if it is not soon. When her coffee was finished she took a cup into the living room and sat down on the couch where Mrs. Jones had been sitting, and thought, it will have to be soon; there's no food for the weekend, after all, and I would have to send my dress to the cleaners on Monday if I were here, and another week's rent due tomorrow. The pound of coffee would be the only detail unattended to.

She had finished her fourth cup of coffee—drinking by now hastily and even desperately—when she heard her husband's step on the stairs. They were still a little embarrassed with one another, so that she hesitated about going to meet him just long enough for him to open the door, and then she came over to him awkwardly and, not knowing still whether he wanted to kiss her when he came home, stood expectantly until he came politely over to her and kissed her cheek.

"Where have you been?" she asked, although it was not at all the sort of thing she wanted to say to him, and she knew as she spoke that he would not tell her.

"Shopping," he said. He had an armful of packages, one of which he selected and gave to her.

"Thank you," she said politely before she opened it; it was, she knew by the feel and the drugstore wrapping, a box of candy, and with a feeling which, when she felt it again later, she knew to be triumph, she thought, of course, it's supposed to be left over, it's to prove the new husband still brings presents to his bride. She opened the box, wanted to take a candy, thought: not before dinner, and then thought, it probably doesn't matter, tonight.

"Will you have one?" she said to him, and he took one.

His manner did not seem strange, or nervous, but when she said, "Mrs. Jones was up here this afternoon," he said quickly, "What did she want, the old busybody?"

"I think she was jealous," Mrs. Smith said. "It's been a long time since *her* husband has taken any interest in her."

"I can imagine," he said.

"Shall I start dinner?" Mrs. Smith asked. "Would you like to rest for a while first?"

"I'm not hungry," he said.

Now, for the first time, he seemed awkward, and Mrs. Smith thought quickly, I was right about the food for the weekend, I guessed right; he did not ask if she was hungry because—and each of them knew now that the other knew—it really did not matter.

Mrs. Smith told herself it would ruin everything to say anything now, and she sat down on the couch next to her husband and said, "I'm a little tired, I think."

"A week of marriage was too much for you," he said, and patted her hand. "We'll have to see that you get more rest."

Why does it take so long, why *does* it take so long? Mrs. Smith thought; she stood up again and walked across the room nervously to look out the window; Mr. Jones was just coming up the front steps and he looked up and saw her and waved. Why does it take so long? she thought again, and turned and said to her husband, "Well?"

"I suppose so," Mr. Smith said, and got up wearily from the couch.

The Story We Used to Tell

This is the story that Y and I used to tell, used to tell in the quiet of the night, in the hours of the quiet of the night, and the moonlight would come, moving forward, moving close; used to whisper to each other in the night . . .

And I, Y would say, had to go first. With the moonlight making white patterns in her hair, she would shake her head and say: I had to go first. Remember, she would say. In this very house. That night. Remember? And the picture, and the moonlight, and the way we laughed.

We had sat on the foot of the bed, the way we used to when we roomed together in school, talking together and laughing sometimes in spite of the grief that filled Y's great house. It was only a month or so after her husband's funeral, I remember, and yet being together again, just the two of us, was somehow enough to make Y smile sometimes, and even occasionally laugh again. I had been wise enough not to remark on the fact that Y had closed off the rooms of the house in which she had lived with her husband, and had moved into an entire new wing of the old place. But I liked her little bedroom, quiet and bare, with no room for books, and only the one picture on the wall.

"It's a picture of the house . . ." Y said to me. "See, you can barely see the windows of this very room. It's before my grandfather-in-law remodeled it, which is why the new wing isn't there."

"It's a beautiful old place," I said. "I almost wish he hadn't changed it so much."

"Plumbing," Y said. "There's nothing wrong with plumbing."

"No," I said, "but I'm glad you've reopened the old wing . . . it must have been a gorgeous place in—say—your grandfather-in-law's time."

And we looked at the picture of the old old house, standing dark and tall against the sky, with the windows of this very room shining faintly through the trees, and the steep winding road coming through the gates and down to the very edge of the picture.

"I'm glad the glass is there," I said, giggling. "I'd hate to have a landslide start on that mountain and come down into our laps!"

"Into my bed, you mean," Y said. "I don't know if I'll be able to sleep, with the old place overhead."

"Grandpop's probably still in it, too," I said. "He's wandering around in a nightcap with a candle in the old barn."

"Plotting improvements." Y pulled the covers up over her head.

I told her, "God save us from all reformers," and went across the hall to my own room, pulled the heavy curtains to shut out the moonlight, and went to bed.

And the next morning Y was gone.

I woke up late, had breakfast downstairs with a first assistant footman or something of the sort presiding (even Y, married for four years into a butler-keeping establishment, had never found out which one to send for to bring tea in the afternoons, and had finally given up completely and taken to serving sherry, which she could pour herself from a decanter on the sideboard), and finally settled down to read, believing that Y would sleep late and come down in her own sweet time.

One o'clock was a little late, however, and when the menagerie began announcing lunch to me, I went after Y.

She wasn't in her room, the bed had been slept in, and none of the menagerie knew where she was. More than that, no one had seen or heard of her since I had left her the night before; everyone else had thought, as I did, that she was sleeping late.

By late afternoon I had decided to call Y's family lawyer, John, who lived on an adjoining estate and had been a close friend of Y's husband, and a kind adviser to Y. And by evening Y's lawyer had decided to call the police.

At the end of a week, nothing had been heard from or of Y, and the police had changed their theory of kidnapping to one of suicide. The lawyer came to me one of those afternoons with a project for closing up the house.

"I dread saying it, Katharine, but—" He shook his head. "I'm afraid she's dead."

"How can she be?" I kept crying out, I remember. "I tell you I was with her all that evening. We talked, and she was happier than she has been for weeks—since her husband died . . ."

"That's why I think she's dead," he said. "She was heartbroken. She had nothing to keep her alive."

"She had plans . . . she was going to sell this house, and travel! She was going to live abroad for a while—meet people, try to start life over again—why, I was going with her! We talked about it that night . . . and we laughed about the house . . . she said the picture would fall on her bed!!" My voice trailed off. It was, I know certainly, the first time I had thought of the picture since I had left Y in her room, with the moonlight coming in and shining on her pale hair on the pillow. And I began to think.

"Wait until tomorrow," I begged him. "Don't do anything for a day or two. Why . . . she might come back tonight!"

He shook his head at me despairingly, but he went away and left me alone in the house. I called the menagerie, and ordered my things moved into Y's room.

The full moon had turned into a lopsided creature, but there was still moonlight enough to fill the room with a haunted light when I lay down in Y's bed, looking into the empty windows in the picture of a house. I fell asleep thinking miserably of Y's cheerful conviction that the old man was loose in the picture, plotting improvements.

The moonlight was still there when I woke up, and so was the old woman. She was hanging on the inside of the glass of the picture, gibbering out at me, and she looked twenty feet high, standing in front of that picture of the house. I sat up in bed and backed as far away from the picture as I could, realizing, in the one lucid moment I had before the cold terror of that thing hit me, that she was on the inside of the glass, and couldn't get out.

Then suddenly she moved aside and I could see the road leading down from the house, and, while I watched, Y came through the gates, running, and waving desperately at me. I could feel my eyes getting wider and wider and the back of my neck getting colder and colder, and then I knew that I had been right and that Y had been caught in some malevolence of the old house, and I began sobbing in thankfulness that I had found her in time.

I picked up my slipper and smashed the glass of the picture and held out my hands to Y to hurry her on toward me. And then I saw that the old woman, no longer hanging on to the inside of the glass, was now free, and in the room with me, and I could hear her laughing. I fell back on the bed in a wild attempt to shove the old woman back into the picture and I could just see Y, dropping her hands in helpless grief, turn around and start slowly back up the road to the house. Then the room went out from under me, and the glass on the picture closed around me.

"I was waving at you to go away," Y was saying over and over. "You should have left me here and gone away. We can't ever get out now—either of us. You should have gone away."

I opened my eyes and looked around. I was in the dining room of the house, but so changed and gloomy! It was dark, and there was no furniture, no ornamentation. The place was still, and damp.

"No plumbing, either," Y said dryly, noticing the bewilderment on my face. "This picture was painted before the improvements were put in."

"But—" I said.

"Hide!" Y whispered. She pushed me into a corner, out of the light of the one candle on the floor.

"Oh my God," I said, and grabbed Y's hands.

Through the doorway came the old man, giggling and pulling at his beard. He was followed by the old woman, silent now, but with a glittering grin, and half waltzing.

"Young ladies!" the old man called in a shrill, cracked voice, looking eagerly about the room. He picked up the candle and began going to the corners with it. "Young ladies," he cried, "come out! We are going to celebrate! Tonight there is to be a ball!"

"Y!" I said. He was coming toward us.

"There you are, there you are. Lovely young ladies, shy over their first ball! Come ahead, young ladies!"

Y gave me one look, and then moved slowly forward. The old man waved the candle at me, calling, "Come along, don't be too demure, no partners then, you know!" and I followed Y into the room. The old man waved at the woman then, saying, "Let the musicians start now," and our first ball began. The music did not materialize, but the old man danced solemnly, first with Y and then with me, while the old crone sat dreamily in the corner, swinging the candle in time.

While the old man was dancing with Y, he would wave at me roguishly as they passed, calling out, "Wallflower!" and something that was very like a grin would come over Y. And once when he was dancing with me and we passed Y, sitting on the floor in abject misery, he cried out sternly: "Come now, look gay! Honey catches more flies than vinegar, you know!" And Y actually began to laugh.

No one could possibly say that I enjoyed myself at my first ball. But, you see, I still thought I was lying on Y's bed, dreaming of the picture. Later, when the old man had limped off to bed, after kissing our hands gallantly, Y and I sat on the dining room floor and talked about it. In spite of the icy touch of the old man's fingers which lingered on our hands, in spite of the chill of the stone floor and the memory of the old crone's cackling, we sat there in the dark together and told each other that it was all a horrible dream.

Y said: "I've been here for a long time. I don't know how long. But every night there's been a ball."

I shivered. "He's a lovely dancer," I said.

"Isn't he though," Y agreed. "I know who he is," she said after a few minutes. "He's grandpop-in-law. He died in this house, crazy."

"You might have told me before I came to visit you," I said.

"I thought he'd stay dead," Y said.

We sat there, not talking, until finally the room began to grow lighter, and the dusk in the house was brightened with sunlight. I ran to the window, but Y laughed. "Wait," she said gloomily.

Outside the window I could see the trees that surrounded the old house, and the road down to the gates. Beyond the gates the trees prevented my seeing much, but I did manage to make out light, and color, and . . . the outlines of Y's bed.

Y came over to the window and stood beside me. "Now do you know why I keep saying I'm dreaming?" she demanded.

"But . . ." I turned around and looked at her. "But you aren't," I said.

"No," Y replied after a minute. "I'm not."

We stood close together then, looking out over the trees and the gate, and beyond them, ridiculously, maddeningly, to the room that would mean freedom.

"Y," I said finally, "this isn't true. It's—" I began to laugh, at last. "It's outrageous!" I shouted. And Y began to laugh, too.

And for a time Y and I, hidden away among the trees around the house, planned an escape. "We're completely helpless unless someone comes into the room," Y said, "and we're completely helpless as long as these two old wrecks wander around loose."

"Remember how I thought you were waving me on when I couldn't hear you through the glass," I said.

"But if the old woman hadn't been there . . ."

We looked at each other. "Why is she here?" I said finally. Y shook her head. "It's not as though she wasn't already dead," I began, and finished weakly—"probably . . ."

And that night, while the old man prepared the room for the ball, Y asked him who the woman was. And, "One of your aunts, my dear," he chuckled, pinching Y's cheek, and, "And I never saw a prettier girl, at that." He shook his head sadly. "She's aged a good deal since we've lived here, though. Not so pretty nowadays, are you, old hag!" he screamed suddenly, and ran over to the old woman to give her a shove that sent her rocking back and forth, giggling wildly and nodding her head.

"Has she been here long?" Y asked timidly, but the old man skipped back and forth, pirouetting with exaggerated grace. "No questions, young ladies, no questions! Pretty heads should be empty, you know!"

That was what decided Y and me. The next day our plans were made, and it all had to be done fast. I do not like to remember what we did, and Y swears now that it is all gone from her mind, but I know as well as she does that we stuffed a pillow over the old man's face while he slept, and hanged him to a tree afterward, in an ecstasy of hatred which spent itself on him, and left us little eagerness for the old woman. But we finished it, and never went back to the forest behind the castle, where the two bodies still hang, for all I know. It's as Y said, then: "We don't know if we can kill them, but we do know that if they're not dead, they're still tied up . . ."

And then, weak and happy and laughing, we lay all day in the sun near the gates, waiting for someone to come into the room.

"How long has it been, Y, that we've been held here?"

"A year, I guess—" This muffled, from Y's face hidden in her arms. "Or maybe more."

"It hasn't been more than a week," I said.

"It's been years," Y said again.

And how much longer was it that we waited? The room, which we could see from the gates, had been dismantled. How bitterly we repented of the time spent away from the view of the room, the time lost while someone had taken up the carpets in the room, had taken away the linen and the mattress from the bed, had taken down the curtains and stripped the room bare of everything but dust! Where had we been, and who would come now to an empty and forsaken room? But it was Y, as always, who thought of it first.

"Why didn't they take the picture down, then?" she said. "They've emptied the room and left the picture still hanging!"

"They must know something! They must believe that the picture has something to do with us!"

"They'd know the room was haunted, since two of us disappeared from there . . ." Y began.

"And no one will ever come into it for that reason," I finished.

We were there long enough for the ivy on the house to grow a quarter inch before someone came to rescue us.

We had often speculated as to who would come. Both of us had believed that it would be a stranger, come to see for himself if he could solve the secret of the room, but when our rescuer finally arrived one evening, it was John. I saw him first, while Y slept, and when I woke her to tell her it was John, she cried for the first time since we had given up hope. We lay in the grass before the gates, waiting for the moon to rise so John could see us and let us out.

We watched him put down a blanket on the empty bed, and lie down to stare directly into the picture. In the half-darkness that meant the moon was rising, we saw him lying there, watching for us. And as the moon rose slowly, coming toward the picture, we stood by the gates, clinging to each other and trembling with excitement.

Even before the full light was upon us, we were racing down the road to him, to the glass that he must break. I remember falling once, and stumbling to my feet to run on, with blood on my face and hands, crying out to John, and I believe now that it was during that moment wasted in getting to my feet that I knew exactly, because I heard Y's voice calling, "Come, John, come on, John, come on!" And I knew that I was screaming, too, and shrieking at the top of my lungs.

And John was sitting up in the bed, and screaming, too, and he put up his foot and kicked at the glass and broke it—at last.

And that is how we tell it, Y and I, in the quiet of the night, in the hours of the quiet of the night, with the moonlight moving close, while we wait in the secret of the night, and John runs constantly about the house, screaming and beating the walls. For I have no partner now, in the evenings, and Y and John do not like to dance alone.

The Sorcerer's Apprentice

Miss Matt was at least partially conscious that she looked like the teacher everyone has had for English in first-year high school; she was small and pretty, in a rice-powder fashion, with a great mass of soft dark hair that tried to stay on top of her head and straggled instead down over her ears; her voice was low and turned pleading instead of sharp; any presentable fourteen-year-old bully could pass her course easily. She had read *Silas Marner* aloud almost daily for the past ten years, marked tests in a dainty blue pencil, and still blushed dreadfully at the age of thirty-four.

The year she was twenty-eight she had gone from New York to San Francisco through the Panama Canal with two other teachers from her high school (Gym and General Science), but none of them had found husbands. With her meekest expectations still unsatisfied, Miss Matt lived quietly alone in an inexpensive two-room apartment, with a tiny kitchenette and a Cézanne print over the sofa. She knew her landlady fairly well; they had a cup of tea together occasionally, two refined ladies, in the landlady's first-floor apartment, but in the six years she had lived in her apartment, Miss Matt had not met any of her neighbors.

On Wednesday afternoons, freed early from the high school, Miss Matt came home and straightened her apartment and washed her hair, and then, her head wrapped in a towel, wearing a Chinese silk housecoat, Miss Matt sat down with a peaceful cup of tea and played *Afternoon of a Faun* and *The Sorcerer's Apprentice* on her small portable phonograph. Sometimes, when it had been a hard day at school and the future looked unusually dark, Miss Matt would permit herself to cry luxuriously for half an hour; afterward she would wash her face, and dress and go out to some nice restaurant for dinner.

Miss Matt was crying on the afternoon that Krishna came to see her. There was a sudden vigorous knock on the door, and while Miss Matt was still holding her handkerchief before her in surprise, the door opened a little and a small pretty head hooked curiously around the edge of the door and stayed, regarding Miss Matt.

After a minute Miss Matt walked over to the phonograph and turned off *The Sorcerer's Apprentice*, averting her head so the tears were not completely visible. "Were you looking for me?" Miss Matt asked finally, then added "Dear?" as the visitor was undeniably a female child.

"Marian said I could come in here," the child said.

Miss Matt collected herself and touched the handkerchief delicately to her eyes. "What did you want me for?" she asked. It was the first time in years Miss Matt had spoken to a child younger than the first year of high school, and she felt free to end a sentence with a preposition.

The child opened the door wider and slipped through, closing it behind her. She was carrying a large album of phonograph records, which she deposited carefully on Miss Matt's maple end table.

"Are those *your* records?" Miss Matt asked hesitantly.

"Marian said I could come and ask you if it is all right for me to play them here on your phonograph," the child said. "What's that?" She pointed at the Cézanne.

"It's a picture," Miss Matt said.

"We have pictures too," the child said. "We have pictures of my daddy."

"Won't you sit down?"

The child turned and looked at Miss Matt for a long minute. "All right," she said finally. "What's your name?"

"Miss Matt," Miss Matt said. "You may call me Miss Matt."

"Mine's Krishna," the child said.

"Krishna." Miss Matt sat down and picked up her cup of tea. "Krishna?"

"Krishna Raleigh," the child said. "I'm six years old and I live just downstairs and right underneath here." Both she and Miss Matt looked down at the floor, and then Krishna went on, "Marian said I could come and play my records here."

"Who is Marian?" Miss Matt asked, "and why should she give you permission to come up here?"

"That's my mother, Marian," Krishna said impatiently.

"I think it's all right." Miss Matt tried to make her voice sound a little doubtful, as though she felt enough authority to deny Krishna if she wanted to, but she realized almost immediately that all Krishna thought was that possibly Miss Matt did not own the phonograph either. "What records are they?" Miss Matt asked quickly.

"My daddy's records," Krishna said proudly. "My daddy made them for me and Marian, and you can listen to them if you want to."

Miss Matt stood up and reached for the album, but Krishna said "I'll do it" and ran across the room to put an arm protectingly over the album. "They're *my* records," she said.

"May I look at them?" Miss Matt asked coldly.

"No," Krishna said. She opened the album lovingly and took out the first record. "This is my daddy playing the piano," she said. "Take that other record off the phonograph." Miss Matt went silently and removed *The Sorcerer's Apprentice* and changed the needle while Krishna stood by, impatiently holding her record. "I play the phonograph all the time at home, but now it's broken," she said, "so Marian said I could come and ask you if you would let me hear my daddy's records."

The edge of Krishna's chin came just to the level of the turntable; she was forced, reluctantly, to yield the record to Miss Matt to have it put on the phonograph, and Miss Matt inspected it carefully, turning it over and over, before she placed it onto the turntable. It was a private recording, labeled TOWN HALL, and then, in ink underneath, "James Raleigh, Shostakovich Polka, June, 1940." The other side was smooth and ungrooved; Miss Matt ran her hand over it before she set it down.

"Come *on*," Krishna said finally. "This record has where my daddy talks on it." She waited, her face just at the edge of the phonograph, and when Miss Matt started to put the phonograph arm down on the record, Krishna giggled and said, "*These* records start from the inside, dopey." Miss Matt put the arm down at the center of the record and waited. First there was the sound of applause, and then a short wait, and then a man's voice said faintly ". . . by Shostakovich," and then more applause. "That's my daddy talking," Krishna said. Miss Matt waited respectfully until the piano started and then said, "Is that your father playing?"

"He played all these records," Krishna said. "He plays the piano in concerts." Her voice rose defiantly. "He's the best piano player who ever lived."

Miss Matt sat down on the straight chair next to the phonograph. "Would you like to sit on the couch?" she asked Krishna.

Krishna went over solemnly and sat down on the edge of the couch, and Miss Matt, with the music loud beside her, watched the child curiously. She was a very pretty child, with blond curls and a sweet smile; Miss Matt wondered fleetingly if her father was blond. "Where is your father now?" she asked.

"Shhh," Krishna said, pointing to the phonograph. "He's in the Army."

Miss Matt nodded sympathetically.

"He kills people," Krishna said. "He's over killing Nazis now." She sighed theatrically. "He used to play the piano, and when he's killed all the Nazis he's going to come home and play the piano again."

"He plays beautifully," Miss Matt said softly.

"It's all right," Krishna said. Her eyes wandered around the room and came to rest finally. "What's that thing?"

Miss Matt stood up and lifted the arm of the phonograph from the record. "I thought you wanted to hear your daddy playing," she said.

"What's that thing?" Krishna repeated.

Miss Matt turned. "It's a doll," she said with annoyance. "Do you want to hear the records or not?"

"I want that doll," Krishna said. She slid off the couch and scampered across the room to the doll.

"I bought that doll in a place called Panama," Miss Matt said. "I bought it from a little girl about your age whose mother made lots of dolls like that. I like that doll as well as almost anything I own." She raised her voice slightly. "Shall I continue with the records?"

Krishna was trying to reach for the doll high in the bookcase where Miss Matt kept it; finally she put her foot on the lower shelf, pushing the books back, and reached up on her toes to seize the doll triumphantly. It was a limp thing, with a gourd for a head and a scrap of red silk for a dress. "I'm going to take this doll home," Krishna said.

"That's my doll." Miss Matt forced herself to stand by the phonograph. "Your mother wouldn't like to have you take someone else's things."

"She doesn't care," Krishna said.

"Krishna," Miss Matt said, "You may not have that doll. Put it back, please."

Krishna turned and looked at Miss Matt in surprise. "I want it," she said.

"I won't let you play your daddy's records on the phonograph," Miss Matt warned.

"All right." Krishna was pulling interestedly at the doll's head, twisting the red silk dress. "I heard them lots of times."

Miss Matt walked over and put her hand firmly on the doll. "Give that to me," she demanded.

Krishna began to laugh. She snatched the doll away from Miss Matt and retreated with it across the room. "You're a crazy old woman," she said. "You're an old crazy old woman."

"Go home," Miss Matt said. She took a deep breath to calm herself, and lifted her head. "Go right home. Go home immediately."

"No," Krishna said. "You're a crazy old woman, crazy, crazy." Deliberately holding the doll out in front of her, she ripped off the silk dress and let it fall onto the floor, then snapped off the head. Miss Matt watched Krishna for a minute, her chin trembling, and then she went over to the phonograph and lifted the record off and smashed it onto the floor. "You don't deserve to have a father like that," she said.

Krishna began to laugh again. "Wait till I tell Marian," she said. "Wait till I tell Marian a crazy old woman broke my daddy's best record where he was talking."

"You can tell Marian anything you like," Miss Matt said. For the first time in her life her voice was shrill. "Now you take the rest of these records and get out." She seized Krishna quickly by the shoulder, pinching as hard as she could, and began to push her toward the door, slapping her hands to make her drop the pieces of the doll.

Krishna, still laughing, clung stubbornly to the door frame, bracing her feet against Miss Matt's furious shoving. Miss Matt finally got her into the hall and slammed the door, then took the album of records and set them quickly outside, slamming the door again before Krishna could get back in. Krishna was still laughing when Miss Matt slammed the door for the second time and turned the key, but when the child realized that the door had shut for the last time, her laughter turned suddenly into howls of anger. Miss Matt, leaning against the door on the inside, distinguished the phrase, repeated over and over, "I want that doll!" Finally Miss Matt heard the crying fade away toward the stairs, and the child's voice crying, "Mommy, make her give me that doll!"

I've got to hurry, Miss Matt thought. She stepped quickly around the broken record on the floor to the broken doll, scooped up the dress and then the other pieces, and hesitated, looking around. Finally she went into the kitchenette and opened the cupboard under the sink, and put the pieces of the doll behind the boxes of soap and the dusting cloths. I'll tell them that awful child did it, she was thinking. If I hurry, I can say that child did it all. Still hurrying, she took a brush and a dustpan and went back to the broken record. It had shattered into small pieces, and it took Miss Matt a few precious seconds to gather them up into the dustpan. I'll tell them I'll sue, she was thinking. She emptied the dustpan into a paper bag and put the bag into the sink cupboard with the doll, and then, her house straightened, with no sign left of Krishna's presence, she fluffed up the pillows of the couch and went into her little bedroom, where she dressed hurriedly and carelessly, repeating to herself incoherently: "I'll tell them the child did it, I'll say I'll sue."

She pulled on a hat over her still-damp hair, tucking the straggling ends up under the hat and holding them there with many hairpins. When she put her coat on, she turned up the collar and ducked her head down so her face would be hidden. Then she picked up her pocketbook and went out, closing the door behind her quietly. Go to the movies where it's dark, she was thinking. When she got down the first flight of stairs and was near the door of the apartment directly under hers, she hesitated for a minute before she ran down the hall to the next flight of stairs. Come back later, she thought, when they're all tired of looking for me.

Jack the Ripper

The man hesitated on the corner under the traffic light, then started off down the side street, walking slowly and watching the few people who passed him. It was long past midnight, and the streets were as nearly deserted as they ever get; as the man went down the dark street he stopped for a minute, thinking he saw a dead girl on the sidewalk. She was nearly against the wall of a building; a few feet beyond her was the small sign of a bar, and seeing that, the man started to walk on, and then turned back to the girl.

She was so drunk that when he shook her and tried to sit her up she sagged backward, her eyes half-closed and her hands rolling on the sidewalk. The man stood and looked at her for a minute, and then turned again and went down to the bar. When he opened the door and went in he saw that the place was nearly empty, with only a group of three or four sailors at the farther end of the bar, and the bartender with them, talking and laughing. There was one man standing at the bar near the doorway, and after looking around for a minute, the man who had come in walked over and stood at the end of the bar.

"Listen," he said, "there's a girl lying out on the street outside."

The man farther down the bar looked at him quietly.

"I just happened to be passing down this way," the man who had just come in went on more urgently, "and I saw her, and I think something had better be done. She can't stay out there." The man farther down the bar went on looking. "She isn't but about seventeen."

"There's a phone out back," the man standing down the bar said. "Call the mayor."

The bartender came easily down to the end of the bar, the smile leaving his face as he came. When he got to the end of the bar, beside the man who had just come in, he stood unsmiling, waiting.

"Listen," the man said again, "there's a girl sixteen, seventeen lying outside in the street. We better get her inside."

"Call the mayor," the man down the bar said, "his number's in the book."

"I was just walking by," the man said, "and she was lying there."

"I know," the bartender said.

"Mention my name," the man down the bar said. "Tell him I told you to call."

"I saw that she was nice and comfortable," the bartender said, "and I put her pocketbook beside her, all nice and convenient." He smiled tenderly. "I hope you didn't disturb her," he said.

The man raised his voice slightly. "She can't keep on lying there," he said. "You're not going to say you intend to leave her there?"

"He'll remember me all right," the man down the bar said, nodding. "He won't forget me in a hurry."

"She likes it there," the bartender said. "Sleeps there nearly every night."

"But a girl fifteen, sixteen!" the man cried.

The bartender's voice became harder; he put both hands on the edge of the bar and leaned over toward the man. "Anytime she likes," he said, "she can get up and go home. She doesn't have to stay there. Let her get up and walk home."

"Not in any sort of a hurry he won't," the man down the bar said.

"Comes in here every night and gets drunk," the bartender went on. "I let her have a beer now and then without money, do you want I should rent her a room, too?" He leaned back again and his voice softened. "Sleeps like a baby, don't she?" He turned around abruptly and walked back down the bar to the sailors. "Another drunk," he said to them.

The man turned to the door and opened it, still hesitating. Then he went out. "Don't forget to tell him what I told you," the man down the bar called after him.

When he got back to the girl he saw that she still lay in the same position, face against the sidewalk, with her knees against the wall. Her pocketbook lay on the sidewalk beside her, and the man picked it up and opened it. There was no money; there was a lipstick from the five and ten, and a key, a comb, and a little notebook. The man put everything back except the notebook; he opened it and found, on the first page, the girl's name and address. When he turned the first page he found a list of about twenty bars, with addresses and, in some cases, names of the bartenders. A few pages later he found another list, this time of sailors, each name followed by the name of a ship, and a date, apparently the date of the last time the ship was in New York. The entries were written in a big, childish writing, with uncrossed T's and an occasional misspelling. Toward the end of the notebook, a picture had been put between the pages. It showed the girl with two sailors, one on each side, their heads together, and all three smiling. The girl in the picture looked pleased and unattractive; lying on the ground, she seemed thin and almost lovely. The man put the picture back into the notebook and the notebook back into the pocketbook, and then, carrying the pocketbook, walked down to the corner and waved down a taxi. With the taxi waiting, he went back to the girl, lifted her, and put her in, and then got in after her. The girl was sprawled out on the seat, and the man had to sit on a corner to give her room. He gave the driver the address he had seen in the notebook, and the driver, after raising his eyes once to the mirror to look at the man, shrugged and drove off.

The house was in a bad neighborhood, old and dirty, and the driver, stopping the taxi, said: "This is it, mister." He turned and looked at the girl, and added doubtfully, "Do I help you?"

The man pulled the girl out of the taxi by taking hold of her legs and dragging her until he could put her feet on the ground, and then taking her by the waist and swinging her over his shoulder. He held her over his shoulder while he took change from his pocket to pay the driver, and then, still holding her by the legs, he went into the house.

The hall was lighted by gaslights, and the stairway was incredibly narrow and steep. The man knocked on the first door, first with his knuckles, and then, grimly, with the girl's shoes, swinging her legs back and forth.

From somewhere on the other side of the door, a woman's voice asked, "What is it?" and finally the door opened a crack and the woman put her face out. It was too dark for the man to see what she looked like, but she said: "Who is it? Rose? She lives on the sixth floor. Last door on the right." The door closed again. The man surveyed the stairway and thought. There was no room in the hallway to put the girl down, so he tightened his grip on her legs and started up the stairs. He stopped for breath on every landing, but by the time he reached the sixth floor he was breathing heavily and moving slowly, putting both feet on each step. He leaned against the wall at the top for a minute, trying to shift the girl's weight, and then went down to the last door on the right. Putting the girl down on the floor, he opened her pocketbook and took out the key and opened the door. It was too dark in the hall to see what was in the room, so he lighted a match and went in, trying to find some light. After lighting three matches he found a candle, which he lit and set on the dresser in its own wax. The room was large enough for a cot and the dresser; on the back of the door were three hooks, on which were hanging a torn silk kimono and a pair of dirty stockings. The bed had a blanket on it, over the mattress, and a dirty, uncovered pillow. On the dresser were a few bobby pins and a package of matches. The man opened the four dresser drawers; all of them were empty except for the top one, which contained a bottle opener and a couple of beer bottle caps. When he had examined the room, the man went outside, where he had left the girl, and picked her up under the arms and dragged her into the room. He dumped her onto the bed and threw the blanket over her. He opened her pocketbook and took out the notebook, glancing through it until he found the picture, which he put in his pocket. He put the key on the dresser and the pocketbook beside it, and then, just before blowing out the candle, took out his knife. It had a polished bone handle, and a long and incredibly sharp blade.

*

He took a taxi on the corner near the tenement, giving the driver an address in the east seventies, and was home in a few minutes. When he got out of the elevator in his apartment house he stopped for a minute, looked at his hands and down at his shoes, and carefully took a piece of lint off his sleeve. He let himself into his apartment with his key, and walked softly into the bedroom. When he turned on the light his wife stirred in her bed, and then opened her eyes. "What time is it?" she murmured.

"Late," he said. He went over and kissed her.

"What kept you so long?" she asked.

"I stopped and had a few drinks after the meeting," he said. He went over to the dresser to put down his keys, and looked at his wife's picture in the tall plastic frame. Reaching in his pocket, he found the picture of the girl with the two sailors and thought for a minute; then he went to his wife's dressing table, and with her plastic-handled nail scissors cut the two sailors out of the picture, leaving the girl alone. This fragment of picture he put into the lower corner of the frame holding his wife's picture. He lighted a cigarette and stood looking at it.

"Aren't you coming to bed?" his wife asked sleepily.

"No," he said. "Believe I'll take a bath."

The Beautiful Stranger

What might be called the first intimation of strangeness occurred at the railroad station. She had come with her children, Smalljohn and her baby girl, to meet her husband when he returned from a business trip to Boston. Because she had been oddly afraid of being late, and perhaps even seeming uneager to encounter her husband after a week's separation, she dressed the children and put them into the car at home a long half-hour before the train was due. As a result, of course, they had to wait interminably at the station, and what was to have been a charmingly staged reunion, family embracing husband and father, became at last an ill-timed and awkward performance. Smalljohn's hair was mussed, and he was sticky. The baby was cross, pulling at her pink bonnet and her dainty lace-edged dress, whining. The final arrival of the train caught them in mid-movement, as it were; Margaret was tying the ribbons on the baby's bonnet, Smalljohn was half over the back of the car seat. They scrambled out of the car, cringing from the sound of the train, hopelessly out of sorts.

John Senior waved from the high steps of the train. Unlike his wife and children, he looked utterly prepared for his return, as though he had taken some pains to secure a meeting at least pain-less, and had, in fact, stood just so, waving cordially from the steps of the train, for perhaps as long as half an hour, ensuring that he should not be caught half-ready, his hand not lifted so far as to over-emphasize the extent of his delight in seeing them again.

His wife had an odd sense of lost time. Standing now on the platform with the baby in her arms and Smalljohn beside her, she could not for a minute remember clearly whether he was coming home, or whether they were yet standing here to say good-by to him. They had been quarreling when he left, and she had spent the week of his absence determining to forget that in his presence she had been frightened and hurt. This will be a good time to get things straight, she had been telling herself; while John is gone I can try to get hold of myself again. Now, unsure at last whether this was an arrival or a departure, she felt afraid again, straining to meet an unendurable tension. This will not do, she thought, believing that she was being honest with herself, and as he came down the train steps and walked toward them she smiled, holding the baby tightly against her so that the touch of its small warmth might bring some genuine tenderness into her smile.

This will not do, she thought, and smiled more cordially and told him "hello" as he came to her. Wondering, she kissed him and then when he held his arm around her and the baby for a minute the baby pulled back and struggled, screaming. Everyone moved in anger, and the baby kicked and screamed, "No, no, no."

"What a way to say hello to Daddy," Margaret said, and she shook the baby, half-amused, and yet grateful for the baby's sympathetic support. John turned to Smalljohn and lifted him, Smalljohn kicking and laughing helplessly. "Daddy, Daddy," Smalljohn shouted, and the baby screamed, "No, no."

Helplessly, because no one could talk with the baby screaming so, they turned and went to the car. When the baby was back in her pink basket in the car, and Smalljohn was settled with another lollipop beside her, there was an appalling quiet which would have to be filled as quickly as possible with meaningful words. John had taken the driver's seat in the car while Margaret was quieting the baby, and when Margaret got in beside him she felt a little chill of animosity at the sight of his hands on the wheel; I can't bear to relinquish even this much, she thought; for a week no one has driven the car except me. Because she could see so clearly that this was unreasonable—John owned half the car, after all—she said to him with bright interest, "And how was your trip? The weather?"

"Wonderful," he said, and again she was angered at the warmth in his tone; if she was unreasonable about the car, he was surely unreasonable to have enjoyed himself quite so much. "Everything went very well. I'm pretty sure I got the contract, everyone was very pleasant about it, and I go back in two weeks to settle everything."

The stinger is in the tail, she thought. He wouldn't tell it all so hastily if he didn't want me to miss half of it; I am supposed to be pleased that he got the contract and that everyone was so pleasant, and the part about going back is supposed to slip past me painlessly.

"Maybe I can go with you, then," she said. "Your mother will take the children."

"Fine," he said, but it was much too late; he had hesitated notice-ably before he spoke.

"I want to go too," said Smalljohn. "Can I go with Daddy?"

They came into their house, Margaret carrying the baby, and John carrying his suitcase and arguing delightedly with Smalljohn over which of them was carrying the heavier weight of it. The house was ready for them; Margaret had made sure that it was cleaned and emptied of the qualities which attached so surely to her posi-tion of wife alone with small children; the toys which Smalljohn had thrown around with unusual freedom were picked up, the baby's clothes (no one, after all, came to call when John was gone) were taken from the kitchen radiator where they had been drying. Aside from the fact that the house gave no impression of waiting for any particular people, but only for anyone well-bred and clean enough to fit within its small trim walls, it could have passed for a home, Margaret thought, even for a home where a happy family lived in domestic peace. She set the baby down in the playpen and turned with the baby's bonnet and jacket in her hand and saw her husband, head bent gravely as he listened to Smalljohn. Who? she wondered suddenly; is he taller? That is not my husband.

She laughed, and they turned to her, Smalljohn curious, and her husband with a quick bright recognition; she thought, why, it is *not* my husband, and he knows that I have seen it. There was no astonishment in her; she would have thought perhaps thirty seconds before that such a thing was impossible, but since it was now clearly possible, surprise would have been meaningless. Some other emotion was necessary, but she found at first only peripheral manifestations of one. Her heart was beating violently, her hands were shaking, and her fingers were cold. Her legs felt weak and she took hold of the back of a chair to steady herself. She found that she was still laughing, and then her emotion caught up with her and she knew what it was: it was relief.

"I'm glad you came," she said. She went over and put her head against his shoulder. "It was hard to say hello in the station," she said.

Smalljohn looked on for a minute and then wandered off to his toybox. Margaret was thinking, this is not the man who enjoyed seeing me cry; I need not be afraid. She caught her breath and was quiet; there was nothing that needed saying.

For the rest of the day she was happy. There was a constant delight in the relief from her weight of fear and unhappiness, it was pure joy to know that there was no longer any residue of suspicion and hatred; when she called him "John" she did so demurely, knowing that he participated in her secret amusement; when he answered her civilly there was, she thought, an edge of laughter behind his words. They seemed to have agreed soberly that mention of the subject would be in bad taste, might even, in fact, endanger their pleasure.

They were hilarious at dinner. John would not have made her a cocktail, but when she came downstairs from putting the children to bed the stranger met her at the foot of the stairs, smiling up at her, and took her arm to lead her into the living room where the cocktail shaker and glasses stood on the low table before the fire.

"How nice," she said, happy that she had taken a moment to brush her hair and put on fresh lipstick, happy that the coffee table which she had chosen with John and the fireplace which had seen many fires built by John and the low sofa where John had slept sometimes, had all seen fit to welcome the stranger with grace. She sat on the sofa and smiled at him when he handed her a glass; there was an odd illicit excitement in all of it; she was "entertaining" a man. The scene was a little marred by the fact that he had given her a martini with neither olive nor onion; it was the way she preferred her martini, and yet he should not have, strictly, known this, but she reassured herself with the thought that naturally he would have taken some pains to inform himself before coming.

He lifted his glass to her with a smile; he is here only because I am here, she thought.

"It's nice to be here," he said. He had, then, made one attempt to sound like John, in the car coming home. After he knew that she had recognized him for a stranger, he had never made any attempt to say words like "coming home" or "getting back," and of course she could not, not without pointing her lie. She put her hand in his and lay back against the sofa, looking into the fire.

"Being lonely is worse than anything in the world," she said.

"You're not lonely now?"

"Are you going away?"

"Not unless you come too." They laughed at his parody of John.

They sat next to each other at dinner; she and John had always sat at formal opposite ends of the table, asking one another politely to pass the salt and the butter.

"I'm going to put in a little set of shelves over there," he said, nodding toward the corner of the dining room. "It looks empty here, and it needs things. Symbols."

"Like?" She liked to look at him; his hair, she thought, was a little darker than John's, and his hands were stronger; this man would build whatever he decided he wanted built.

"We need things together. Things we like, both of us. Small delicate pretty things. Ivory."

With John she would have felt it necessary to remark at once that they could not afford such delicate pretty things, and put a cold finish to the idea, but with the stranger she said, "We'd have to look for them; not everything would be right."

"I saw a little creature once," he said. "Like a tiny little man, only colored all purple and blue and gold."

She remembered this conversation; it contained the truth like a jewel set in the evening. Much later, she was to tell herself that it was true; John could not have said these things.

★

She was happy, she was radiant, she had no conscience. He went obediently to his office the next morning, saying good-by at the door with a rueful smile that seemed to mock the present necessity for doing the things that John always did, and as she watched him go down the walk she reflected that this was surely not going to be permanent; she could not endure having him gone for so long every day, although she had felt little about parting from John; moreover, if he kept doing John's things he might grow imperceptibly more like John. We will simply have to go away, she thought. She was pleased, seeing him get into the car; she would gladly share with him—indeed, give him outright—all that had been John's, so long as he stayed her stranger.

She laughed while she did her housework and dressed the baby. She took satisfaction in unpacking his suitcase, which he had abandoned and forgotten in a corner of the bedroom, as though prepared to take it up and leave again if she had not been as he thought her, had not wanted him to stay. She put away his clothes, so disarmingly like John's, and wondered for a minute at the closet; would there be a kind of delicacy in him about John's things? Then she told herself no, not so long as he began with John's wife, and laughed again.

The baby was cross all day, but when Smalljohn came home from nursery school his first question was—looking up eagerly— "Where is Daddy?"

"Daddy has gone to the office," and again she laughed, at the moment's quick sly picture of the insult to John.

Half a dozen times during the day she went upstairs, to look at his suitcase and touch the leather softly. She glanced constantly as she passed through the dining room into the corner where the small shelves would be someday, and told herself that they would find a tiny little man, all purple and blue and gold, to stand on the shelves and guard them from intrusion.

When the children awakened from their naps she took them for a walk and then, away from the house and returned violently to her former lonely pattern (walk with the children, talk meaninglessly of Daddy, long for someone to talk to in the evening ahead, restrain herself from hurrying home: he might have telephoned), she began to feel frightened again; suppose she had been wrong? It could not be possible that she was mistaken; it would be unutterably cruel for John to come home tonight.

Then, she heard the car stop and when she opened the door and looked up she thought, no, it is not my husband, with a return of gladness. She was aware from his smile that he had perceived her doubts, and yet he was so clearly a stranger that, seeing him, she had no need of speaking.

She asked him, instead, almost meaningless questions during that evening, and his answers were important only because she was storing them away to reassure herself while he was away. She asked him what was the name of their Shakespeare professor in college, and who was that girl he liked so before he met Margaret. When he smiled and said that he had no idea, that he would not recognize the name if she told him, she was in delight. He had not bothered to master all of the past, then; he had learned enough (the names of the children, the location of the house, how she liked her cocktails) to get to her, and after that, it was not important, because either she would want him to stay, or she would, calling upon John, send him away again.

"What is your favorite food?" she asked him. "Are you fond of fishing? Did you ever have a dog?"

"Someone told me today," he said once, "that he had heard I was back from Boston, and I distinctly thought he said that he heard I was dead in Boston."

He was lonely, too, she thought with sadness, and that is why he came, bringing a destiny with him: now I will see him come every evening through the door and think, this is not my husband, and wait for him remembering that I am waiting for a stranger.

"At any rate," she said, "*you* were not dead in Boston, and nothing else matters."

She saw him leave in the morning with a warm pride, and she did her housework and dressed the baby; when Smalljohn came home from nursery school he did not ask, but looked with quick searching eyes and then sighed. While the children were taking their naps she thought that she might take them to the park this afternoon, and then the thought of another such afternoon, another long afternoon with no one but the children, another afternoon of widowhood, was more than she could submit to; I have done this too much, she thought, I must see something today beyond the faces of my children. No one should be so much alone.

Moving quickly, she dressed and set the house to rights. She called a high school girl and asked if she would take the children to the park; without guilt, she neglected the thousand small orders regarding the proper jacket for the baby, whether Smalljohn might have popcorn, when to bring them home. She fled, thinking, I must be with people.

She took a taxi into town, because it seemed to her that the only possible thing to do was to seek out a gift for him, her first gift to him, and she thought she would find him, perhaps, a little creature all blue and purple and gold.

She wandered through the strange shops in the town, choosing small lovely things to stand on the new shelves, looking long and critically at ivories, at small statues, at brightly colored meaningless expensive toys, suitable for giving to a stranger.

It was almost dark when she started home, carrying her packages. She looked from the window of the taxi into the dark streets, and thought with pleasure that the stranger would be home before her, and look from the window to see her hurrying to him; he would think, this is a stranger, I am waiting for a stranger, as he saw her coming. "Here," she said, tapping on the glass, "right here, driver." She got out of the taxi and paid the driver, and smiled as he drove away. I must look well, she thought, the driver smiled back at me.

She turned and started for the house, and then hesitated; surely she had come too far? This is not possible, she thought, this cannot be; surely our house was white?

The evening was very dark, and she could see only the houses going in rows, with more rows beyond them and more rows beyond that, and somewhere a house which was hers, with the beautiful stranger inside, and she lost out here.

All She Said Was Yes

What can you do? Howard and Dorrie are always telling me I'm too sensitive, and let myself get worked up about things, but really, even Howard had to admit that the Lansons' accident just couldn't have happened at a worse time. It sounds awful when you come right out and say it, but I'd always rather be frank and open than mealy-mouthed, and even though it was a dreadful thing to happen *any*time, it really made me *furious* to have our trip to Maine ruined.

We'd lived next door to Don and Helen Lanson for sixteen years, since before our Dorrie and their Vicky were born, and of course, living next door and with the girls growing up together, we'd always been friendly enough, even though you don't have to get along with people *all* the time, and frankly, some of the crowd the Lansons knew were a little too fancy for us. Besides, they were never secret about things and expected us to be the same, and it bothered me sometimes when I stopped to think that for sixteen years we hadn't had a day's privacy; I like friendly neighbors as well as the next one, but it was a little too much, sometimes. I used to tell Howard that Helen Lanson always knew what we were having for dinner, and of course it worked the other way around, too; whenever the Lansons had one of their fights we had to close the windows and go down to the cellar to keep from hearing, and even then Helen Lanson was sure to be over the next morning to cry on my shoulder. I hope the new neighbors are a little more—well—reticent.

Howard and I felt terrible when it happened, naturally. Howard went out with the State Police, and I offered to go over and tell Vicky. It wasn't the kind of thing I relished, you can imagine, but someone had to do it, and I'd known her since she was born. I was thankful that Dorrie was away at camp, because *she* would have been heartbroken, living next door to them all her life. When I went over to ring the doorbell that night I really couldn't think how the child was going to take it; I never did think much of parents going out and leaving a fifteen-year-old girl alone in the house—you read all the time about men breaking into houses where girls are alone—but I supposed Helen always figured Vicky was all right with us home next door; we certainly don't go out nearly every night like the Lansons did.

But then, Vicky was never much of a one for minding things, anyway; I know that she opened the door that night right away, without even asking who it was or making sure it wasn't some man; I never let Dorrie open the door at night unless she knows who is on the other side. Well, I might as well come right out with it—I don't *like* Vicky. Even that night, with all the trouble ahead for her, I couldn't make myself like her. I was terribly sorry for her, certainly, and at the same time all I could keep thinking was what I was going to do when she heard the news. She was so big and clumsy and ugly that I really couldn't face the thought of having to put my arms around her and comfort her—I hated the idea of patting her hand, or stroking her hair, and yet I was the only person to do it. All the way over from our house I had been wondering how I was going to say it, and then when she opened the door and just stood there looking at me—and never a "hello" or anything from her; she just wasn't the kind who offered things, if you know what I mean—I almost lost my courage. Finally I asked her if I could come in, because I had to talk to her, and she only opened the door wider and stood away, and I came in and she closed the door behind me and stood there waiting. Well, I know that house almost as well as I know my own, and so I walked into the living room and sat down and she came along after me and sat down, too, and looked at me.

Well, there was nothing like getting right to it, so I tried to say something gentle first; what I finally settled on was looking very serious and saying, "Vicky, you're going to have to be brave."

I must say she didn't help me much. She just sat there looking at me, and I suddenly thought that maybe all the unusual excitement, with Howard driving off in the middle of the night like that, and all the lights on in our house and my coming over the way I did, might have let on to her that something was wrong, and she might even have guessed already that it had to do with her parents, so the sooner she heard the truth, the better, I thought, and I said, "There's been an accident, Vicky. Corporal Atkins of the State Police phoned us a few minutes ago, because he knew you were alone here and he wanted someone to be with you." It wasn't much of a way to go about it, I know, but I would much rather have sat there talking all around the subject than tell her what I had to say next. I took a deep breath and said, "It's your mother and father, Vicky. There's been an accident."

Well, so far she hadn't said a word, not a single word since I came through the door, and now all she said was, "Yes."

I thought it must be shock, and I was glad that Howard had thought to call Doctor Hart before he left, to come and help me with Vicky, and I began to wonder how long it would be before the doctor came, because I'm simply no good with sick people, and would be sure to do the wrong thing. I was thinking about the doctor, and I said, "They always drove too fast—" and she said, "I know." I sat there waiting for her to cry, or whatever a girl like that does when she finds out her parents have been killed, and then I remembered that she didn't know yet that they were killed, but only that they had been in an accident, so I took another deep breath and said, "They're both—" I couldn't say it, though, just couldn't bring out the word. Finally I said, "Gone."

"I know," she said. So I needn't have worried.

"We're so sorry, Vicky," I said, wondering if now was the time to go over and pat her head.

"Do you think they really believed they were going to die?" she asked me.

"Well, I guess no one ever really *believes* . . ." I started to say, but she wasn't listening to me; she was looking down at her hands and shaking her head. "I told them, you know," she said. "I told my mother a couple of months ago that it was going to happen, the accident and their dying, but she wouldn't listen to me, no one ever does. She said it was an adolescent fantasy."

Well, that was Helen Lanson for you, of course. *Adolescent fantasy* is the way she talked, and pretended she was being honest with the child. It wasn't any of my business, of course, but I can tell you that Dorrie got spanked when she did something wrong, and none of this psychological jargon to make her think it was my fault, either. "I guess everybody told them," I said to Vicky. "You can't drive the way they did without asking for trouble. I spoke to Helen about it once myself—"

"That's when I got over being sad," she said, as though she thought she ought to excuse herself. "I told her, and she wouldn't believe me. I even told her I'd have to go and live with Aunt Cynthia in London, England." She smiled at me. "I'm going to like London, England; I'll go to a big school there and study hard."

Well, as far as I knew, Aunt Cynthia in London, England, hadn't even been notified yet, but if this child could sit there coolly not five minutes after hearing that her parents had been killed in an accident and make plans for her future—well, all I could say is that maybe some of Helen Lanson's psychology paid off, in a way she might not like so much, and I just hope that if ever anything happens to me, *my* daughter will have the grace to sit there and shed a tear. Although it's probably kinder to believe that Vicky was in shock.

"It's a terrible thing," I said, wondering how long before the doctor could make it.

"Aunt Cynthia will get here on Tuesday," she said to me. "The first plane will have to turn back because of engine trouble. I'm sorry about your trip to Maine."

I was touched. Here was this girl, after the most terrible disaster that can happen to a child, and she could spare a thought for our trip to Maine. It was certainly just the worst luck in the world for us, but you can't always expect a child to see things from a grown-up's point of view, and even if the news about her parents didn't bring a tear, I was pleased to see that the girl could still feel for somebody.

"Try not to worry about it," I told her. Of course we just couldn't take off for Maine the morning after our next-door neighbors had been killed in an accident, but there was no point in Vicky's bothering about that, too. "Please don't be upset," I said.

"You won't be able to go later in the year because it will be too cold at the lodge. You'll have to go somewhere else, but please don't go on a boat. Please?"

"Of course not," I said; I didn't want the doctor to come in and find us talking about my worries, so I said, "You'll come over and stay with us until your aunt comes."

"In Dorrie's room," she said.

Well, I hadn't really planned anything yet, but of course Dorrie's room was the best place for her; you never know when you're going to need the guest room for company, and Dorrie would be away at camp for the next two weeks. "We'll pretend that you're my little girl for a while," I said, and wondered if it was the right thing to say—it certainly sounded silly enough—and then thought that after all, I had had as much of a shock as she had, and then I heard the doctor's car outside and I confess it was a relief. I still don't think it was natural for a child to sit there and listen to news like that and not even jump.

I left her with the doctor and went upstairs—as I say, I know that house as well as I know my own—and tried to find some things for her to bring over with her; I could come over in the morning and get anything she wanted, of course, so I just took a pair of clean pajamas out of the drawer and one of her good school dresses out of the closet; she was going to have to see a good many people in the next day or so and there was no harm in her looking as neat and clean as I could make her. I got her toothbrush out of the bathroom—and I'm no stickler for housework, but I'd be ashamed to keep a bathroom the way Helen Lanson did—and then I thought that maybe she had some kind of a toy dog or doll or something to comfort her; Dorrie may be fifteen years old, but she still has a little blue lion I gave her when she was small, and you can always tell when Dorrie's upset about something because she takes her blue lion to bed with her. But in this girl's room there was nothing.

You would have been shocked. Books, of course, and a picture of her mother and father, and a set of paints and a game or so, but nothing . . . well, soft. I finally lifted her pillow and underneath it was a little notebook with a red cover, like a school notebook or something, and since it was under her pillow I thought it must be something she valued—I've seen Dorrie's diary under her pillow, like that, and even though of course I've never looked inside it I know how excited she gets if she thinks someone's gotten to it. I thought maybe Vicky might want to keep this little book safe, so I folded it in with the nightgown and a pair of clean socks, and after thinking for a minute (after all, wouldn't I want someone to do the same for Dorrie?) I took the picture of her mother and father and put that in, too. When I went downstairs she was still sitting there and the doctor was sitting with her, and when I came in he looked at me and shrugged, so I suppose he hadn't gotten any more tears from her than I had. I went out into the hall with the doctor and he said he had given her a sedative and I said I was taking her right next door and would put her to sleep in Dorrie's bed. "She doesn't seem to care one way or another," I told him.

"Sometimes it takes a while," he said. "It's a terrible thing; too much, probably, for her mind to take in all at once. I expect that by tomorrow she'll be feeling it more, and I'll stop in and see her in the morning."

Well, I saw that all the lights were turned out and the doors locked and then I took Vicky's things and we went next door and it was a relief to me to be back in my own house, even though I admit I felt a good twinge when I saw our suitcases all packed and standing in the hall. We had planned to get a good early start in the morning, and now here I had to unpack everything again. I asked Vicky if she would like a cup of cocoa and she said yes—I never did see that girl when she wouldn't eat—so I left her in the kitchen with her cocoa and a piece of my good chocolate cake and I went upstairs and fixed up Dorrie's room for her. I took out a lot of Dorrie's things because somehow—and I don't want to sound nasty, but it's true—you couldn't think of that great dull girl sleeping with Dorrie's pretty little pictures and dolls and necklaces and dance souvenirs all around her; she fit in Dorrie's room like Dorrie would fit in a dollhouse. I made the bed all neat, and I put on Dorrie's blue comforter, because it would have to be cleaned anyway before Dorrie came home, and then I brought her upstairs and waited while she got undressed. When I went in to tuck her in I had made up my mind of course that I wasn't going to be hesitant or anything, and I was going to kiss her good night, because after all the girl was alone in the world now, except for the kindness of neighbors who took her in. When I came in she was in bed and I think the doctor's sedative—or my hot cocoa—was affecting her, because she looked sleepy and kind of full, like a big cat that's had a mouse. She looked much too big for Dorrie's bed, I can tell you that. She was trying to be brave, though; when she turned her head on the pillow and looked at me she gave a little smile, and I thought maybe she was getting ready to cry, but she only said, "I *did* tell them. I've known about it for two months."

"I'm sure of it," I said. "Try not to think about it anymore tonight."

"They wouldn't believe me."

"Well, it certainly wasn't your fault, and it won't do you any good to keep brooding on it; right now you've got to sleep."

"I knew all about it," she said.

"Shh," I said. I turned out the light, and went over to kiss her good night and she looked up at me and said, "Don't go in any boats." She had some strange connection in that odd mind between me and boats; she must have mentioned it half a dozen times during those first few days, when her thoughts were so confused and dazed. I suppose she had heard something, or perhaps Helen and Don had said something—maybe one of the last things they said to her; people always remember something like that—and it could have been about me; they talked about us enough, heaven knows. Anyway, I told her not to worry about boats anymore, that everything was going to be all right, and I finally leaned over and gave her a little kiss on that big white forehead and said, "Good night."

"Good night," she said. I turned on Dorrie's night-light in case she should wake up in the night and forget she was in Dorrie's room and then closed the door and came downstairs to wait for Howard.

When he came in he was feeling pretty awful, so I made him some cocoa and while he had it we sat and talked about our trip to Maine. "There's certainly no chance of it *now*," I told him. "The girl's right upstairs. We can't do a thing until the aunt comes."

"They notified the aunt," Howard said. "Sent a cable from the police station."

"What makes me hopping mad is having to unpack the bags. And my nice green sweater I bought just for the trip."

"Well, it wouldn't look very good if we just took off and left the girl alone."

"No," I said. "It's a terrible thing," I told him, "a terrible thing to happen *anytime*, of course, but wouldn't you just *know* they'd go and do it now?"

"No help for it. We'll have to try and plan something else. Is she asleep?"

"I think she must be. I gave her some cocoa. You know, that's another thing that bothers me. That girl hasn't cried a single tear."

"Kids like that sometimes feel it worse inside."

"Maybe," but I didn't think so. "No early start tomorrow, I guess."

I really felt like crying, seeing Howard take those suitcases upstairs, but he told me to cheer up. "It's rotten bad luck," he said, "but we'll think of something else."

There was a lot to do the next day. First, I had to unpack those suitcases and put everything away so it wouldn't wrinkle. Also, I thought I kind of ought to go over to the Lansons' and straighten up—Helen Lanson always left things in a mess, and I certainly wouldn't have been surprised to find her dinner dishes still dirty in her sink; that girl wouldn't lift a finger to wash them, I know now, after having her in my house. Not one thing did she do. I can't quite picture Helen Lanson picking up after her, so I guess Vicky kept that room of hers at home looking so swept and bare, but in my house she never made Dorrie's bed once, never got out of her chair to take a dish to the kitchen, never offered to dust or vacuum even though half the mess was on her account.

I had to forgive her, of course, because of the sad blow she'd had, but I'd just like to see my Dorrie act like that no matter *what* happened. I mean, even if I was dead it would give me comfort to know that my daughter didn't forget her training, and the nice manners I taught her.

Half the time Vicky never bothered to answer at all when she was spoken to. That morning I asked her what she wanted me to bring her back from her own house and she just looked at me. Maybe there was nothing there she wanted. I just decided the aunt would have to look over everything. Helen Lanson had some lovely china, and a set of wineglasses I would have given my right arm to own; she'd inherited them from her grandmother, and you'd think even a child like Vicky would have some sense of their value, but when I mentioned them and said how much I coveted them, she only stared at me. I straightened things up around the Lansons' house and got some clothes for Vicky, and then locked everything up tight and brought the keys home and set them on the mantel, where I could find them right away when the aunt came. If I had been another kind of person, I could have those wineglasses today and no one would ever have known.

I was pretty sure that along during the day people would be coming in; the Lansons being as popular as they were, it seemed a lot of their friends might drop over to see if Vicky was all right and I wasn't starving her or beating her or something. You'd think with all the friends the Lansons had, someone might have come forward to take the girl so we wouldn't be tied down with her, but of course we were right on the spot when someone was needed, and as Howard said, it still wouldn't look right to go off so soon. The doctor said Vicky was fine; she spent most of the morning up in Dorrie's room reading Dorrie's books, and after lunch I told her to dress nicely and comb her hair and come downstairs to sit. I just wanted her there looking proper if anyone came; lucky she had a dark dress to wear. Mrs. Wright came by early; she lived down the street and had only just heard. She was kind of sniffling, with a handkerchief over her face most of the time, and she patted Vicky's hand and said it was heartbreaking, just heartbreaking, and Vicky looked at her. After a minute or so of this she gave up and followed me out to the kitchen to get a cup of tea and said, "Has she been like this ever since *it* happened?"

"No," I said. "All night she was asleep."

"Has she been crying?"

"Not a single tear."

I got the cups out; one thing about Mrs. Wright, you don't get off easy. Tea and chocolate cake were the least she expected, and I supposed if the Lansons' fancy friends dropped around later it would mean cocktails and potato chips and crackers and olives and whatnot. "It's a heartbreaking thing," Mrs. Wright kept saying, "simply heartbreaking. Were they killed instantly?"

"I suppose so. I don't know anything about it." I knew what she wanted to ask me, but I wasn't going to help her out. It's not good for people to think about such things; I never asked Howard a word about it and he never offered to tell me, because I always think that a person has enough everyday troubles without going looking for the horrible details of what happens to other people. "They hit a truck," I said. "That's all I know."

"Anyway, it will be in the paper tonight. That poor little girl. Who told her? You? How did she take it?"

"About as you'd expect," I said. I didn't want Mrs. Wright blaming *me* for the way Vicky acted; she might think I'd broken the news wrong, or something, so I started back into the living room with the tea tray and of course she had to follow me and couldn't ask any more about it with Vicky sitting right there. She tried to make bright conversation instead, I guess to cheer Vicky a little, although I could have told her to save her breath.

She told about Mrs. Haven at the grocery forgetting her lamb chops and how the grocer had to come down from his dinner and open the store for her and she told about the Actons' cat getting run over, but she stopped herself in the middle of that and looked at Vicky to see if she had said anything wrong and then she started quickly to tell about her grandson, who just got admitted to medical school.

"He's going to be a doctor," she explained.

"He'll be caught with a girl in his room and expelled pretty soon," Vicky said suddenly.

"Vicky!" I said. I couldn't think of anything decent to say; I mean, I couldn't punish her, her not being my child and all, but I did think I ought to do something, with Mrs. Wright sitting there with her mouth open. "Young ladies should speak politely in company, Vicky," I said. Dorrie would never have said a thing like that about Mrs. Wright's grandson.

"I'll overlook it," Mrs. Wright said, "considering your present circumstances, Vicky, although you ought not to have that kind of thought with your parents lying there—" She stopped, and took out her handkerchief again, and Vicky stared at the wall, and I thought it would be a pleasure to tan that young lady's hide.

Later some of the Lansons' friends did come, as I expected, and it was cocktails and potato chips and crackers and pickles and everything; we could have had a party of our own, and invited our own friends, for what it cost us to entertain the Lansons' friends, although I must say that one of the men took the Lansons' keys and went over and got a bottle of gin because, he said, it was the least the Lansons would want us to do, and I thought that was probably true. Everyone tried to say something nice to Vicky, but it was hard. I heard one conversation that shocked me, because if I heard Dorrie talking like that to her elders, I would have washed her mouth out with soap. A Mr. Sherman, whom I hadn't met before, was telling her what a fine man her father had been—I suppose he thought he ought to, although anyone who knew Don Lanson knew better—and Vicky came right out and said, in that flat voice of hers, "Your wife finally has the evidence to divorce you." You can imagine how that sounded, right to an old friend of her father's, and he was surprised to hear it, you could tell; I don't think my Dorrie even knows the *word* divorce. Later I heard her telling her father's lawyer that the papers in his office were going to be burned up in a big fire; he had been talking to her about her father's will, and I suppose somehow the idea of a will got through to her—a little thing like that will, sometimes, you know—so she reacted like a spiteful baby. I thought it was extremely rude of her, driving her father's friends out of my house like that, and I was going to tell her so, but there was always someone there talking to her, patting her hand and telling her to be brave. Tell Vicky to be brave—tell the ocean to keep rolling.

Well, it was like that till her aunt came. She was delayed getting here—some trouble with the plane—and so she missed the funeral, but I saw that Vicky was there in a dark-blue dress and black shoes and her hair combed, and all, and never a tear did that child shed. They had a nice attendance, I must say. You would have thought the Lansons were the most popular people in town, but I suppose people thought it was a friendly gesture to Vicky, and of course since Howard and I were kind of in charge, I guess a lot of people came out of courtesy to us. Once during the ceremony Vicky leaned over toward me and whispered, "You see that man over there, the one with the bald head and the gray suit? He stole some money and they're going to put him in jail," which I thought a disrespectful and silly remark to make during her parents' own funeral, particularly since a lot of people thought she was getting overcome and looked to see if I was going to have to take her out.

The day the aunt arrived was the day of the big fire downtown that destroyed almost a whole block of offices, so I didn't have a chance to introduce her to many of the people who had been dropping in nearly every day. I had Vicky's clothes all clean and neat—I could hardly send her home dirty, after all—and packed ready to take back. I must say I wasn't sorry to see that girl turned over to her own relatives; it was hard, having her in Dorrie's room all the time, and Howard was getting so he could hardly eat, looking at her sitting there at the dinner table every night and stuffing herself. The night before she went to her aunt—they were going to stay next door for a day or so, arranging for things to be sold and to be stored and to be given away, and I must say I had half an idea that the aunt might have thought of me when it came to the wineglasses, Vicky knowing how I wanted them so much, and after all I'd done—the night before she left, when I went in to say good night, she gave me her little red notebook. "This is for you," she said. "I want you to have it because you've been so kind to me."

Well, it was the only word of thanks I was ever to get. Not one word was ever said about those wineglasses. I knew she prized the little book and thought she was giving me something precious, so I took it. "Stay away from boats," she said, and I laughed at her, I really had to, and then she told me to take good care of the little book and of course I promised her I would.

"I'll remember you when I'm in London, England," she said. "Tell Dorrie to write to me sometimes."

"I surely will," I said. Dorrie is the sweetest child in the world, and if she thought it would give Vicky any pleasure to get a letter from her, she'd sit right down. "Now, good night," I said. I had gotten used to kissing her good night, but I never looked forward to it.

"Good night," she said, and went right off to sleep, as she always did. Well, they left, and I hear the house has been sold and someone new was coming to live there. I took a look at Vicky's little red notebook, thinking it might be a little book of poems like Dorrie gave me once, or even pictures of something, but I was disappointed; the child had been amusing herself writing gossipy little paragraphs about her neighbors and her parents' friends—although what else would you expect, considering the way Don and Helen used to talk about people?—and horror tales about atom bombs and the end of the world, not at all the kind of thing you like to think about a child dwelling on; I wouldn't have Dorrie thinking about things like that, and I threw the little book in the furnace. She must have been a very lonely child, I thought, to spend her time writing sad little stories. I hope she's as happy in London as she expected to be, and meanwhile we've decided what we're going to do to make up for our lost trip to Maine. We'll keep Dorrie out of school for a couple of weeks—she's always at the top; she can miss a little work—and we're all going to go on a cruise.

What a Thought

Dinner had been good. Margaret sat with her book on her lap and watched her husband digesting, an operation to which he always gave much time and thought. As she watched he put his cigar down without looking and used his free hand to turn the page of his paper. Margaret found herself thinking with some pride that unlike many men she had heard about, her husband did not fall asleep after a particularly good dinner.

She flipped the pages of her book idly; it was not interesting. She knew that if she asked her husband to take her to a movie, or out for a ride, or to play gin rummy, he would smile at her and agree; he was always willing to do things to please her, still, after ten years of marriage. An odd thought crossed her mind: she would pick up the heavy glass ashtray and smash her husband over the head with it.

"Like to go to a movie?" her husband asked.

"I don't think so, thanks," Margaret said. "Why?"

"You look sort of bored," her husband said.

"Were you watching me?" Margaret asked. "I thought you were reading."

"Just looked at you for a minute." He smiled at her, the smile of a man who is still, after ten years of marriage, very fond of his wife.

The idea of smashing the glass ashtray over her husband's head had never before occurred to Margaret, but now it would not leave her mind. She stirred uneasily in her chair, thinking: what a terrible thought to have, whatever made me think of such a thing? Probably a perverted affectionate gesture, and she laughed.

"Funny?" her husband asked.

"Nothing," Margaret said.

She stood up and crossed the room to the hall door, without purpose. She was very uneasy, and looking at her husband did not help. The cord that held the curtains back made her think: strangle him. She told herself: it's not that I don't love him, I just feel morbid tonight. As though something bad were going to happen. A telegram coming, or the refrigerator breaking down. Drown him, the goldfish bowl suggested.

Look, Margaret told herself severely, standing just outside the hall door so that her husband would not see her if he looked up from his paper, look, this is perfectly ridiculous. The idea of a grown woman troubling herself with silly fears like that—it's like being afraid of ghosts, or something. *Nothing* is going to happen to him, Margaret, she said almost aloud; *nothing* can happen to hurt either you or your husband or anyone you love. You are perfectly safe.

"Margaret?" her husband called.

"Yes?"

"Is something wrong?"

"No, dear," Margaret said. "Just getting a drink of water."

Poison him? Push him in front of a car? A train?

I don't *want* to kill my husband, Margaret said to herself. I never *dreamed* of killing him. I want him to live. Stop it, stop it.

She got her drink of water, a little formality she played out with herself because she had told him she was going to do it, and then wandered back into the living room and sat down. He looked up as she entered.

"You seem very restless tonight," he said.

"It's the weather, I guess," Margaret said. "Heat always bothers me."

"Sure you wouldn't like to go to a movie?" he said. "Or we could go for a ride, cool off."

"No, thanks," she said. "I'll go to bed early."

"Good idea," he said.

What would I do without him? she wondered. How would I live, who would ever marry me, where would I go? What would I do with all the furniture, crying when I saw his picture, burning his old letters? I could give his suits away, but what would I do with the house? Who would take care of the income tax? I love my husband, Margaret told herself emphatically; I *must* stop thinking like this. It's like an idiot tune running through my head.

She got up again to turn the radio on; the flat voice of the announcer offended her and she turned the radio off again, passing beyond it to the bookcase. She took down a book and then another, leafing through them without seeing the pages, thinking: it isn't as though I had a motive; they'd never catch me. Why would I kill my husband? She could see herself saying tearfully to an imaginary police lieutenant: "But I loved him—I can't *stand* his being dead!"

"Margaret," her husband said. "Are you worried about something?"

"No, dear," she said. "Why?"

"You really seem terribly upset tonight. Are you feverish?"

"No," she said. "A chill, if anything."

"Come over here and let me feel your forehead."

She came obediently, and bent down for him to put his hand on her forehead. At his cool touch she thought, Oh, the dear, good man; and wanted to cry at what she had been thinking.

"You're right," he said. "Your head feels cold. Better go on off to bed."

"In a little while," she said. "I'm not tired yet."

"Shall I make you a drink?" he asked. "Or something like lemonade?"

"Thank you very much, dear," she said. "But no thanks."

They say if you soak a cigarette in water overnight the water will be almost pure nicotine by morning, and deadly poisonous. You can put it in coffee and it won't taste.

"Shall I make *you* some coffee?" she asked, surprising herself.

He looked up again, frowning. "I just had two cups for dinner," he said. "But thanks just the same."

I'm brave enough to go through with it, Margaret thought; what will it all matter a hundred years from now? I'll be dead, too, by then, and who cares about the furniture?

She began to think concretely. A burglar. First call a doctor, then the police, then her brother-in-law and her own sister. Tell them all the same thing, her voice broken with tears. It would not be necessary to worry about preparations; the more elaborately these things were planned, the better chance of making a mistake. She could get out of it without being caught if she thought of it in a broad perspective and not as a matter of small details. Once she started worrying about things like fingerprints she was lost. Whatever you worry about catches you, every time.

"Have you any enemies?" she asked her husband, not meaning to.

"Enemies," he said. For a moment he took her seriously, and then he smiled and said, "I suppose I have hundreds. Secret ones."

"I didn't mean to ask you that," she said, surprising herself again.

"Why would I have enemies?" he asked, suddenly serious again, and setting down his paper. "What makes you think I have enemies, Margaret?"

"It was silly of me," she said. "A silly thought." She smiled and after a minute he smiled again.

"I suppose the milkman hates me," he said. "I always forget to leave the bottles out."

The milkman would hardly do; he knew it, and he would not help her. Her glance rested on the glass ashtray, glittering and colored in the light from the reading lamp; she had washed the ashtray that morning and nothing had occurred to her about it then. Now she thought: it ought to be the ashtray; the first idea is always the best.

She rose for the third time and came around to lean on the back of his chair; the ashtray was on the table to her right, now, and she bent down and kissed the top of his head.

"I never loved you more," she said, and he reached up without looking to touch her hair affectionately.

Carefully she took his cigar out of the ashtray and set it on the table. For a minute he did not notice and then, as he reached for his cigar, he saw that it was on the table and picked it up quickly, touching the table underneath to see if it had burned. "Set fire to the house," he said casually. When he was looking at the paper again she picked up the ashtray silently.

"I don't want to," she said as she struck him.

The Bus

Old Miss Harper was going home, although the night was wet and nasty. Miss Harper disliked traveling at any time, and she particularly disliked traveling on this dirty small bus which was her only way of getting home; she had frequently complained to the bus company about their service because it seemed that no matter where she wanted to go, they had no respectable bus to carry her. Getting away from home was bad enough—Miss Harper was fond of pointing out to the bus company—but getting home always seemed very close to impossible. Tonight Miss Harper had no choice: if she did not go home by this particular bus she could not go for another day. Annoyed, tired, depressed, she tapped irritably on the counter of the little tobacco store which served also as the bus station. Sir, she was thinking, beginning her letter of complaint, although I am an elderly lady of modest circumstances and must curtail my fondness for travel, let me point out that your bus service falls far below . . .

Outside, the bus stirred noisily, clearly not anxious to be moving; Miss Harper thought she could already hear the weary sound of its springs sinking out of shape. I just can't make this trip again, Miss Harper thought, even seeing Stephanie isn't worth it, they really go out of their way to make you uncomfortable. "Can I get my ticket, please?" she said sharply, and the old man at the other end of the counter put down his paper and gave her a look of hatred.

Miss Harper ordered her ticket, deploring her own cross voice, and the old man slapped it down on the counter in front of her and said, "You got three minutes before the bus leaves."

He'd love to tell me I missed it, Miss Harper thought, and made a point of counting her change.

The rain was beating down, and Miss Harper hurried the few exposed steps to the door of the bus. The driver was slow in opening the door and as Miss Harper climbed in she was thinking, Sir, I shall never travel with your company again. Your ticket salesmen are ugly, your drivers are surly, your vehicles indescribably filthy . . .

There were already several people sitting in the bus, and Miss Harper wondered where they could possibly be going; were there really this many small towns served only by this bus? Were there really other people who would endure this kind of trip to get somewhere, even home? I'm very out of sorts, Miss Harper thought, very out of sorts; it's too strenuous a visit for a woman of my age; I need to get home. She thought of a hot bath and a cup of tea and her own bed, and sighed. No one offered to help her put her suitcase on the rack, and she glanced over her shoulder at the driver sitting with his back turned and thought, he'd probably rather put me off the bus than help me, and then, perceiving her own ill nature, smiled. The bus company might write a letter of complaint about *me*, she told herself and felt better. She had providentially taken a sleeping pill before leaving for the bus station, hoping to sleep through as much of the trip as possible, and at last, sitting near the back, she promised herself that it would not be unbearably long before she had a bath and a cup of tea, and tried to compose the bus company's letter of complaint. Madam, a lady of your experience and advanced age ought surely to be aware of the problems confronting a poor but honest little company which wants only . . .

She was aware that the bus had started, because she was rocked and bounced in her seat, and the feeling of rattling and throbbing beneath the soles of her shoes stayed with her even when she slept at last. She lay back uneasily, her head resting on the seat back, moving back and forth with the motion of the bus, and around her other people slept, or spoke softly, or stared blankly out the windows at the passing lights and the rain.

Sometime during her sleep Miss Harper was jostled by someone moving into the seat behind her, her head was pushed and her hat disarranged; for a minute, bewildered by sleep, Miss Harper clutched at her hat, and said vaguely, "Who?"

"Go back to sleep," a young voice said, and giggled. "I'm just running away from home, that's all."

Miss Harper was not awake, but she opened her eyes a little and looked up to the ceiling of the bus. "That's wrong," Miss Harper said as clearly as she could. "That's wrong. Go back."

There was another giggle. "Too late," the voice said. "Go back to sleep."

Miss Harper did. She slept uncomfortably and awkwardly, her mouth a little open. Sometime, perhaps an hour later, her head was jostled again and the voice said, "I think I'm going to get off here. 'By now."

"You'll be sorry," Miss Harper said, asleep. "Go back."

Then, still later, the bus driver was shaking her. "Look, lady," he was saying, "I'm not an alarm clock. Wake up and get off the bus."

"What?" Miss Harper stirred, opened her eyes, felt for her pocketbook.

"I'm not an alarm clock," the driver said. His voice was harsh and tired. "I'm not an alarm clock. Get off the bus."

"What?" said Miss Harper again.

"This is as far as you go. You got a ticket to here. You've arrived. And I am not an alarm clock waking up people to tell them when it's time to get off; you got here, lady, and it's not part of my job to carry you off the bus. I'm not—"

"I intend to report you," Miss Harper said, awake. She felt for her pocketbook and found it in her lap, moved her feet, straightened her hat. She was stiff and moving was difficult.

"Report me. But from somewhere else. I got a bus to run. Now will you please get off so I can go on my way?"

His voice was loud, and Miss Harper was sickeningly aware of faces turned toward her from along the bus, grins, amused comments. The driver turned and stamped off down the bus to his seat, saying, "She thinks I'm an alarm clock," and Miss Harper, without assistance and moving clumsily, took down her suitcase and struggled with it down the aisle. Her suitcase banged against seats, and she knew that people were staring at her; she was terribly afraid that she might stumble and fall.

"I'll certainly report you," she said to the driver, who shrugged.

"Come on, lady," he said. "It's the middle of the night and I got a bus to run."

"You ought to be *ashamed* of yourself," Miss Harper said wildly, wanting to cry.

"Lady," the driver said with elaborate patience, "please get off my bus."

The door was open, and Miss Harper eased herself and her suitcase onto the steep step. "She thinks everyone's an alarm clock, got to see she gets off the bus," the driver said behind her, and Miss Harper stepped onto the ground. Suitcase, pocketbook, gloves, hat; she had them all. She had barely taken stock when the bus started with a jerk, almost throwing her backward, and Miss Harper, for the first time in her life, wanted to run and shake her fist at someone. I'll report him, she thought, I'll see that he loses his job, and then she realized that she was in the wrong place.

Standing quite still in the rain and the darkness Miss Harper became aware that she was not at the bus corner of her town where the bus should have left her. She was on an empty crossroads in the rain. There were no stores, no lights, no taxis, no people. There was nothing, in fact, but a wet dirt road under her feet and a signpost where two roads came together. Don't panic, Miss Harper told herself, almost whispering, don't panic; it's all right, it's all right, you'll see that it's all right, don't be frightened.

She took a few steps in the direction the bus had gone, but it was out of sight and when Miss Harper called falteringly, "Come back," and, "Help," there was no answer to the shocking sound of her own voice out loud except the steady drive of the rain. I sound old, she thought, but I will not panic. She turned in a circle, her suitcase in her hand, and told herself, don't panic, it's all right.

There was no shelter in sight, but the signpost said RICKET'S LANDING; so that's where I am, Miss Harper thought, I've come to

Ricket's Landing and I don't like it here. She set her suitcase down next to the signpost and tried to see down the road; perhaps there might be a house, or even some kind of a barn or shed where she could get out of the rain. She was crying a little, and lost and hopeless, saying Please, won't someone come? when she saw headlights far off down the road and realized that someone was really coming to help her. She ran to the middle of the road and stood waving, her gloves wet and her pocketbook draggled. "Here," she called, "here I am, please come and help me."

Through the sound of the rain she could hear the motor, and then the headlights caught her and, suddenly embarrassed, she put her pocketbook in front of her face while the lights were on her. The lights belonged to a small truck, and it came to an abrupt stop beside her and the window near her was rolled down and a man's voice said furiously, "You want to get killed? You trying to get killed or something? What you doing in the middle of the road, trying to get killed?" The young man turned and spoke to the driver. "It's some dame. Running out in the road like that."

"Please," Miss Harper said, as he seemed almost about to close the window again, "please help me. The bus put me off here when it wasn't my stop and I'm lost."

"Lost?" The young man laughed richly. "First I ever heard anyone getting lost in Ricket's Landing. Mostly they have trouble *finding* it." He laughed again, and the driver, leaning forward over the steering wheel to look curiously at Miss Harper, laughed too. Miss Harper put on a willing smile, and said, "Can you take me somewhere? Perhaps a bus station?"

"No bus station." The young man shook his head profoundly. "Bus comes through here every night, stops if he's got any passengers."

"Well," Miss Harper's voice rose in spite of herself; she was suddenly afraid of antagonizing these young men; perhaps they might even leave her here where they found her, in the wet and dark. "Please," she said, "can I get in with you, out of the rain?"

The two young men looked at each other. "Take her down to the old lady's," one of them said.

"She's pretty wet to get in the truck," the other one said.

"Please," Miss Harper said, "I'll be glad to pay you what I can."

"We'll take you to the old lady," the driver said. "Come on, move over," he said to the other young man.

"Wait, my suitcase." Miss Harper ran back to the signpost, no longer caring how she must look, stumbling about in the rain, and brought her suitcase over to the truck.

"That's awful wet," the young man said. He opened the door and took the suitcase from Miss Harper. "I'll just throw it in the back," he said, and turned and tossed the suitcase into the back of the truck; Miss Harper heard the sodden thud of its landing, and wondered what things would look like when she unpacked; my bottle of cologne, she thought despairingly. "Get *in*," the young man said, and, "My God, you're wet."

Miss Harper had never climbed up into a truck before, and her skirt was tight and her gloves slippery from the rain. Without help from the young man she put one knee on the high step and somehow hoisted herself in; this cannot be happening to me, she thought clearly. The young man pulled away fastidiously as Miss Harper slid onto the seat next to him.

"You are pretty wet," the driver said, leaning over the wheel to look around at Miss Harper. "Why were you out in the rain like that?"

"The bus driver." Miss Harper began to peel off her gloves; somehow she had to make an attempt to dry herself. "He told me it was my stop."

"That would be Johnny Talbot," the driver said to the other young man. "He drives that bus."

"Well, I'm going to report him," Miss Harper said. There was a little silence in the truck, and then the driver said, "Johnny's a good guy. He means all right."

"He's a bad bus driver," Miss Harper said sharply.

The truck did not move. "You don't want to report old Johnny," the driver said.

"I most certainly—" Miss Harper began, and then stopped. Where am I? she thought, what is happening to me? "No," she said at last, "I won't report old Johnny."

The driver started the truck, and they moved slowly down the road, through the mud and the rain. The windshield wipers swept back and forth hypnotically, there was a narrow line of light ahead from their headlights, and Miss Harper thought, what is happening to me? She stirred, and the young man next to her caught his breath irritably and drew back. "She's soaking wet," he said to the driver. "I'm wet already."

"We're going down to the old lady's," the driver said. "She'll know what to do."

"What old lady?" Miss Harper did not dare to move, even turn her head. "Is there any kind of a bus station? Or even a taxi?"

"You could," the driver said consideringly, "you could wait and catch that same bus tomorrow night when it goes through. Johnny'll be driving her."

"I just want to get home as soon as possible," Miss Harper said. The truck seat was dreadfully uncomfortable, she felt steamy and sticky and chilled through, and home seemed so far away that perhaps it did not exist at all.

"Just down the road a mile or so," the driver said reassuringly.

"I've never heard of Ricket's Landing," Miss Harper said. "I can't imagine how he came to put me off there."

"Maybe somebody else was supposed to get off there and he thought it was you by mistake." This deduction seemed to tax the young man's mind to the utmost, because he said, "See, someone else might of been supposed to get off instead of you."

"Then *he's* still on the bus," said the driver, and they were both silent, appalled.

Ahead of them a light flickered, showing dimly through the rain, and the driver pointed and said, "There, that's where we're going." As they came closer Miss Harper was aware of a growing dismay. The light belonged to what seemed to be a roadhouse, and Miss Harper had never been inside a roadhouse in her life. The house itself was only a dim shape looming in the darkness, and the light, over the side door, illuminated only a sign, hanging crooked, which read BEER BAR & GRILL.

"Is there anywhere else I could go?" Miss Harper asked timidly, clutching her pocketbook. "I'm not at all sure, you know, that I ought—"

"Not many people here tonight," the driver said, turning the truck into the driveway and pulling up in the parking lot which had once, Miss Harper was sad to see, been a garden. "Rain, probably."

Peering through the window and the rain, Miss Harper felt, suddenly, a warm stir of recognition, of welcome; it's the house, she thought, why, of course, the house is lovely. It had clearly been an old mansion once, solidly and handsomely built, with the balance and style that belonged to a good house of an older time. "Why?" Miss Harper asked, wanting to know why such a good house should have a light tacked on over the side door, and a sign hanging crooked but saying BEER BAR & GRILL; "Why?" asked Miss Harper, but the driver said, "This is where you wanted to go. Get her suitcase," he told the other young man.

"In here?" asked Miss Harper, feeling a kind of indignation on behalf of the fine old house, "into this saloon?" Why, I used to live in a house like this, she thought, what are they doing to our old houses?

The driver laughed. "You'll be safe," he said.

Carrying her suitcase and her pocketbook Miss Harper followed the two young men to the lighted door and passed under the crooked sign. Shameful, she thought, they haven't even bothered to take care of the place; it needs paint and tightening all around and probably a new roof, and then the driver said, "Come on, come on," and pushed open the heavy door.

"I used to live in a house like this," Miss Harper said, and the young men laughed.

"I bet you did," one of them said, and Miss Harper stopped in the doorway, staring, and realized how strange she must have sounded. Where there had certainly once been comfortable rooms, high-ceilinged and square, with tall doors and polished floors, there was now one large dirty room, with a counter running along one side and half a dozen battered tables; there was a jukebox in a corner and torn linoleum on the floor. "Oh, no," Miss Harper said. The room smelled unpleasant, and the rain slapped against the bare windows.

Sitting around the tables and standing around the jukebox were perhaps a dozen young people, resembling the two who had brought Miss Harper here, all looking oddly alike, all talking and laughing flatly. Miss Harper leaned back against the door; for a minute she thought they were laughing about her. She was wet and disheartened and these noisy people did not belong at all in the old house. Then the driver turned and gestured to her. "Come and meet the old lady," he said, and then, to the room at large, "Look, we brought company."

"Please," Miss Harper said, but no one had given her more than a glance. With her suitcase and her pocketbook she followed the two young men across to the counter; her suitcase bumped against her legs and she thought, I must not fall down.

"Belle, Belle," the driver said, "look at the stray cat we found."

An enormous woman swung around in her seat at the end of the counter, and looked at Miss Harper; looking up and down, looking at the suitcase and Miss Harper's wet hat and wet shoes, looking at Miss Harper's pocketbook and gloves squeezed in her hand, the woman seemed hardly to move her eyes; it was almost as though she absorbed Miss Harper without any particular effort. "Hell you say," the woman said at last. Her voice was surprisingly soft. "Hell you say."

"She's wet," the second young man said; the two young men stood one on either side of Miss Harper, presenting her, and the enormous woman looked her up and down. "Please," Miss Harper said; here was a woman at least, someone who might understand and sympathize, "please, they put me off my bus at the wrong stop and I can't seem to find my way home. Please."

"Hell you say," the woman said, and laughed, a gentle laugh. "She sure is wet," she said.

"Please," Miss Harper said.

"You'll take care of her?" the driver asked. He turned and smiled down at Miss Harper, obviously waiting, and, remembering, Miss

Harper fumbled in her pocketbook for her wallet. How much, she was wondering, not wanting to ask, it was such a short ride, but if they hadn't come I might have gotten pneumonia, and paid all those doctor's bills; I have caught cold, she thought with great clarity, and chose two five-dollar bills from her wallet. They can't argue over five dollars each, she thought, and sneezed. The two young men and the large woman were watching her with great interest, and all of them saw that after Miss Harper took out the two five-dollar bills there were a single and two tens left in the wallet. The money was not wet. I suppose I should be grateful for that, Miss Harper thought, moving slowly. She handed a five-dollar bill to each young man and felt that they glanced at one another over her head.

"Thanks," the driver said; I could have gotten away with a dollar each, Miss Harper thought. "Thanks," the driver said again, and the other young man said, "Say, thanks."

"Thank *you*," Miss Harper said formally.

"I'll put you up for the night," the woman said. "You can sleep here. Go tomorrow." She looked Miss Harper up and down again. "Dry off a little," she said.

"Is there anywhere else?" Then, afraid that this might seem ungracious, Miss Harper said, "I mean, is there any way of going on tonight? I don't want to impose."

"We got rooms for rent." The woman half turned back to the counter. "Cost you ten for the night."

She's leaving me bus fare home, Miss Harper thought; I suppose I should be grateful. "I'd better, I guess," she said, taking out her wallet again. "I mean, thank you."

The woman accepted the bill and half turned back to the counter. "Upstairs," she said. "Take your choice. No one's around." She glanced sideways at Miss Harper. "I'll see you get a cup of coffee in the morning. I wouldn't turn a dog out without a cup of coffee."

"Thank you." Miss Harper knew where the staircase would be, and she turned and, carrying her suitcase and her pocketbook, went to what had once been the front hall and there was the staircase, so lovely in its still proportions that she caught her breath. She turned back and saw the large woman staring at her, and said, "I used to live in a house like this. Built about the same time, I guess. One of those good old houses that were made to stand forever, and where people—"

"Hell you say," the woman said, and turned back to the counter.

The young people scattered around the big room were talking; in one corner a group surrounded the two who had brought Miss Harper and now and then they laughed. Miss Harper was touched with a little sadness now, looking at them, so at home in the big ugly room which had once been so beautiful. It would be nice, she thought, to speak to these young people, perhaps even become their friend, talk and laugh with them; perhaps they might like to know that this spot where they came together had been a lady's drawing room. Hesitating a little, Miss Harper wondered if she might call "Good night," or "Thank you" again, or even "God bless you all." Then, since no one looked at her, she started up the stairs. Halfway there was a landing with a stained-glass window, and Miss Harper stopped, holding her breath. When she had been a child the stained-glass window on the stair landing in her house had caught the sunlight, and scattered it on the stairs in a hundred colors. Fairyland colors, Miss Harper thought, remembering; I wonder why we don't live in these houses now. I'm lonely, Miss Harper thought, and then she thought, but I must get out of these wet clothes; I really am catching cold.

Without thinking she turned at the top of the stairs and went to the front room on the left; that had always been her room. The door was open and she glanced in; this was clearly a bedroom for rent, and it was ugly and drab and cheap. The light turned on with a cord hanging beside the door, and Miss Harper stood in the doorway, saddened by the peeling wallpaper and the sagging floor; what have they done to the house, she thought; how can I sleep here tonight?

At last she moved to cross the room and set her suitcase on the bed. I must get dry, she told herself, I must make the best of things. The bed was correctly placed, between the two front windows, but the mattress was stiff and lumpy, and Miss Harper was frightened at the faint smell of dark couplings and a remote echo in the springs; I will not think about such things, Miss Harper thought, I will not let myself dwell on any such thing; this might be the room where I slept as a girl. The windows were almost right—two across the front, two at the side—and the door was placed correctly; how they did build these old places to a square-cut pattern, Miss Harper thought, how they did put them together; there must be a thousand houses all over the country built exactly like this. The closet, however, was on the wrong side. Some oddness of construction had set the closet to Miss Harper's right as she sat on the bed, when it ought really to have been on her left; when she was a girl the big closet had been her playhouse and her hiding place, but it had been on the left.

The bathroom was wrong, too, but that was less important. Miss Harper had thought wistfully of a hot tub before she slept, but a glance at the bathtub discouraged her; she could simply wait until she got home. She washed her face and hands, and the warm water comforted her. She was further comforted to find that her bottle of cologne had not broken in her suitcase and that nothing inside had gotten wet. At least she could sleep in a dry nightgown, although in a cold bed.

She shivered once in the cold sheets, remembering a child's bed. She lay in the darkness with her eyes open, wondering at last where she was and how she had gotten here: first the bus and then the truck, and now she lay in the darkness and no one knew where she was or what was to become of her. She had only her suitcase and a little money in her pocketbook; she did not know where she was. She was very tired and she thought that perhaps the sleeping pill she had taken much earlier had still not quite worn off; perhaps the sleeping pill had been affecting all her actions, since she had been following docilely, bemused, wherever she was taken; in the morning, she told herself sleepily, I'll show them I can make decisions for myself.

The noise downstairs which had been a jukebox and adolescent laughter faded softly into a distant melody; my mother is singing in the drawing room, Miss Harper thought, and the company is sitting on the stiff little chairs listening; my father is playing the piano. She could not quite distinguish the song, but it was one she had heard her mother sing many times; I could creep out to the top of the stairs and listen, she thought, and then became aware that there was a rustling in the closet, but the closet was on the wrong side, on the right instead of the left. It is more a rattling than rustling, Miss Harper thought, wanting to listen to her mother singing, it is as though something wooden were being shaken around. Shall I get out of bed and quiet it so I can hear the singing? Am I too warm and comfortable, am I too sleepy?

The closet was on the wrong side, but the rattling continued, just loud enough to be irritating, and at last, knowing she would never sleep until it stopped, Miss Harper swung her legs over the side of the bed and, sleepily, padded barefoot over to the closet door, reminding herself to go to the right instead of the left.

"What are you doing in there?" she asked aloud, and opened the door. There was just enough light for her to see that it was a wooden snake, head lifted, stirring and rattling itself against the other toys. Miss Harper laughed. "It's my snake," she said aloud, "it's my old snake, and it's come alive." In the back of the closet she could see her old toy clown, bright and cheerful, and as she watched, enchanted, the toy clown flopped languidly forward and back, coming alive. At Miss Harper's feet the snake moved blindly, clattering against a doll house where the tiny people inside stirred, and against a set of blocks, which fell and crashed. Then Miss Harper saw the big beautiful doll sitting on a small chair, the doll with long golden curls and wide-lashed blue eyes and a stiff organdy party dress; as Miss Harper held out her hands in joy the doll opened her eyes and stood up.

"Rosabelle," Miss Harper cried out, "Rosabelle, it's me."

The doll turned, looking widely at her, smile painted on. The red lips opened and the doll quacked, outrageously, a flat slapping voice coming out of that fair mouth. "Go away, old lady," the doll said, "go away, old lady, go away."

Miss Harper backed away, staring. The clown tumbled and danced, mouthing at Miss Harper, the snake flung its eyeless head viciously at her ankles, and the doll turned, holding her skirts, and her mouth opened and shut. "Go away," she quacked, "go away, old lady, go away."

The inside of the closet was all alive; a small doll ran madly from side to side, the animals paraded solemnly down the gangplank of Noah's ark, a stuffed bear wheezed asthmatically. The noise was louder and louder, and then Miss Harper realized that they were all looking at her hatefully and moving toward her. The doll said "Old lady, old lady," and stepped forward; Miss Harper slammed the closet door and leaned against it. Behind her the snake crashed against the door and the doll's voice went on and on. Crying out, Miss Harper turned and fled, but the closet was on the wrong side and she turned the wrong way and found herself cowering against the far wall with the door impossibly far away while the closet door slowly opened and the doll's face, smiling, looked for her.

Miss Harper fled. Without stopping to look behind she flung herself across the room and through the door, down the hall and on down the wide lovely stairway. "Mommy," she screamed, "Mommy, Mommy."

Screaming, she fled out the door. "Mommy," she cried, and fell, going down and down into darkness, turning, trying to catch onto something solid and real, crying.

"Look, lady," the bus driver said. "I'm not an alarm clock. Wake up and get off the bus."

"You'll be sorry," Miss Harper said distinctly.

"Wake up," he said, "wake up and get off the bus."

"I intend to report you," Miss Harper said. Pocketbook, gloves, hat, suitcase.

"I'll certainly report you," she said, almost crying.

"This is as far as you go," the driver said.

The bus lurched, moved, and Miss Harper almost stumbled in the driving rain, her suitcase at her feet, under the sign reading RICKET'S LANDING.

Family Treasures

Anne Waite was a most unfortunate girl, although she was, of all the girls living in the small women's dormitory, the only one who might not be persuaded to agree that she was unfortunate. More than any of the other girls in the house, Anne felt herself to be free and unconfined, accepting the ordinary regulations of institutional community life as a concession to the authorities, rather than as an imposed obligation. The university was large, and Anne was small, yet the university was more strictly bound by iron rules than Anne, and was, on the whole, Anne would have said, more unfortunate. The university authorities had been brought to recognize Anne particularly because of the death of her mother during the last term of her freshman year; Anne, returning to college as a sophomore, was without one surviving relative except for the university. Her college education had been paid for in advance, along with a regular, although small, allowance, that duly provided for—in case the university should not extend its paternal benevolence—the purchase of Anne's clothes.

The university provided Anne with a small, fairly well-maintained room in one of its more comfortable living centers, where, as did fifteen other girls, Anne had a bed and a chair and a desk and a dresser. She was required to present herself for breakfast at seven, arrive promptly upon call at fire drill, and be in the house with the front door locked behind her no later than eleven on weeknights, twelve on Saturdays. She was also required to be reasonably friendly with the other girls, a friendship in no cases to extend to extreme devotion, pointed whispering in the dining hall, or sleeping two in one bed; she was expected to rise when the house mother entered the room, and be decently civil to the maids.

Anne's mother had died shortly after the end of the football season, and long before the season of spring dances, and although Anne was at that time a shy and rather friendless girl, everyone in the house, from the house mother to the three girls on the first floor who had received permission to set up a darkroom in the first-floor bathroom for developing photographs, had sought Anne out either in the gloomy weather before she had set out for home, or in the bright warm days that followed immediately after her return, to offer both sympathy and a quick, friendly curiosity for details of the funeral. Anne had a vague comprehension, although naturally she could never investigate the fact fully, that several of the girls—Helena, for instance, on the second floor, and Cheryl, who was of course the house president—who had sat with her, choking up and saying "I know how I'd feel if it was *my* moth—" before dissolving into tears with her, had gone directly from Anne to dates with well-dressed boys who parked their cars, as a matter of hallowed custom, on the hill near the lake, where Cheryl certainly, and Helena probably, had sat laughing, and drinking beer, and what else?, Anne wondered.

Anne minded none of this particularly; what she did mind, and found insulting, was the immediate decrease of her value in the eyes of the other girls in the house shortly after her mother was buried. It was no longer in good taste to commiserate with Anne, because, as was generally known, Anne was Trying to be Brave. With her bravery clearly established by her anonymity, Anne faded back into the colorless girl on the third floor who lived alone, had no friends, and rarely spoke.

It was too much to hope, naturally, that Cheryl and Helena would introduce Anne to any of their young men just because her mother had died, or that the three girls on the first floor would allow her to develop pictures in their bathroom darkroom, but Anne had cherished a hope, along with so many other people to whom sudden and unusual things have happened, that after it was all over she might be changed—her face a little prettier, perhaps, or her hair a more decided color, or at *least* an interesting sadness in her manner, and the ability to think quickly and effortlessly of things to say when she passed the other girls in the hall.

At the beginning, then, of her sophomore year at the university, Anne was doing as well as might be expected in her studies, had an unblemished record at fire drill, could certainly not be accused of any disproportionate friendships, and was, in fact, very little better off after her mother's death at all.

It did not take long for Anne to recognize this, since she was, in her silent and veiled manner, very agile; consequently it was in only about the third week of the school year that Anne stole Helena's ankle bracelet and hid it in her mother's trunk. It went under her mother's books and papers and the ancient fur cape, which was of no value but had become Anne's in the disposal of Anne's mother's private things, during which the bank holding all of Anne's money had, with the air of an impersonal machine humanizing itself through a sentimental understanding of a small detail, sent it neatly wrapped to Anne as a memento.

Helena's ankle bracelet was of solid gold, and had been given to Helena by a young man in whom she no longer had any profitable interest. Anne had seen it during the glorious days of her bereavement, in a blue china trinket box on Helena's dresser, where it would be difficult to discover its loss casually out of the mess of necklaces and compacts and odd little items donated to Helena by various young men whose names Helena could remember easily when she looked over their honorary insignia in the box on her dresser, although in most cases she had forgotten the occasions when she had received her trophies. The ankle bracelet was neither the greatest nor the least of Helena's treasures, and Anne, stealing it and hiding it safely away, was confident that in all the mixture of young men's gifts in the box, Helena would forever be unable to recall the name on the ankle bracelet without its presence to remind her.

One evening, several days after the ankle bracelet had joined Anne's mother's fur cape in the trunk in Anne's closet, Anne passed Helena's room, full of noise and chatter, with six or seven girls inside, and after hesitating for a minute in the doorway, she slipped inside and sat down on the floor near the door. Although everyone noticed her and greeted her amiably enough, no one asked her any questions or addressed any particular remarks to her; nor did the tenor of their conversation change materially with her entrance. While Anne was there, Helena several times consulted the trinket box, twice to put things away and once to determine the year in which a young man under discussion had made the university's scholastic honorary society. Not in all this evening did Helena notice that she no longer had one of her gold ankle bracelets.

The day on which a notice appeared on the dormitory bulletin board announcing the date of the university's winter dance, Anne went quietly, in her slippers, into Cheryl's room while she was in class. In the top drawer of Cheryl's desk—Anne had seen it before—was an inexpensive black pen-and-pencil set, which, in its particular box, had been awarded to Cheryl when she graduated from high school by the members of her class, whom, as class president, she had inspired to be exactly the same as every other class graduated from that academy. Anne had heard Cheryl telling about the pen-and-pencil set (the pen no longer worked) with becoming modesty: they had voted her most likely to succeed, and given her the pen-and-pencil set, and there were shy little jokes about the great books she had been expected to write with the pen and the great pictures she had been expected to sketch with the pencil but how, as a matter of fact, she used neither, although she was the house president and a member of the senior council of the university. Along with her name, on both the pen and pencil, was written "Voted Most Likely to Succeed."

Anne put the pen-and-pencil set with the ankle bracelet, on the bottom of her mother's trunk, and if Cheryl noticed that it was gone, she said nothing to Anne about it, although Anne had taken of late to joining the other girls in the living room after the house was closed for the night, where, in pajamas and bathrobes, they drank Cokes ordered from a neighboring drugstore and ate sandwiches barely inferior to the college food.

There was a girl named Maggie, who was accounted a great wit, and from her room Anne stole a stuffed gray bear that Maggie ordinarily kept securely hidden under her pillow; by the time the bear had settled comfortably into Anne's mother's trunk, Maggie had probably discovered her loss but, after a noble battle with herself, had apparently decided to say nothing about it, but to sharpen her sarcasms against the world until her errant bear should return, wending his individual way back as he had taken his secret way of going.

Anne's usual method was to watch, pressing herself softly against the slight crack in the door of her third-floor room, or leaning back beside a window with the curtain before her, until the girl whose room she had chosen to violate had left the house. Then, wearing felt slippers and usually a bathrobe over her clothes, and sometimes carrying a bath towel to avert suspicion and to cover any bulky objects, Anne would move softly out of her room, her heart shaking deliciously, biting her lips to keep from smiling. In the early afternoons, when the house was most quiet, Anne could go from one floor to the next by the backstairs, without being seen or attracting attention if she were. If anyone noticed her, she could say that the tub on the third floor was occupied and she had come to the second floor to take a bath, or to the first floor to answer the phone; if she were seen coming out of someone's room—which never, to her knowledge, had happened—she could say, with perfect truth, that she was looking for something.

Before the snow had fully melted, in the inexorable round of the university year, Anne had, besides the ankle bracelet and the pen-and-pencil set and the gray teddy bear, a black satin slip she had found on the floor of a closet and washed carefully and folded neatly before setting it away in her mother's trunk; she had a carbon copy of a sonnet, neatly typed and dated (it had been sent away, Anne knew, to a poetry magazine not long before, but the rejection notice was not attached to the carbon), and a small leather-covered notebook, virgin except for the first page, on which was written largely: "BUY ASPIRIN. WRITE HOME. GET SPANISH ASSGNMT. DRESS FROM CLEANERS."

Also by this time, of course, many of the losses had been discovered. Cheryl, going one day to her desk drawer to make a shy point about her own worth, was not able to find her pen-and-pencil set inscribed "Voted Most Likely to Succeed," and after much thought and consideration, she mentioned the fact cautiously to several of her friends.

"Not that I think it's been *stolen*, or anything," Cheryl insisted over and over again. "I don't think anyone in the house *steals*. I just can't imagine where my pen-and-pencil set has gone."

"Perhaps you left it somewhere," one of the girls might suggest incautiously, to which Cheryl would reply with indignation, "*Naturally* I'd never take it anywhere—not with 'Voted Most Likely to Succeed' written all over it. But I just *know* it hasn't been *stolen*."

When the loss of the black satin slip became a topic of conversation, Cheryl's apprehensions became "But who around here *steals*?" and "I just can't *believe* it of anyone in the house." Maggie, who had lost the gray teddy bear, never mentioned it, although she did say she was almost positive that a silver signet ring was gone from her top right-hand drawer, and she was fairly certain that she had seen one of the maids hovering near the dresser shortly before she'd discovered that the ring was gone. The girl whose carbon copy of a sonnet was missing admitted blushingly that she could not say for sure how many copies of the sonnet she had made. One of the girls managed to recall that at one time she had owned a compact with her name on it, which she was no longer able to find; another believed that the yellow blouse she had blamed the laundry for losing had most likely been stolen. Anne softly contributed, during one discussion, the additional fact that she herself had lost a couple of things, but no one noticed particularly, probably on the theory that Anne's possessions were so anonymous anyway that loss of any of them would be superfluous.

"I can't believe it of the *maids*," Cheryl was saying by now. "Surely not the *maids*."

"Someone must have come in from outside, then," said the girl who had lost the black satin slip. "Imagine, if anyone sneaked into the house and went through our *clothes*." She shivered delightedly.

"I don't think anyone could have come in," Helena said firmly.

They circled joyfully around the fact that it might be one of themselves, and eyed one another with pleased suspicion. There was a group, made up of Helena, Cheryl, and several of the others, who believed excitedly that Maggie was doing it, and Cheryl said feelingly, "I can't believe it of *Maggie*."

"Well," someone offered hesitantly, "she doesn't have a lot of money, you know. She could have sold some of the jewelry."

"She has a new sweater," Helena said. "You know—the red one. And you can take my word for it, that sweater cost a lot more than anything Maggie's ever worn before."

"Of course," Cheryl said thoughtfully, "she wouldn't *dare* wear any of those things—*you* know. But still, I *can't*—"

There was another group, made up of Maggie and several others, including the three girls with the bathroom darkroom, who believed Cheryl was responsible.

"Of course," Maggie said charitably, "if it *was* Cheryl, you couldn't really blame her. I mean, sometimes people have something wrong with them and they've *got* to steal."

"Dipsomania," one of the darkroom girls contributed knowingly. "It can only be cured by psychoanalysis."

The girls moved closer to one another, listening, and someone offered, softly, "Do you suppose her family knows? And let her come back to college?"

"*Her* family," Maggie said, "probably they don't want her stealing *their* stuff."

There was still another group, of course, with shifting ringleaders, who believed that Helena had done it. "She can't *stand* anyone having something she doesn't have," one girl said. "It drives her crazy just to see one of us with a new coat or something."

"Not that she doesn't have *enough*, as it is," said another. "I can't really *imagine* Helena touching anything that didn't belong to her. Except, of course, she's really *terribly* jealous."

The remaining girls, who believed that the three girls with the bathroom darkroom had stolen the property, based their case on incontrovertible facts: 1) that people who have permission to turn a first-floor bathroom into a photographic darkroom think they own the world, anyway; 2) no one could really tell whether they were in their darkroom at any given time, no matter what they *said*; they could be anywhere in the house; and 3) one of the three girls had been heard expressing a most enthusiastic admiration of a china cat on the dresser of another girl in the house, and although the china cat was not missing yet, a pack of cigarettes she had put down next to it was, and anyone could get rattled and grab the first thing she saw.

No one, for a minute, suspected Anne. Anne, in all of the suspicion and confusion, went from one to another of the little talking groups, offering her disregarded opinions, and at night, when the house was quiet, she took out her treasures and counted them over, setting the teddy bear next to the sonnet and the ankle bracelet next to the leather notebook, weighing the pen-and-pencil set in her hands and regarding its motto until she could have drawn from memory the peculiar angular script of it; trying on the black satin slip and walking silently around her room, with its door never locked.

Eventually, it was Anne who brought a formal complaint to the house mother.

It had occurred to Anne that the house mother, whose name was Miss McBride, had worn at various times a pair of dangling jet earrings, which Anne knew were kept in a cardboard box in Miss McBride's dresser. As a result, one afternoon, in her bathrobe and carrying her towel, Anne approached the quiet, bookless room that Miss McBride had only just vacated to go shopping, and had, fortunately, only just stepped inside when Miss McBride returned unexpectedly. In the still atmosphere of the room Anne was speechless for a minute, as Miss McBride looked at her, and then Anne, making the best of her situation, said urgently, "Miss McBride, I was looking for you."

"Yes?" Miss McBride said, not prepared to commit herself. She was a fairly young, well-set-up, incredibly romantic woman, and was fond of the big-sisterly admiration she received from her girls; she was partial to sympathetic smiles and knowing nods, and allowed the rumor to circulate uncontradicted that she had permitted—even encouraged—one of her girls to elope several years before with an extremely wealthy chemistry major. Although she had heard the stories of thievery, and was completely aware of the many rumors going around in her house, she was not yet prepared to commit herself on the subject, and did not intend to take any action until she knew better what kind to take without offending anyone. By telling her precipitately, Anne would force her to do something immediately, and so Miss McBride's tone when she said "Yes?" again to Anne was cold, and almost ominous.

"Miss McBride," Anne said, allowing her words to come almost in a rush, so that later, when Miss McBride questioned her, the easygoing mind would remember only her emotionality, "Miss McBride, I don't know what to do. Really, it's *awful*. I couldn't have *believed* it of her," Anne said, borrowing freely from Cheryl; "it must be some kind of a mental disease, or something," borrowing freely from Maggie. "I mean, when I *saw* her I tried to think of something to say, and she looked so guilty. So I came right down to tell you and ask you what to do." Anne hesitated for a minute, then added plaintively, "Please, can't we sort of keep it quiet, not have a scandal?"

"Who?" Miss McBride said, having fastened accurately on the one essential fact.

Anne dropped her eyes. "I'd rather not say, please, Miss McBride."

"You won't tell me?" Miss McBride's voice rose. Anne blushed and remained silent.

"Of course," Miss McBride said, embarrassed for a minute at her own forwardness. There was no further attempt made by either of them to discuss the thievery. After a few minutes' thought Miss McBride said, "I'll post a notice on the bulletin board, for a house meeting tonight."

By some odd coincidence every girl at the house meeting—in fact, every girl in the house—knew by the time Cheryl called the meeting to order that Miss McBride knew who the thief was, or had a clue, or meant to find out that night. Delicious apprehension made each girl tremble separately; many of them hoped that their most intimate friends would prove to be innocent; if a vote had been taken, the most likely candidate would have been Cheryl herself, just as she had been elected president of the house. As she stood in the center of the room, with the other girls around her draped over chairs and lying on the sofas and sitting on the floor, Cheryl knew perfectly well that each girl watching her imagined she saw some sign of guilt on her face.

Miss McBride spoke, soberly and earnestly. "Look, kids," she said, "this is a terrible thing. Everyone, all over campus, knows about it by now. They're beginning to talk about us, how we've got someone in this house who borrows things that don't belong to her and then forgets to return them. It's not good for any of you. I know you all want to protect your own reputations, and all together we want to keep this a clean and decent house. I think that the girl who is responsible for all this doesn't quite realize that she is hurting all of us by not stepping forward." Miss McBride stopped for a minute, but no one came forward, hand raised. "Do you think," Miss McBride went on, "that if I said we'd all go to our rooms quietly, and then I'd wait in mine until the girl came to me—do you think that would do any good?"

There was a silence, and then one of the girls in a corner, who wanted action, said, "Not if she's gotten away with it this far, she won't."

"I think I ought to tell you," Miss McBride said significantly, "that the name of the girl is known."

There was a dead silence of anticipation.

"I'm not going to tell you her name," Miss McBride said firmly. "And I'm not going to tell you who saw her. All I'm going to say is that I'm going to take steps to stop this business, once and for all."

There was another silence; Miss McBride was the one who had to take action. Miss McBride took a deep breath. "I'm going to search every room in this house," she said with relish. "Tonight."

There was another long silence, finally broken when one of the girls said timidly, "I don't think you have the right to do that, Miss McBride."

"Anyone who has anything to hide," Miss McBride said emphatically, settling the matter once and for all, "can easily see the position she puts herself in."

Anne, unappalled, hugged herself secretly. This was the best of all; she was perhaps the only person who had read the diary in Cheryl's desk, seen the letters in Helena's dresser, penetrated the secrets buried in handkerchief boxes, under beds, in the darkest corners of closets, the secrets known to be there, yet believed inviolate until a good excuse made them common currency, sometimes shocking, sometimes laughable.

"You can start with *my* room," Cheryl said with dignity. There was a strong shift of sentiment toward Cheryl after this statement—unless, several of the girls wondered privately, Cheryl, as house president, had had warning of the search?

Miss McBride rose purposefully and went to the stairs, where she stopped again. "Kids," she said, her voice lacking eagerness, "isn't there some other way of doing this?" As she spoke, she started up the stairs. Cheryl first, and then the whole roomful of girls, followed her. Miss McBride went up to the second floor and then, after another minute's thought, up to the third floor. Here there lived only Anne and three others.

"Whose room shall I start with?" Miss McBride asked indecisively.

"Mine," Anne said firmly. Miss McBride, looking at Anne across the line of girls standing still in the hall, tried to make her glance meaningful. "Anne," she was trying to say, "I know it's all right, you're not the thief because you won't tell me who is; I've got to search your room." Miss McBride's gesturing eyebrows tried to say eloquently, "But we know, you and I, that it's only a formal gesture." She looked at Anne until all the other girls looked at her too, and then, unseen, Miss McBride shrugged helplessly at Anne.

Miss McBride, with the advice and the occasional help of the other girls, searched quickly and ineffectually. All of the drawers in the dresser and the desk were opened and their contents stirred around. "Some of the stuff was too big to really *hide*," one of the girls contributed, and Miss McBride, adopting this theory into her concept of searching, made only perfunctory gestures at the bookcase and the bedcovers, although she lifted the mattress to look underneath, and one of the girls took the pillow out of its case. Anne, standing near the door, watched the girls showing curiosity about her for the second time in her life, saw a girl whom she rather admired poke hastily and surreptitiously at Anne's dresses in the closet, saw another girl stop by the desk to read a letter Anne was writing to a high school friend. Miss McBride, at the lid of Anne's mother's trunk, said superfluously, "This yours, Anne?"

"My mother's," Anne said quietly. Miss McBride let the corner of the fur cape fall immediately from her fingers, and said questioningly to the other girls "I don't think . . . ?"

"Of course not," someone said uncomfortably, and the girl who had been reading Anne's letter hurriedly dropped it back onto the desk.

"Well," Miss McBride said, and smiled at Anne. "That's that," she said. She moved with purpose out of the room, and the girls followed her in a flock. Although Miss McBride moved into the next room on the floor, some of the girls separated themselves from her and could be heard, farther down the hall, instituting a search of their own in another room. Miss McBride, her searching growing more and more haphazard, went through all the rooms on the third floor; by the time she had done all four rooms she was only opening drawers and glancing into closets, but the rest of the girls were going over the rooms like locusts, reading, confusing, examining everything they could find. Talk was circulating among the group ("Did you *see* what they found—" "I should think she'd *die*—"), but the girls held together. Miss McBride said occasionally, "Now, let's play fair, kids. No one running off to her own room." And always, when she said this, she counted them, rapidly, at a glance.

On the second floor, Cheryl's diary turned up, and a collection of scandalous love letters in Helena's room, and a locket in which another girl had pasted a picture of one of her professors. The owner of the room always, without exception, stood by the door while her room was searched, ready to run if anything too awkward (something she never knew she had? perhaps something she had borrowed and not returned? perhaps something everyone would find unanimously, irresistibly funny? the stolen things, perhaps?) or too shaming turned up.

Naturally the darkroom was not searched, but Miss McBride insisted on having the girls go through *her* room, which, carefully prepared, disclosed nothing except a picture of a handsome young man whom Miss McBride blushingly refused to identify as either a brother or a fiancé.

When the search was over and they were all gathered together in the living room again, Miss McBride gave voice to the prevailing suspicion by saying, "Well, kids, it looks like one of you was warned in time and got rid of the stuff. But, as I told you before, we know who it is. *Now* I am going to say that if the girl who took these things that didn't belong to her will come to me secretly in my room tonight, nothing more will be said." She started for her room and then stopped to turn back and add, "Needless to say, if nothing comes of this tonight I shall have to take further steps. I had hoped"—she sighed lightly—"I had hoped to settle this here among ourselves, but if that is not possible I shall have to take further steps." She took herself with dignity into her own room, and the girls, knowing more now than they did before, separated and went silently off to their own. No one cared to speak; each one knew the secrets of all the others; no one was inviolate any longer. It would be a long and painful process to build new privacies, secure them safely against intrusion, learn to trust one another again; there was a great destruction that went on in the house that night, of ruined treasures being burned, torn, cut with nail scissors. The wastebaskets taken out the next day were filled with loose torn pages and destroyed photographs, and for many days after that the girls in the house spoke rarely, and very politely, to one another.

When the house was finally quiet, Anne took out her ankle bracelet, her teddy bear and her sonnet, her pen-and-pencil set, her black slip and her leather notebook, added to them Miss McBride's dangling jet earrings, which she had slipped into her pocket while helping search Miss McBride's room, and set them in a row on her bed. All together, they were barely enough to fill a tiny overnight bag, so Anne stopped off in the house living room to slip three or four metal ashtrays into the bag with them. She stood for a minute just inside the front door, surveying the house, which was silent, with all its doors shut; it was her first minute of unalloyed pleasure since her mother's funeral. Then she slipped quickly out the front door and down the street, carrying the overnight bag; mighty, armed.

A Visit
(for Dylan Thomas)

I

The house in itself was, even before anything had happened there, as lovely a thing as she had ever seen. Set among its lavish grounds, with a park and a river and a wooded hill surrounding it, and carefully planned and tended gardens close upon all sides, it lay upon the hills as though it were something too precious to be seen by everyone; Margaret's very coming there had been a product of such elaborate arrangement, and such letters to and fro, and such meetings and hopings and wishings, that when she alighted with Carla Rhodes at the doorway of Carla's home, she felt that she too had come home, to a place striven for and earned. Carla stopped before the doorway and stood for a minute, looking first behind her, at the vast reaching gardens and the green lawn going down to the river, and the soft hills beyond, and then at the perfect grace of the house, showing so clearly the long-boned structure within, the curving staircases and the arched doorways and the tall thin lines of steadying beams, all of it resting back against the hills, and up, past rows of windows and the flying lines of the roof, on, to the tower—Carla stopped, and looked, and smiled, and then turned and said, "Welcome, Margaret."

"It's a lovely house," Margaret said, and felt that she had much better have said nothing.

The doors were opened and Margaret, touching as she went the warm head of a stone faun beside her, passed inside. Carla, following, greeted the servants by name, and was welcomed with reserved pleasure; they stood for a minute on the rose-and-white-tiled floor. "Again, welcome, Margaret," Carla said.

Far ahead of them the great stairway soared upward, held to the hall where they stood by only the slimmest of carved balustrades; on Margaret's left hand a tapestry moved softly as the door behind was closed. She could see the fine threads of the weave, and the light colors, but she could not have told the picture unless she went far away, perhaps as far away as the staircase, and looked at it from there; perhaps, she thought, from halfway up the stairway this great hall, and perhaps the whole house, is visible, as a complete body of story together, all joined and in sequence. Or perhaps I shall be allowed to move slowly from one thing to another, observing each, or would that take all the time of my visit?

"I never saw anything so lovely," she said to Carla, and Carla smiled.

"Come and meet my mama," Carla said.

They went through doors at the right, and Margaret, before she could see the light room she went into, was stricken with fear at meeting the owners of the house and the park and the river, and as she went beside Carla she kept her eyes down.

"Mama," said Carla, "this is Margaret, from school."

"Margaret," said Carla's mother, and smiled at Margaret kindly. "We are very glad you were able to come."

She was a tall lady wearing pale green and pale blue, and Margaret said as gracefully as she could, "Thank you, Mrs. Rhodes; I am very grateful for having been invited."

"Surely," said Mrs. Rhodes softly, "surely my daughter's friend Margaret from school should be welcome here; surely we should be grateful that she has come."

"Thank you, Mrs. Rhodes," Margaret said, not knowing how she was answering, but knowing that she was grateful.

When Mrs. Rhodes turned her kind eyes on her daughter, Margaret was at last able to look at the room where she stood next to her friend; it was a pale-green and a pale-blue long room with tall windows that looked out onto the lawn and the sky, and thin colored china ornaments on the mantel. Mrs. Rhodes had left her needlepoint when they came in and from where Margaret stood she could see the pale sweet pattern from the underside; all soft colors it was, melting into one another endlessly, and not finished. On the table nearby were books, and one large book of sketches that were most certainly Carla's; Carla's harp stood next to the windows, and beyond one window were marble steps outside, going shallowly down to a fountain, where water moved in the sunlight. Margaret thought of her own embroidery—a pair of slippers she was working for her friend—and knew that she should never be able to bring it into this room, where Mrs. Rhodes's long white hands rested on the needlepoint frame, soft as dust on the pale colors.

"Come," said Carla, taking Margaret's hand in her own, "Mama has said that I might show you some of the house."

They went out again into the hall, across the rose and white tiles which made a pattern too large to be seen from the floor, and through a doorway where tiny bronze fauns grinned at them from the carving. The first room that they went into was all gold, with gilt on the window frames and on the legs of the chairs and tables, and the small chairs standing on the yellow carpet were made of gold brocade with small gilded backs, and on the wall were more tapestries showing the house as it looked in the sunlight with even the trees around it shining, and these tapestries were let into the wall and edged with thin gilded frames.

"There is so much tapestry," Margaret said.

"In every room," Carla agreed. "Mama has embroidered all the hangings for her own room, the room where she writes her letters. The other tapestries were done by my grandmamas and my great-grandmamas and my great-great-grandmamas."

The next room was silver, and the small chairs were of silver brocade with narrow silvered backs, and the tapestries on the walls of this room were edged with silver frames and showed the house in moonlight, with the white light shining on the stones and the windows glittering.

"Who uses these rooms?" Margaret asked.

"No one," Carla said.

They passed then into a room where everything grew smaller as they looked at it: the mirrors on both sides of the room showed the door opening and Margaret and Carla coming through, and then, reflected, a smaller door opening and a small Margaret and a smaller Carla coming through, and then, reflected again, a still smaller door and Margaret and Carla, and so on, endlessly, Margaret and Carla diminishing and reflecting. There was a table here and nesting under it another lesser table, and under that another one, and another under that one, and on the greatest table lay a carved wooden bowl holding within it another carved wooden bowl, and another within that, and another within that one. The tapestries in this room were of the house reflected in the lake, and the tapestries themselves were reflected, in and out, among the mirrors on the wall, with the house in the tapestries reflected in the lake.

This room frightened Margaret rather, because it was so difficult for her to tell what was in it and what was not, and how far in any direction she might easily move, and she backed out hastily, pushing Carla behind her. They turned from here into another doorway which led them out again into the great hall under the soaring staircase, and Carla said, "We had better go upstairs and see your room; we can see more of the house another time. We have *plenty* of time, after all," and she squeezed Margaret's hand joyfully.

They climbed the great staircase, and passed, in the hall upstairs, Carla's room, which was like the inside of a shell in pale colors, with lilacs on the table, and the fragrance of the lilacs followed them as they went down the halls.

The sound of their shoes on the polished floor was like rain, but the sun came in on them wherever they went. "Here," Carla said, opening a door, "is where we have breakfast when it is warm; here," opening another door, "is the passage to the room where Mama does her letters. And that—" nodding "—is the stairway to the tower, and *here* is where we shall have dances when my brother comes home."

"A real tower?" Margaret said.

"And *here*," Carla said, "is the old schoolroom, and my brother and I studied here before he went away, and I stayed on alone studying here until it was time for me to come to school and meet *you*."

"Can we go up into the tower?" Margaret asked.

"Down here, at the end of the hall," Carla said, "is where all my grandpapas and my grandmamas and my great-great-grandpapas and grandmamas live." She opened the door to the long gallery, where pictures of tall old people in lace and pale waistcoats leaned down to stare at Margaret and Carla. And then, to a walk at the top of the house, where they leaned over and looked at the ground below and the tower above, and Margaret looked at the gray stone of the tower and wondered who lived there, and Carla pointed out where the river ran far below, far away, and said they should walk there tomorrow.

"When my brother comes," she said, "he will take us boating on the river."

In her room, unpacking her clothes, Margaret realized that her white dress was the only one possible for dinner, and thought that she would have to send home for more things; she had intended to wear her ordinary gray downstairs most evenings before Carla's brother came, but knew she could not when she saw Carla in light blue, with pearls around her neck. When Margaret and Carla came into the drawing room before dinner Mrs. Rhodes greeted them very kindly, and asked had Margaret seen the painted room or the room with the tiles?

"We had no time to go near that part of the house at all," Carla said.

"After dinner, then," Mrs. Rhodes said, putting her arm affectionately around Margaret's shoulders, "we will go and see the painted room and the room with the tiles, because they are particular favorites of mine."

"Come and meet my papa," Carla said.

The door was just opening for Mr. Rhodes, and Margaret, who felt almost at ease now with Mrs. Rhodes, was frightened again of Mr. Rhodes, who spoke loudly and said, "So this is m'girl's friend from school? Lift up your head, girl, and let's have a look at you." When Margaret looked up blindly, and smiled weakly, he patted her cheek and said, "We shall have to make you look bolder before you leave us," and then he tapped his daughter on the shoulder and said she had grown to a monstrous fine girl.

They went in to dinner, and on the walls of the dining room were tapestries of the house in the seasons of the year, and the dinner service was white china with veins of gold running through it, as though it had been mined and not molded. The fish was one Margaret did not recognize, and Mr. Rhodes very generously insisted upon serving her himself without smiling at her ignorance. Carla and Margaret were each given a glassful of pale spicy wine.

"When my brother comes," Carla said to Margaret, "we will not dare be so quiet at table." She looked across the white cloth to Margaret, and then to her father at the head, to her mother at the foot, with the long table between them, and said, "My brother can make us laugh all the time."

"Your mother will not miss you for these summer months?" Mrs. Rhodes said to Margaret.

"She has my sisters, ma'am," Margaret said, "and I have been away at school for so long that she has learned to do without me."

"We mothers never learn to do without our daughters," Mrs. Rhodes said, and looked fondly at Carla. "Or our sons," she added with a sigh.

"When my brother comes," Carla said, "you will see what this house can be like with life in it."

"When does he come?" Margaret asked.

"One week," Mr. Rhodes said, "three days, and four hours."

When Mrs. Rhodes rose, Margaret and Carla followed her, and Mr. Rhodes rose gallantly to hold the door for them all.

That evening Carla and Margaret played and sang duets, although Carla said that their voices together were too thin to be appealing without a deeper voice accompanying, and that when her brother came they should have some splendid trios. Mrs. Rhodes complimented their singing, and Mr. Rhodes fell asleep in his chair.

Before they went upstairs Mrs. Rhodes reminded herself of her promise to show Margaret the painted room and the room with the tiles, and so she and Margaret and Carla, holding their long dresses up away from the floor in front so that their skirts whispered behind them, went down a hall and through a passage and down another hall, and through a room filled with books and then through a painted door into a tiny octagonal room where each of the sides was paneled and painted, with pink and blue and green and gold small pictures of shepherds and nymphs, lambs and fauns, playing on the broad green lawns by the river, with the house standing lovely behind them. There was nothing else in the little room, because seemingly the paintings were furniture enough for one room, and Margaret felt surely that she could stay happily and watch the small painted people playing, without ever seeing anything more of the house. But Mrs. Rhodes led her on, into the room of the tiles, which was not exactly a room at all, but had one side all glass window looking out onto the same lawn of the pictures in the octagonal room. The tiles were set into the floor of this room, in tiny bright spots of color which showed, when you stood back and looked at them, that they were again a picture of the house, only now the same materials that made the house made the tiles, so that the tiny windows were tiles of glass, and the stones of the tower were chips of gray stone, and the bricks of the chimneys were chips of brick.

Beyond the tiles of the house Margaret, lifting her long skirt as she walked, so that she should not brush a chip of the tower out of place, stopped and said, "What is *this*?" And stood back to see, and then knelt down and said, "*What* is this?"

"Isn't she enchanting?" said Mrs. Rhodes, smiling at Margaret, "I've always loved her."

"I was wondering what Margaret would say when she saw it," said Carla, smiling also.

It was a curiously made picture of a girl's face, with blue-chip eyes and a red-chip mouth, staring blindly from the floor, with long light braids made of yellow stone chips going down evenly on either side of her round cheeks.

"She is pretty," said Margaret, stepping back to see her better. "What does it say underneath?"

She stepped back again, holding her head up and back to read the letters, pieced together with stone chips and set unevenly in the floor. "Here was Margaret," it said, "who died for love."

2

There was, of course, not time to do everything. Before Margaret had seen half the house, Carla's brother came home. Carla came running up the great staircase one afternoon calling "Margaret, Margaret, he's come," and Margaret, running down to meet her, hugged her and said, "I'm so glad."

He had certainly come, and Margaret, entering the drawing room shyly behind Carla, saw Mrs. Rhodes with tears in her eyes and Mr. Rhodes standing straighter and prouder than before, and Carla said, "Brother, here is Margaret."

He was tall and haughty in uniform, and Margaret wished she had met him a little later, when she had perhaps been to her room again, and perhaps tucked up her hair. Next to him stood his friend, a captain, small and dark and bitter, and smiling bleakly upon the family assembled. Margaret smiled back timidly at them both, and stood behind Carla.

Everyone then spoke at once. Mrs. Rhodes said "We've missed you so," and Mr. Rhodes said "Glad to have you back, m'boy," and Carla said "We shall have such times—I've promised Margaret—" and Carla's brother said "So this is Margaret?" and the dark captain said "I've been wanting to come."

It seemed that they all spoke at once, every time; there would be a long waiting silence while all of them looked around with joy at being together, and then suddenly everyone would have found something to say. It was so at dinner: Mrs. Rhodes said "You're not eating enough," and "You used to be more fond of pome-granates," and Carla said "We're to go boating," and "We'll have a dance, won't we?" and "Margaret and I insist upon a picnic," and "I saved the river for my brother to show to Margaret." Mr. Rhodes puffed and laughed and passed the wine, and Margaret hardly dared lift her eyes. The black captain said "Never realized what an attractive old place it could be, after all," and Carla's brother said "There's much about the house I'd like to show Margaret."

After dinner they played charades, and even Mrs. Rhodes did Achilles with Mr. Rhodes, holding his heel and both of them laughing and glancing at Carla and Margaret and the captain. Carla's brother leaned on the back of Margaret's chair and once she looked up at him and said, "No one ever calls you by name. Do you actually have a name?"

"Paul," he said.

The next morning they walked on the lawn, Carla with the captain and Margaret with Paul. They stood by the lake, and Margaret looked at the pure reflection of the house and said, "It almost seems as though we could open a door and go in."

"There," said Paul, and he pointed with his stick at the front entrance, "There is where we shall enter, and it will swing open for us with an underwater crash."

"Margaret," said Carla, laughing, "you say odd things, sometimes. If you tried to go into *that* house, you'd be in the lake."

"Indeed, and not like it much, at all," the captain added.

"Or would you have the side door?" asked Paul, pointing with his stick.

"I think I prefer the front door," said Margaret.

"But you'd be drowned," Carla said. She took Margaret's arm as they started back toward the house, and said, "We'd make a scene for a tapestry right now, on the lawn before the house."

"Another tapestry?" said the captain, and grimaced.

They played croquet, and Paul hit Margaret's ball toward a wicket, and the captain accused her of cheating prettily. And they played word games in the evening, and Margaret and Paul won, and everyone said Margaret was so clever. And they walked endlessly on the lawns before the house, and looked into the still lake, and watched the reflection of the house in the water, and Margaret chose a room in the reflected house for her own, and Paul said she should have it.

"That's the room where Mama writes her letters," said Carla, looking strangely at Margaret.

"Not in our house in the lake," said Paul.

"And I suppose if you like it she would lend it to you while you stay," Carla said.

"Not at all," said Margaret amiably. "I think I should prefer the tower anyway."

"Have you seen the rose garden?" Carla asked.

"Let me take you there," said Paul.

Margaret started across the lawn with him, and Carla called to her, "Where are you off to now, Margaret?"

"Why, to the rose garden," Margaret called back, and Carla said, staring, "You are really very odd, sometimes, Margaret. And it's growing colder, far too cold to linger among the roses," and so Margaret and Paul turned back.

Mrs. Rhodes's needlepoint was coming on well. She had filled in most of the outlines of the house, and was setting in the windows. After the first small shock of surprise, Margaret no longer wondered that Mrs. Rhodes was able to set out the house so well without a pattern or a plan; she did it from memory and Margaret, realizing this for the first time, thought "How amazing," and then "But of course; how else *would* she do it?"

To see a picture of the house, Mrs. Montague needed only to lift her eyes in any direction, but, more than that, she had of course never used any other model for her embroidery; she had of course learned the faces of the house better than the faces of her children. The dreamy life of the Rhodeses in the house was most clearly shown Margaret as she watched Mrs. Rhodes surely and capably building doors and windows, carvings and cornices, in her embroidered house, smiling tenderly across the room to where Carla and the captain bent over a book together, while her fingers almost of themselves turned the edge of a carving Margaret had forgotten or never known about until, leaning over the back of Mrs. Rhodes's chair, she saw it form itself under Mrs. Rhodes's hands.

The small thread of days and sunlight, then, that bound Margaret to the house, was woven here as she watched. And Carla, lifting her head to look over, might say, "Margaret, do come and look, here. Mother is always at her work, but my brother is rarely home."

They went for a picnic, Carla and the captain and Paul and Margaret, and Mrs. Rhodes waved to them from the doorway as they left, and Mr. Rhodes came to his study window and lifted his hand to them. They chose to go to the wooded hill beyond the house, although Carla was timid about going too far away—"I always like to be where I can see the roofs, at least," she said—and sat among the trees, on moss greener than Margaret had ever seen before, and spread out a white cloth and drank red wine.

It was a very proper forest, with neat trees and the green moss, and an occasional purple or yellow flower growing discreetly away from the path. There was no sense of brooding silence, as there sometimes is with trees about, and Margaret realized, looking up to see the sky clearly between the branches, that she had seen this forest in the tapestries in the breakfast room, with the house shining in the sunlight beyond.

"Doesn't the river come through here somewhere?" she asked, hearing, she thought, the sound of it through the trees. "I feel so comfortable here among these trees, so at home."

"It is possible," said Paul, "to take a boat from the lawn in front of the house and move without sound down the river, through the trees, past the fields and then, for some reason, around past the house again. The river, you see, goes almost around the house in a great circle. We are very proud of that."

"The river *is* nearby," said Carla. "It goes almost completely around the house."

"Margaret," said the captain. "You must not look rapt on a picnic unless you are contemplating nature."

"I was, as a matter of fact," said Margaret. "I was contemplating a caterpillar approaching Carla's foot."

"Will you come and look at the river?" said Paul, rising and holding his hand out to Margaret. "I think we can see much of its great circle from near here."

"Margaret," said Carla as Margaret stood up. "You are *always* wandering off."

"I'm coming right back," Margaret said, with a laugh. "It's only to look at the river."

"Don't be away long," Carla said. "We must be getting back before dark."

The river as it went through the trees was shadowed and cool, broadening out into pools where only the barest movement disturbed the ferns along its edge, and where small stones made it possible to step out and see the water all around, from a precarious island, and where without sound a leaf might be carried from the limits of sight to the limits of sight, moving swiftly but imperceptibly and turning a little as it went.

"Who lives in the tower, Paul?" asked Margaret, holding a fern and running it softly over the back of her hand. "I know someone lives there, because I saw someone moving at the window once."

"Not *lives* there," said Paul, amused. "Did you think we kept a political prisoner locked away?"

"I thought it might be the birds, at first," Margaret said, glad to be describing this to someone.

"No," said Paul, still amused. "There's an aunt, or a great-aunt, or perhaps even a great-great-great-aunt. She doesn't live there, at all, but goes there because she says she cannot *endure* the sight of tapestry." He laughed. "She has filled the tower with books, and a huge old cat, and she may practice alchemy there, for all anyone knows. The reason you've never seen her would be that she has one of her spells of hiding away. Sometimes she is downstairs daily."

"Will I ever meet her?" Margaret asked wonderingly.

"Perhaps," Paul said. "She might take it into her head to come down formally one night to dinner. Or she might wander carelessly up to you where you sat on the lawn, and introduce herself. Or you might never see her, at that."

"Suppose I went up to the tower?"

Paul glanced at her strangely. "I suppose you could, if you wanted to," he said. "*I've* been there."

"Margaret," Carla called through the woods. "Margaret, we shall be late if you do not give up brooding by the river."

All this time, almost daily, Margaret was seeing new places in the house: the fan room, where the most delicate filigree fans had been set into the walls with their fine ivory sticks painted in exquisite miniature; the small room where incredibly perfect wooden and glass and metal fruits and flowers and trees stood on glittering glass shelves, lined up against the windows. And daily she passed and repassed the door behind which lay the stairway to the tower, and almost daily she stepped carefully around the tiles on the floor which read "Here was Margaret, who died for love."

It was no longer possible, however, to put off going to the tower. It was no longer possible to pass the doorway several times a day and do no more than touch her hand secretly to the panels, or perhaps set her head against and listen, to hear if there were footsteps going up or down, or a voice calling her. It was not possible to pass the doorway once more, and so in the early morning Margaret set her hand firmly to the door and pulled it open, and it came easily, as though relieved that at last, after so many hints and insinuations, and so much waiting and such helpless despair, Margaret had finally come to open it.

The stairs beyond, gray stone and rough, were, Margaret thought, steep for an old lady's feet, but Margaret went up effortlessly, though timidly. The stairway turned around and around, going up to the tower, and Margaret followed, setting her feet carefully upon one step after another, and holding her hands against the warm stone wall on either side, looking forward and up, expecting to be seen or spoken to before she reached the top; perhaps, she thought once, the walls of the tower were transparent and she was clearly, ridiculously visible from the outside, and Mrs. Rhodes and Carla, on the lawn—if indeed they ever looked upward to the tower—might watch her and turn to one another with smiles, saying "There is Margaret, going up to the tower at last," and, smiling, nod to one another.

The stairway ended, as she had not expected it would, in a heavy wooden door, which made Margaret, standing on the step below to find room to raise her hand and knock, seem smaller, and even standing at the top of the tower she felt that she was not really tall.

"Come in," said the great-aunt's voice, when Margaret had knocked twice; the first knock had been received with an expectant silence, as though inside someone had said inaudibly, "Is that someone knocking at *this* door?" and then waited to be convinced by a second knock—and Margaret's knuckles hurt from the effort of knocking to be heard through a heavy wooden door. She opened the door awkwardly from below—how much easier this all would be, she thought, if I knew the way—went in, and said politely, before she looked around, "I'm Carla's friend. They said I might come up to the tower to see it, but of course if you would rather I went away I shall." She had planned to say this more gracefully, without such an implication that invitations to the tower were issued by the downstairs Rhodeses, but the long climb and her being out of breath forced her to say everything at once, and she had really no time for the sounding periods she had composed.

In any case the great-aunt said politely—she was sitting at the other side of the round room, against a window, and she was not very clearly visible—"I am amazed that they told you about me at all. However, since you are here I cannot pretend that I really object to having you; you may come in and sit down."

Margaret came obediently into the room and sat down on the stone bench which ran all the way around the tower room, under the windows which of course were on all sides and open to the winds, so that the movement of the air through the tower room was insistent and constant, making talk difficult and even distinguishing objects a matter of some effort.

As though it were necessary to establish her position in the house emphatically and immediately, the old lady said, with a gesture and a grin, "My tapestries," and waved at the windows. She seemed to be not older than a great-aunt, although perhaps too old for a mere aunt, but her voice was clearly able to carry through the sound of the wind in the tower room and she seemed compact and strong beside the window, not at all as though she might be dizzy from looking out, or tired from the stairs.

"May I look out the window?" Margaret asked, almost of the cat, which sat next to her and regarded her without friendship, but without, as yet, dislike.

"Certainly," said the great-aunt. "Look out the windows, by all means."

Margaret turned on the bench and leaned her arms on the wide stone ledge of the window, but she was disappointed. Although the tops of the trees did not reach halfway up the tower, she could see only branches and leaves below and no sign of the wide lawns or the roofs of the house or the curve of the river.

"I hoped I could see the way the river went, from here."

"The river doesn't *go* from here," said the old lady, and laughed.

"I mean," Margaret said, "they told me that the river went around in a curve, almost surrounding the house."

"Who told you?" said the old lady.

"Paul."

"I see," said the old lady. "*He's* back, is he?"

"He's been here for several days, but he's going away again soon."

"And what's *your* name?" asked the old lady, leaning forward.

"Margaret."

"I see," said the old lady again. "That's my name, too," she said.

Margaret thought that "How nice" would be an inappropriate reply to this, and something like "Is it?" or "Just imagine" or "What a coincidence" would certainly make her feel more foolish than she believed she really was, so she smiled uncertainly at the old lady and dismissed the notion of saying "What a lovely name."

"He should have come and gone sooner," the old lady went on, as though to herself. "Then we'd have it all behind us."

"Have all *what* behind us?" Margaret asked, although she felt that she was not really being included in the old lady's conversation with herself, a conversation that seemed—and probably was—part of a larger conversation which the old lady had with herself constantly and on larger subjects than the matter of Margaret's name, and which even Margaret, intruder as she was, and young, could not be allowed to interrupt for very long. "Have all *what* behind us?" Margaret asked insistently.

"I say," said the old lady, turning to look at Margaret, "he should have come and gone already, and we'd all be well out of it by now."

"I see," said Margaret. "Well, I don't think he's going to be here much longer. He's talking of going." In spite of herself, her voice trembled a little. In order to prove to the old lady that the trembling in her voice was imaginary, Margaret said almost defiantly, "It will be very lonely here after he has gone."

"We'll be well out of it, Margaret, you and I," the old lady said. "Stand away from the window, child, you'll be wet."

Margaret realized with this that the storm, which had—she knew now—been hanging over the house for long sunny days had broken, suddenly, and that the wind had grown louder and was bringing with it through the windows of the tower long stinging rain. There were drops on the cat's black fur, and Margaret felt the side of her face wet. "Do your windows close?" she asked. "If I could help you—?"

"I don't mind the rain," the old lady said. "It wouldn't be the first time it's rained around the tower."

"I don't mind it," Margaret said hastily, drawing away from the window. She realized that she was staring back at the cat, and added nervously, "Although, of course, getting wet is—" She hesitated and the cat stared back at her without expression. "I mean," she said apologetically, "some people don't *like* getting wet."

The cat deliberately turned its back on her and put its face closer to the window.

"What were you saying about Paul?" Margaret asked the old lady, feeling somehow that there might be a thin thread of reason tangling the old lady and the cat and the tower and the rain, and even, with abrupt clarity, defining Margaret herself and the strange hesitation which had caught at her here in the tower. "He's going away soon, you know."

"It would have been better if it were over with by now," the old lady said. "These things don't take really long, you know, and the sooner the better, I say."

"I suppose *that's* true," Margaret said intelligently.

"After all," said the old lady dreamily, with raindrops in her hair, "we don't always see ahead, into things that are going to happen."

Margaret was wondering how soon she might politely go back downstairs and dry herself off, and she meant to stay politely only so long as the old lady seemed to be talking, however remotely, about Paul. Also, the rain and the wind were coming through the window onto Margaret in great driving gusts, as though Margaret and the old lady and the books and the cat would be washed away, and the top of the tower cleaned of them.

"I *would* help you if I could," the old lady said earnestly to Margaret, raising her voice almost to a scream to be heard over the wind and the rain. She stood up to approach Margaret, and Margaret, thinking she was about to fall, reached out a hand to catch her. The cat stood up and spat, the rain came through the window in a great sweep, and Margaret, holding the old lady's hands, heard through the sounds of the wind the equal sounds of all the voices in the world, and they called to her saying "Good-by, good-by," and "All is lost," and another voice saying "I will always remember you," and still another called, "It is so dark." And, far away from the others, she could hear a voice calling, "Come back, come back." Then the old lady pulled her hands away from Margaret and the voices were gone. The cat shrank back and the old lady looked coldly at Margaret and said, "As I was saying, I would help you if I *could*."

"I'm so sorry," Margaret said weakly. "I thought you were going to fall."

"Good-by," said the old lady.

3

At the ball Margaret wore a gown of thin blue lace that belonged to Carla, and yellow roses in her hair, and she carried one of the fans from the fan room, a daintily painted ivory thing which seemed indestructible, since she dropped it twice, and which had a tiny picture of the house painted on its ivory sticks, so that when the fan was closed the house was gone. Mrs. Rhodes had given it to her to carry, and had given Carla another, so that when Margaret and Carla passed one another dancing, or met by the punch bowl or in the halls, they said happily to one another, "Have you still got your fan? I gave mine to someone to hold for a minute; I showed mine to everyone. Are you still carrying your fan? I've got *mine*."

Margaret danced with strangers and with Paul, and when she danced with Paul they danced away from the others, up and down the long gallery hung with pictures, in and out between the pillars which led to the great hall opening into the room of the tiles. Near them danced ladies in scarlet silk, and green satin, and white velvet, and Mrs. Rhodes, in black with diamonds at her throat and on her hands, stood at the top of the room and smiled at the dancers, or went on Mr. Rhodes's arm to greet guests who came laughingly in between the pillars looking eagerly and already moving in time to the music as they walked. One lady wore white feathers in her hair, curling down against her shoulder; another had a pink scarf over her arms, and it floated behind her as she danced. Paul was in his haughty uniform, and Carla wore red roses in her hair and danced with the captain.

"Are you really going tomorrow?" Margaret asked Paul once during the evening; she knew that he was, but somehow asking the question—which she had done several times before—established a communication between them, of his right to go and her right to wonder, which was sadly sweet to her.

"I *said* you might meet the great-aunt," said Paul, as though in answer; Margaret followed his glance, and saw the old lady of the tower. She was dressed in yellow satin, and looked very regal and proud as she moved through the crowd of dancers, drawing her skirt aside if any of them came too close to her. She was coming toward Margaret and Paul where they sat on small chairs against the wall, and when she came close enough she smiled, looking at Paul, and said to him, holding out her hands, "I am very glad to see you, my dear."

Then she smiled at Margaret and Margaret smiled back, very glad that the old lady held out no hands to her.

"Margaret told me you were here," the old lady said to Paul, "and I came down to see you once more."

"I'm very glad you did," Paul said. "I wanted to see you so much that I almost came to the tower."

They both laughed and Margaret, looking from one to the other of them, wondered at the strong resemblance between them. Margaret sat very straight and stiff on her narrow chair, with her blue lace skirt falling charmingly around her and her hands folded neatly in her lap, and listened to their talk. Paul had found the old lady a chair and they sat with their heads near together, looking at one another as they talked, and smiling.

"You look very fit," the old lady said. "Very fit indeed." She sighed.

"You look wonderfully well," Paul said.

"Oh, well," said the old lady. "I've aged. I've aged, I know it."

"So have I," said Paul.

"Not noticeably," said the old lady, shaking her head and regarding him soberly for a minute. "*You* never will, I suppose."

At that moment the captain came up and bowed in front of Margaret, and Margaret, hoping that Paul might notice, got up to dance with him.

"I saw you sitting there alone," said the captain, "and I seized the precise opportunity I have been awaiting all evening."

"Excellent military tactics," said Margaret, wondering if these remarks had not been made a thousand times before, at a thousand different balls.

"I could be a splendid tactician," said the captain gallantly, as though carrying on his share of the echoing conversation, the words spoken under so many glittering chandeliers, "if my objective were always so agreeable to me."

"I saw you dancing with Carla," said Margaret.

"Carla," he said, and made a small gesture that somehow showed Carla as infinitely less than Margaret. Margaret knew that she had seen him make the same gesture to Carla, probably with reference to Margaret. She laughed.

"I forget what I'm supposed to say now," she told him.

"You're supposed to say," he told her seriously, "'And do you really leave us so soon?'"

"And do you really leave us so soon?" said Margaret obediently.

"The sooner to return," he said, and tightened his arm around her waist. Margaret said, it being her turn, "We shall miss you very much."

"*I* shall miss *you*," he said, with a manly air of resignation.

They danced two waltzes, after which the captain escorted her handsomely back to the chair from which he had taken her, next to which Paul and the old lady continued in conversation, laughing and gesturing. The captain bowed to Margaret deeply, clicking his heels.

"May I leave you alone for a minute or so?" he asked. "I believe Carla is looking for me."

"I'm perfectly all right here," Margaret said. As the captain hurried away she turned to hear what Paul and the old lady were saying.

"I remember, I remember," said the old lady laughing, and she tapped Paul on the wrist with her fan. "I never imagined there would be a time when I should find it funny."

"But it *was* funny," said Paul.

"We were so young," the old lady said. "I can hardly remember."

She stood up abruptly, bowed to Margaret, and started back across the room among the dancers. Paul followed her as far as the doorway and then left her to come back to Margaret. When he sat down next to her he said, "So you met the old lady?"

"I went to the tower," Margaret said.

"She told me," he said absently, looking down at his gloves. "Well," he said finally, looking up with an air of cheerfulness. "Are they *never* going to play a waltz?"

Shortly before the sun came up over the river the next morning they sat at breakfast, Mr. and Mrs. Rhodes at the ends of the table, Carla and the captain, Margaret and Paul. The red roses in Carla's hair had faded and been thrown away, as had Margaret's yellow roses, but both Carla and Margaret still wore their ball gowns, which they had been wearing for so long that the soft richness of them seemed natural, as though they were to wear nothing else for an eternity in the house, and the gay confusion of helping one another dress, and admiring one another, and straightening the last folds to hang more gracefully, seemed all to have happened longer ago than memory, to be perhaps a dream that might never have happened at all, as perhaps the figures in the tapestries on the walls of the dining room might remember, secretly, an imagined process of dressing themselves and coming with laughter and light voices to sit on the lawn where they were woven. Margaret, looking at Carla, thought that she had never seen Carla so familiarly as in this soft white gown, with her hair dressed high on her head—had it really been curled and pinned that way? Or had it always, forever, been so?—and the fan in her hand—had she not always had that fan, held just so?—and when Carla turned her head slightly on her long neck she captured the air of one of the portraits in the long gallery. Paul and the captain were still somehow trim in their uniforms; they were leaving at sunrise.

"Must you really leave this morning?" Margaret whispered to Paul.

"You are all kind to stay up and say good-by," said the captain, and he leaned forward to look down the table at Margaret, as though it were particularly kind of her.

"Every time my son leaves me," said Mrs. Rhodes, "it is as though it were the first time."

Abruptly, the captain turned to Mrs. Rhodes and said, "I noticed this morning that there was a bare patch on the grass before the door. Can it be restored?"

"I had not known," Mrs. Rhodes said, and she looked nervously at Mr. Rhodes, who put his hand quietly on the table and said, "We hope to keep the house in good repair so long as we are able."

"But the broken statue by the lake?" said the captain. "And the tear in the tapestry behind your head?"

"It is wrong of you to notice these things," Mrs. Rhodes said, gently.

"What can I do?" he said to her. "It is impossible not to notice these things. The fish are dying, for instance. There are no grapes in the arbor this year. The carpet is worn to thread near your embroidery frame," he bowed to Mrs. Rhodes, "and in the house itself—" bowing to Mr. Rhodes "—there is a noticeable crack over the window of the conservatory, a crack in the solid stone. Can you repair that?"

Mr. Rhodes said weakly, "It is very wrong of you to notice these things. Have you neglected the sun, and the bright perfection of the drawing room? Have you been recently to the gallery of portraits? Have you walked on the green portions of the lawn, or only watched for the bare places?"

"The drawing room is shabby," said the captain softly. "The green brocade sofa is torn a little near the arm. The carpet has lost its luster. The gilt is chipped on four of the small chairs in the gold room, the silver paint scratched in the silver room. A tile is missing from the face of Margaret, who died for love, and in the great gallery the paint has faded slightly on the portrait of—" bowing again to Mr. Rhodes "—your great-great-great-grandfather, sir."

Mr. Rhodes and Mrs. Rhodes looked at one another, and then Mrs. Rhodes said, "Surely it is not necessary to reproach *us* for these things?"

The captain reddened and shook his head.

"My embroidery is very nearly finished," Mrs. Rhodes said. "I have only to put the figures into the foreground."

"*I* shall mend the brocade sofa," said Carla.

The captain glanced once around the table, and sighed. "I must pack," he said. "We cannot delay our duties even though we have offended lovely women." Mrs. Rhodes, turning coldly away from him, rose and left the table, with Carla and Margaret following.

Margaret went quickly to the tile room, where the white face of Margaret who died for love stared eternally into the sky beyond the broad window. There was indeed a tile missing from the wide white cheek, and the broken spot looked like a tear, Margaret thought; she kneeled down and touched the tile face quickly to be sure that it was not a tear.

Then she went slowly back through the lovely rooms, across the broad rose-and-white-tiled hall, and into the drawing room, and stopped to close the tall doors behind her.

"There really is a tile missing," she said.

Paul turned and frowned; he was standing alone in the drawing room, tall and bright in his uniform, ready to leave. "You are mistaken," he said. "It is not possible that anything should be missing."

"I saw it."

"It is not *true*, you know," he said. He was walking quickly up and down the room, slapping his gloves on his wrist, glancing nervously, now and then, at the door, at the tall windows opening out onto the marble stairway. "The house is the same as ever," he said. "It does not change."

"But the worn carpet . . ." It was under his feet as he walked.

"Nonsense," he said violently. "Don't you think I'd know my own house? I care for it constantly, even when *they* forget; without this house I could not exist; do you think it would begin to crack while I am here?"

"How can you keep it from aging? Carpets *will* wear, you know, and unless they are replaced . . ."

"Replaced?" He stared as though she had said something evil. "What could replace anything in this house?" He touched Mrs. Rhodes's embroidery frame, softly. "All *we* can do is add to it."

There was a sound outside; it was the family coming down the great stairway to say good-by. He turned quickly and listened, and it seemed to be the sound he had been expecting. "I will always remember you," he said to Margaret, hastily, and turned again toward the tall windows. "Good-by."

"It is so dark," Margaret said, going beside him. "You will come back?"

"I will come back," he said sharply. "Good-by." He stepped across the sill of the window onto the marble stairway outside; he was black for a moment against the white marble, and Margaret stood still at the window watching him go down the steps and away through the gardens. "Lost, lost," she heard faintly, and, from far away, "All is lost."

She turned back to the room, and, avoiding the worn spot in the carpet and moving widely around Mrs. Rhodes's embroidery frame, she went to the great doors and opened them. Outside, in the hall with the rose-and-white-tiled floor, Mr. and Mrs. Rhodes and Carla were standing with the captain.

"Son," Mrs. Rhodes was saying, "when will you be back?"

"Don't *fuss* at me," the captain said. "I'll be back when I can."

Carla stood silently, a little away. "Please be careful," she said, and, "Here's Margaret, come to say good-by to you, Brother."

"Don't linger, m'boy," said Mr. Rhodes. "Hard on the women."

"There are so many things Margaret and I planned for you while you were here," Carla said to her brother. "The time has been so short."

Margaret, standing beside Mrs. Rhodes, turned to Carla's brother (*and Paul; who was Paul?*) and said, "Good-by." He bowed to her and moved to go to the door with his father.

"It is hard to see him go," Mrs. Rhodes said. "And we do not know when he will come back." She put her hand gently on Margaret's shoulder. "We must show you more of the house," she said. "I saw you one day try the door of the ruined tower; have you seen the hall of flowers? Or the fountain room?"

"When my brother comes again," Carla said, "we shall have a musical evening, and perhaps he will take us boating on the river."

"And my visit?" said Margaret smiling. "Surely there will be an end to my visit?"

Mrs. Rhodes, with one last look at the door from which Mr. Rhodes and the captain had gone, dropped her hand from Margaret's shoulder and said, "I must go to my embroidery. I have neglected it while my son was with us."

"You will not leave us before my brother comes again?" Carla asked Margaret.

"I have only to put the figures into the foreground," Mrs. Rhodes said, hesitating on her way to the drawing room. "I shall have you exactly if you sit on the lawn near the river."

"We shall be models of stillness," said Carla, laughing. "Margaret, will you come and sit beside me on the lawn?"

The Good Wife

Mr. James Benjamin poured a second cup of coffee for himself, sighed, and reached across the table for the cream. "Genevieve," he said without troubling to turn, "has Mrs. Benjamin had her breakfast tray yet?"

"She's still asleep, Mr. Benjamin. I went up ten minutes ago."

"Poor thing," said Mr. Benjamin, and helped himself to toast. He sighed again, discarded the newspaper as unworthy of notice, and was pleased to find that Genevieve was bringing in the mail.

"Any letters for me?" he asked, more to contribute to some human communication and desire, even so low a one as desiring the mail, than to secure information that he might very well have in a minute; "Anything for me?"

Genevieve was too well bred to turn over the letters, but she said "It's all here, Mr. Benjamin" as though he might have suspected her of abstracting vital letters, about business, perhaps, or from women.

There were of course—it was the third of the month—bills from various department stores, the latest of them dated on the tenth of the previous month, when Mrs. Benjamin had first taken to her room. They were trifling, and Mr. Benjamin set them aside, along with the circulars that advertised underwear, and dishes, and cosmetics, and furniture; it would amuse Mrs. Benjamin to look these over later. There was a bank statement, and Mr. Benjamin threw it irritably away toward the coffeepot, to be looked over later. There were three personal letters—one to himself, from a friend in Italy, praising the weather there at the moment, and two for Mrs. Benjamin. The first of these, which Mr. Benjamin opened without hesitation, was from her mother, and read,

Dear, just a hurried line to let you know that we're leaving on the tenth. I still hope you might come with us and of course up until the minute we leave for the boat we'll be waiting for word from you. You won't even need a trunk—we're planning to do all our shopping in Paris, of course, anyway, and of course you wouldn't need much for the boat. But do as you please. You know how we both counted on your coming and cannot understand your changing your mind at the last minute, but of course if James says so I suppose you have no choice. Anyway, if there's any chance of you and James both joining us later, do let me know. I'll send you our address. Meanwhile, take care of yourself, and remember we are always thinking of you, love, Mother.

Mr. Benjamin set this letter aside to be answered, and opened the other letter addressed to his wife. It was, he assumed, from an old school friend, because he did not know the name, and it read:

Helen, darling, just saw your name in the paper, being married, and how *marvelous*. Do we know the lucky man? Anyway, we always said you'd be the first married and now here you are, the last—at least, Smitty hasn't married yet, but we never counted *her*. Anyway, Doug and I are just *dying* to see you, and now that we're in touch again I'll be waiting for word from you about when you and your new hubby can run up and pay us a visit. Any weekend at *all*, and let us know what train you'll make. Just *loads* of love and congratulations, Joanie.

This letter did not absolutely require an answer, but Mr. Benjamin set it aside anyway. He poured himself a third cup of coffee, and drank it peacefully, regarding the department store advertisements superimposed upon the horrors of the morning paper. When he had finished this cup of coffee, he rose, and collected the advertisements and the paper and said, when he saw Genevieve standing in the kitchen doorway, "I'm finished, thanks, Genevieve. Is Mrs. Benjamin awake?"

"I just took up her tray, Mr. Benjamin," Genevieve said.

"Right," said Mr. Benjamin. "I'll be leaving for the office on the eleven-fifteen train, Genevieve. I'll drive myself to the station, and I'll be back about seven. You and Mrs. Carter will take care of Mrs. Benjamin while I'm gone?"

"Of course, Mr. Benjamin."

"Good." With his little collection of papers, Mr. Benjamin turned resolutely toward the stairs, leaving behind him the breakfast dishes and the coffeepot and Genevieve's incurious eyes.

His wife's room was at the head of the stairs, a heavy oaken door with brass-trimmed knobs and hinges. The key hung always on a hook just beside the doorway, and Mr. Benjamin sighed a third time as he lifted it down and weighed it for a minute in his hand. When he fitted the key to the lock in the door he heard the first split second of stunned silence within, and then the rattle of dishes as his wife set aside her breakfast tray and waited for the door to open. Sighing, Mr. Benjamin turned the key and opened the door.

"Good morning," he said, avoiding looking at her and going instead to the window, which showed him the same view of the garden that he had seen from the dining room, the same flowers a little farther away, the same street beyond, the same rows of houses. "How are you feeling this morning?"

"Very well, thank you."

The lawn, seen from this angle, showed more clearly that it needed trimming, and he said, "Have to get hold of that fellow to do the lawn."

"His name's in the little telephone book," she said. "The one where I keep numbers like the laundry's, and the grocer's." There was the sound of her coffee cup being moved. "Kept," she said.

"It's going to be another nice day," he said, still looking out.

"Splendid. Will you play golf?"

"You know I don't play golf on Mondays," he said, turning to her in surprise; once he had looked at her, even without intending to, he found it not difficult; she was always the same, these mornings now, and it came as more of a shock to him daily to realize that although, throughout the rest of the house, she existed as a presence made up half of recollection and half of intention, here in her room she was the same as always, and not influential at all. She sometimes wore a blue bed jacket and had an egg on her tray, and she sometimes put her hair onto the top of her head with combs instead of letting it fall about her shoulders, and she sometimes sat in the chair next to the window, and she was sometimes reading the books he brought her from the library, but essentially she was the same, and the same woman as the one he had married and probably the same woman that he might one day bury.

Her voice, when she spoke to him, was the one she had used for many years, although recently she had learned to keep it lower and without emotion; at first, that had been because she disliked the thought of Genevieve and Mrs. Carter hearing her, but now it was because it did so little good to shout at him, and frequently drove him away. "Any mail?" she asked.

"A letter from your mother, one from someone named Joanie."

"Joanie?" she said, frowning. "I don't know anyone named Joanie."

"Helen," he said irritably, "will you *please* stop talking like that?"

She hesitated, and then took up her coffee cup again with a gesture that made it clear that whatever she had intended to say, she was persuaded that there was no reason to say it again.

"I don't know her name," he said patiently, "but it was on her letter. She said Smitty wasn't married yet. She said how wonderful that you were married and would you and your hubby visit her soon."

"Joan Morris," she said. "Why didn't you say so instead of letting me—" She stopped.

"There were no other letters," he said deliberately.

"I wasn't expecting any but Mother's."

"Has Mr. Ferguson forgotten you, do you suppose? Or perhaps given up a difficult job?"

"I don't know Mr. Ferguson."

"So easily discouraged . . ." he said. "It could hardly have been a very . . . *passionate* affair."

"I don't know anyone named Ferguson." She kept her voice quiet, as she always did now, but she moved her coffee cup slightly in its saucer, and looked at it with interest, the thin cup moving in a tiny delicate circle on the saucer. "There wasn't any affair."

He went on, speaking as quietly as she did, and watching the coffee cup, but he sounded almost wistful. "You gave him up so easily," he said. "Hardly a word from me, and poor Mr. Ferguson was abandoned. And now he seems to be weakening in his efforts to release you." He thought. "I don't believe there's been a letter for nearly a week," he said.

"I don't know who writes the letters. I don't know anyone named Ferguson."

"Perhaps not. Perhaps he saw you in a bus, or across a restaurant, and had since that magic moment dedicated his life to you; perhaps, even, you succeeded in dropping a note out the window, or Genevieve took pity on you . . . perhaps Genevieve's fur coat was a bribe?"

"It hardly seemed likely that I should be needing a fur coat," she said.

"It was a present from me, originally, was it not? You will be pleased to know that Genevieve came directly to me and offered to return the coat."

"I suppose you *did* take it back?"

"I did," he said. "I prefer not to have Genevieve indebted to you."

He was already tired of her this morning; it was not possible to communicate with her because she would not abandon her coffee cup, and she knew already of course that he had taken the coat and the jewelry away from Genevieve. There was not even the hope between them that he believed she had actually dropped a note from the window, or somehow gotten word to the outside world; there was not even, they both knew, any way in which she might sit down and, hands trembling and with nervous glances at the door, set upon paper any statement of her position which might bring someone to unlock the door and let her out. Even if she had been allowed pencil and paper or had found it possible to scrawl with a lipstick upon a handkerchief, she was not capable anymore of expressions such as "I am kept prisoner by my husband, help me" or "Save an unfortunate woman unjustly confined" or "Get the police" or even "Help"; there had been a period when she had tried to force her way out of the room when the door was opened, but that had been only at first. She had then fallen into a sullen indifference and during that time he had watched her closely, since the (then almost daily) letters from Ferguson had suggested methods for release and he had suspected then that she was trying to communicate with her mother. Now, however, in this fairly new attitude of hers, which had begun when she gave away her clothes to Genevieve and began to stay in bed all day, and the letters from Ferguson were not as frequent, he had become easier in his mind about her, and even allowed her books and magazines, and had once brought her a dozen roses for her room. He did not for a minute believe that she was crafty enough to be planning an escape, or to use this apparent resigned state of mind to deceive him into thinking she had accepted his authority. "You still remember," he asked her, thinking of this, "that you may at any time resume your normal life, and wear your pretty clothes again, and return to normal?"

"I remember it," she said, and laughed.

He came toward her, toward the bed and the coffee cup and toward her blue bed jacket, until he could see clearly the combs on the top of her head and the small hairs that escaped. "Just tell me," he said beggingly. "All you have to do is to tell me—only a few words—tell me about Ferguson, and where you met him and what—" He stopped. "Confess," he said sternly, and she lifted her head to look at him.

"I don't know anyone named Ferguson. I never loved anyone in my life. I never had any affairs. I have nothing to confess. I do not want to wear my pretty clothes again."

He sighed, and turned toward the door. "I wonder why not," he said.

"Don't forget to lock the door," she said, turning to take her book from the table. Mr. Benjamin locked the door behind him and stood for a minute holding the key in his hand before he hung it again on its hook. Then he turned wearily and went down the stairs. Genevieve was dusting the living room and he stopped in the doorway and said, "Genevieve, Mrs. Benjamin would like something light for lunch; perhaps a salad."

"Certainly, Mr. Benjamin," Genevieve said.

"I won't have dinner home," Mr. Benjamin said. "I thought I might, but I believe I'll stay in town after all. I believe Mrs. Benjamin needs new library books; will you take care of that for her?"

"Certainly, Mr. Benjamin," Genevieve said again.

He felt oddly hesitant, almost as though he would rather stand there and talk to Genevieve than go on into his study; perhaps that was because Genevieve would certainly answer "Yes, Mr. Benjamin." He moved abruptly before he could say anything else, and went into his study and closed and locked the door, thinking as he did so, two rooms locked and shut away from the rest of the house, two rooms far apart, and all the house in between not being used, the living room and the dining room and the hall and the stairs and the bedrooms all just lying there, shutting two locked rooms away from each other. He shook his head violently; he was tired. He slept in the bedroom next to his wife's and sometimes at night the temptation to unlock her door and go inside and tell her she was forgiven was very strong for him; he was fortunately kept from this by the frightful recollection of the one time he had unlocked his wife's door during the night and she had driven him out with her fists and had locked the door from the inside, returning the key to him in the morning without a word; he suspected that soon it would not be possible for him to enter her room even by day.

He sat down at his desk and pressed his hand to his forehead irritably. It had to be done, however, and he took a sheet of her monogrammed notepaper and opened his fountain pen. "Dearest Mommy," he wrote, "my mean old finger is still too painful to write with—James says he thinks I may have sprained it, but I think he is just tired of taking dictation from me—as if he had ever done anything else; anyway, we're both just *sick* that we can't join you in Paris after all, but I really think we're wiser not to. After all, we only came back from our honeymoon in July, and James just *has* to spend *some* time at his old office. He says maybe this winter we can fly down to South America for a couple of weeks, and not let anyone know where we're going or when we're coming back or anything. Anyway, have a lovely time in Paris, and buy *lots* of lovely clothes, and *don't* forget to write me." Mr. Benjamin sat and regarded his letter and then, sighing, took up his pen and added, "Love, Helen and James." He sealed and addressed the letter and then, sitting quietly at his desk with his hands folded in front of him, he spent a moment thinking. He reached a sudden decision and opened the bottom drawer of the desk and took out a box of rather cheap notepaper, faintly colored, and a fountain pen filled with brown ink. With a sober air which made his gesture some-how ominous, he took the pen into his left hand and began to write in a bold hand, "My dearest, I have finally thought of a way to get around the jealous old fool. I've spoken to the girl a couple of times at the library and I think she'll help us if she's sure she won't get into trouble. Here's what I want to do . . ."

The Man in the Woods

Wearily, moving his feet because he had nothing else to do, Christopher went on down the road, hating the trees that moved slowly against his progress, hating the dust beneath his feet, hating the sky, hating this road, all roads, everywhere. He had been walking since morning, and all day the day before that, and the day before that, and days before that, back into the numberless line of walking days that dissolved, seemingly years ago, into the place he had left, once, before he started walking. This morning he had been walking past fields, and now he was walking past trees that mounted heavily to the road, and leaned across, bending their great old bodies toward him; Christopher had come into the forest at a crossroads, turning onto the forest road as though he had a choice, looking back once to see the other road, the one he had not chosen, going peacefully on through fields, in and out of towns, perhaps even coming to an end somewhere beyond Christopher's sight.

The cat had joined him shortly after he entered the forest, emerging from between the trees in a quick, shadowy movement that surprised Christopher at first and then, oddly, comforted him, and the cat had stayed beside him, moving closer to Christopher as the trees pressed insistently closer to them both, trotting along in the casual acceptance of human company that cats exhibit when they are frightened. Christopher, when he stopped once to rest, sitting on a large stone at the edge of the road, had rubbed the cat's ears and pulled the cat's tail affectionately, and had said, "Where we going, fellow? Any ideas?" and the cat had closed his eyes meaningfully and opened them again.

"Haven't seen a house since we came into these trees," Christopher remarked once, later, to the cat; squinting up at the sky, he had added, "Going to be dark before long." He glanced apprehensively at the trees so close to him, irritated by the sound of his own voice in the silence, as though the trees were listening to him and, listening, had nodded solemnly to one another.

"Don't worry," Christopher said to the cat. "Road's got to go *some*where."

It was not much later—an hour before dark, probably—that Christopher and the cat paused, surprised, at a turn in the road, because a house was ahead. A neat stone fence ran down to the road, smoke came naturally from the chimneys, the doors and windows were not nailed shut, nor were the steps broken or the hinges sagging. It was a comfortable-looking, settled old house, made of stone like its fence, easily found in the pathless forest because it lay correctly, compactly, at the end of the road, which was not a road at all, of course, but merely a way to the house. Christopher thought briefly of the other way, long before, that he had not followed, and then moved forward, the cat at his heels, to the front door of the house.

The sound of a river came from among the trees. The river knew a way out of the forest, because it moved along sweetly and clearly, over clean stones and, unafraid, among the dark trees.

Christopher approached the house as he would any house, farmhouse, suburban home, or city apartment, and knocked politely and with pleasure on the warm front door.

"Come in, then," a woman said as she opened it, and Christopher stepped inside, followed closely by the cat.

The woman stood back and looked for a minute at Christopher, her eyes searching and wide; he looked back at her and saw that she was young, not so young as he would have liked, but too young, seemingly, to be living in the heart of a forest.

"I've been here for a long time, though," she said, as if she'd read his thoughts. Out of this dark hallway, he thought, she might look older; her hair curled a little around her face, and her eyes were far too wide for the rest of her, as if she were constantly straining to see in the gloom of the forest. She wore a long green dress that was gathered at her waist by a belt made of what he subsequently saw was grass woven into a rope; she was barefoot. While he stood uneasily just inside the door, looking at her as she looked at him, the cat went round the hall, stopping curiously at corners and before closed doors, glancing up, once, into the unlighted heights of the stairway that rose from the far end of the hall.

"He smells another cat," she said. "We have one."

"Phyllis," a voice called from the back of the house, and the woman smiled quickly, nervously, at Christopher and said, "Come along, please. I shouldn't keep you waiting."

He followed her to the door at the back of the hall, next to the stairway, and was grateful for the light that greeted them when she opened it. He was led directly into a great warm kitchen, glowing with an open fire on its hearth, and well lit, against the late-afternoon dimness of the forest, by three kerosene lamps set on table and shelves. A second woman stood by the stove, watching the pots that steamed and smelled maddeningly of onions and herbs; Christopher closed his eyes, like the cat, against the unbelievable beauty of warmth, light, and the smell of onions.

"Well," the woman at the stove said with finality, turning to look at Christopher. She studied him carefully, as the other woman had done, and then turned her eyes to a bare whitewashed area, high on the kitchen wall, where lines and crosses indicated a rough measuring system. "Another day," she said.

"What's your name?" the first woman asked Christopher, and he said "Christopher" without effort and then, "What's yours?"

"Phyllis," the young woman said. "What's your cat's name?"

"I don't know," Christopher said. He smiled a little. "It's not even my cat," he went on, his voice gathering strength from the smell of the onions. "He just followed me here."

"We'll have to name him something," Phyllis said. When she spoke she looked away from Christopher, turning her overlarge eyes on him again only when she stopped speaking. "Our cat's named Grimalkin."

"Grimalkin," Christopher said.

"*Her* name," Phyllis said, gesturing with her head toward the cook. "*Her* name's Aunt Cissy."

"Circe," the older woman said doggedly to the stove. "Circe I was born and Circe I will have for my name till I die."

Although she seemed, from the way she stood and the way she kept her voice to a single note, to be much older than Phyllis, Christopher saw her face clearly in the light of the lamps—she was vigorous and clear-eyed, and the strength in her arms when she lifted the great iron pot easily off the stove and carried it to the stone table in the center of the kitchen surprised Christopher. The cat, who had followed Christopher and Phyllis into the kitchen, leaped noiselessly onto the bench beside the table, and then onto the table; Phyllis looked warily at Christopher for a minute before she pushed the cat gently to drive him off the table.

"We'll have to find a name for your cat," she said apologetically as the cat leaped down without taking offense.

"Kitty," Christopher said helplessly. "I guess I always call cats 'Kitty.'"

Phyllis shook her head. She was about to speak when Aunt Cissy stopped her with a glance, and Phyllis moved quickly to an iron chest in the corner of the kitchen, from which she took a cloth to spread on the table, and heavy stone plates and mugs, which she set on the table in four places. Christopher sat down on the bench, with his back to the table, to indicate clearly that he had no intention of presuming that he was sitting at the table but was on the bench only because he was tired, that he would not swing around to the table until invited warmly and specifically to do so.

"Are we almost ready, then?" Aunt Cissy said. She swept her eyes across the table, adjusted a fork, and stood back, her glance never for a minute resting on Christopher. Then she moved over to the wall beside the door, where she stood, quiet and erect, and Phyllis went to stand beside her. Christopher, turning his head to look at them, had to turn again as footsteps approached from the hall, and after a minute's interminable pause, the door opened. The two women stayed respectfully by the far wall, and Christopher stood up without knowing why, except that it was his host who was entering.

This was a man toward the end of middle age; although he held his shoulders stiffly back, they looked as if they would sag without a constant effort. His face was lined and tired, and his mouth, like his shoulders, appeared to be falling downward into resignation. He was dressed, as the women were, in a long green robe tied at the waist, and he, too, was barefoot. As he stood in the doorway, with the darkness of the hall behind him, his white head shone softly, and his eyes, bright and curious, regarded Christopher for a long minute before they turned, as the older woman's had done, to the crude measuring system on the upper wall.

"We are honored to have you here," he said at last to Christopher; his voice was resonant, like the sound of the wind in the trees. Without speaking again, he took his seat at the head of the stone table and gestured to Christopher to take the place on his right. Phyllis came away from her post by the door and slipped into the place across from Christopher, and Aunt Cissy served them all from the iron pot before taking her own place at the foot of the table.

Christopher stared down at the plate before him, and the rich smell of the onions and meat met him, so that he closed his eyes again for a minute before starting to eat. When he lifted his head he could see, over Phyllis's head, the dark window, the trees pressed so close against it that their branches were bent against the glass, a tangled crowd of leaves and branches looking in.

"What will we call you?" the old man asked Christopher at last.

"I'm Christopher," Christopher said, looking only at his plate or up at the window.

"And have you come far?" the old man said.

"Very far." Christopher smiled. "I suppose it seems farther than it really is," he explained.

"I am named Oakes," the old man said.

Christopher gathered himself together with an effort. Ever since entering this strange house he had been bewildered, as though intoxicated from his endless journey through the trees, and uneasy at coming from darkness and the watching forest into a house where he sat down without introductions at his host's table. Swallowing, Christopher turned to look at Mr. Oakes and said, "It's very kind of you to take me in. If you hadn't, I guess I'd have been wandering around in the woods all night."

Mr. Oakes bowed his head slightly at Christopher.

"I guess I was a little frightened," Christopher said with a small embarrassed laugh. "All those trees."

"Indeed, yes," Mr. Oakes said placidly. "All those trees."

Christopher wondered if he had shown his gratitude adequately. He wanted very much to say something further, something that might lead to an explicit definition of his privileges: whether he was to stay the night, for instance, or whether he must go out again into the woods in the darkness; whether, if he did stay the night, he might have in the morning another such meal as this dinner. When Aunt Cissy filled his plate a second time, Christopher smiled up at her. "This is certainly wonderful," he said to her. "I don't know when I've had a meal I enjoyed this much."

Aunt Cissy bowed her head to him as Mr. Oakes had before.

"The food comes from the woods, of course," Mr. Oakes said. "Circe gathers her onions down by the river, but naturally none of that need concern you."

"I suppose not," Christopher said, feeling that he was not to stay the night.

"Tomorrow will be soon enough for you to see the house," Mr. Oakes added.

"I suppose so," Christopher said, realizing that he was indeed to stay the night.

"Tonight," Mr. Oakes said, his voice deliberately light. "Tonight, I should like to hear about you, and what things you have seen on your journey, and what takes place in the world you have left."

Christopher smiled. Knowing that he could stay the night, could not in charity be dismissed before the morning, he felt relaxed. Aunt Cissy's good dinner had pleased him, and he was ready enough to talk with his host.

"I don't really know quite *how* I got here," he said. "I just took the road into the woods."

"You would have to go through the woods to get here," his host agreed soberly.

"Before *that*," Christopher went on, "I passed a lot of farmhouses and a little town—do you know the name of it? I asked a woman there for a meal and she turned me away."

He laughed now, at the memory, with Aunt Cissy's good dinner warm inside him.

"And before that," he said, "I was studying."

"You are a scholar," the old man said. "Naturally."

"I don't know *why*." Christopher turned at last to Mr. Oakes and spoke frankly. "I don't know why," he repeated. "One day I was there, in college, like everyone else, and then the next day I just left, without any reason except that I did." He glanced from Mr. Oakes to Phyllis to Aunt Cissy; they were all looking at him with blank expectation. He stopped, then said lamely, "And I guess that's all that happened before I came here."

"He brought a cat with him," Phyllis said softly, her eyes down.

"A cat?" Mr. Oakes looked politely around the kitchen, saw Christopher's cat curled up under the stove, and nodded. "One brought a dog," he said to Aunt Cissy. "Do you remember the dog?"

Aunt Cissy nodded, her face unchanging.

There was a sound at the door, and Phyllis said, without moving, "That is our Grimalkin coming for his supper."

Aunt Cissy rose and went over to the outer door and opened it. A cat, tiger-striped where Christopher's cat was black, but about the same size, trotted casually into the kitchen, without a glance at Aunt Cissy, went directly for the stove, then saw Christopher's cat. Christopher's cat lifted his head lazily, widened his eyes, and stared at Grimalkin.

"I think they're going to fight," Christopher said nervously, half rising from his seat. "Perhaps I'd better—"

But he was too late. Grimalkin lifted his voice in a deadly wail, and Christopher's cat spat, without stirring from his comfortable bed under the stove; then Grimalkin moved incautiously and was caught off guard by Christopher's cat. Spitting and screaming, they clung to each other briefly, then Grimalkin ran crying out the door that Aunt Cissy opened for him.

Mr. Oakes sighed. "What is your cat's name?" he inquired.

"I'm *terribly* sorry," Christopher said, with a fleeting fear that his irrational cat might have deprived them both of a bed. "Shall I go and find Grimalkin outside?"

Mr. Oakes laughed. "He was fairly beaten," he said, "and has no right to come back."

"Now," Phyllis said softly, "now we can call your cat Grimalkin. Now we have a name, Grimalkin, and no cat, so we can give the name to your cat."

Christopher slept that night in a stone room at the top of the house, a room reached by the dark staircase leading from the hall. Mr. Oakes carried a candle to the room for him, and Christopher's cat, now named Grimalkin, left the warm stove to follow. The room was small and neat, and the bed was a stone bench, which Christopher, investigating after his host had gone, discovered to his amazement was mattressed with leaves, and had for blankets heavy furs that looked like bearskins.

"This is quite a forest," Christopher said to the cat, rubbing a corner of the bearskin between his hands. "And quite a family."

Against the window of Christopher's room, as against all the windows in the house, was the wall of trees, crushing themselves hard against the glass. "I wonder if that's why they made this house out of stone?" Christopher asked the cat. "So the trees wouldn't push it down?"

All night long the sound of the trees came into Christopher's dreams, and he turned gratefully in his sleep to the cat purring beside him in the great fur coverings.

In the morning, Christopher came down into the kitchen, where Phyllis and Aunt Cissy, in their green robes, were moving about the stove. His cat, who had followed him down the stairs, moved immediately ahead of him in the kitchen to sit under the stove and watch Aunt Cissy expectantly. When Phyllis had set the stone table and Aunt Cissy had laid out the food, they both moved over to the doorway as they had the night before, waiting for Mr. Oakes to come in.

When he came, he nodded to Christopher and they sat, as before, Aunt Cissy serving them all. Mr. Oakes did not speak this morning, and when the meal was over he rose, gesturing to Christopher to follow him. They went out into the hall, with its silent closed doors, and Mr. Oakes paused.

"You have seen only part of the house, of course," he said. "Our handmaidens keep to the kitchen unless called to this hall."

"Where do they sleep?" Christopher asked. "In the kitchen?" He was immediately embarrassed by his own question, and smiled awkwardly at Mr. Oakes to say that he did not deserve an answer, but Mr. Oakes shook his head in amusement and put his hand on Christopher's shoulder.

"On the kitchen floor," he said. And then he turned his head away, but Christopher could see that he was laughing. "Circe," he said, "sleeps nearer to the door from the hall."

Christopher felt his face growing red and, glad for the darkness of the hall, said quickly, "It's a very old house, isn't it?"

"Very old," Mr. Oakes said, as though surprised by the question. "A house was found to be vital, of course."

"Of course," Christopher said, agreeably.

"In here," Mr. Oakes said, opening one of the two great doors on either side of the entrance. "In here are the records kept."

Christopher followed him in, and Mr. Oakes went to a candle that stood in its own wax on a stone table and lit it with the flint that lay beside it. He then raised the candle high, and Christopher saw that the walls were covered with stones, piled up to make loose, irregular shelves. On some of the shelves great, leather-covered books stood, and on other shelves lay stone tablets, and rolls of parchment.

"They are of great value," Mr. Oakes said sadly. "I have never known how to use them, of course." He walked slowly over and touched one huge volume, then turned to show Christopher his fingers covered with dust. "It is my sorrow," he said, "that I cannot use these things of great value."

Christopher, frightened by the books, drew back into the doorway. "At one time," Mr. Oakes said, shaking his head, "there were many more. Many, many more. I have heard that at one time this room was made large enough to hold the records. I have never known how they came to be destroyed."

Still carrying the candle, he led Christopher out of the room and shut the big door behind them. Across the hall another door faced them. As Mr. Oakes led the way in with the candle, Christopher saw that it was another bedroom, larger than the one in which he had slept.

"This, of course," Mr. Oakes said, "is where I have been sleeping, to guard the records."

He held the candle high again and Christopher saw a stone bench like his own, with heavy furs lying on it, and above the bed a long and glittering knife resting upon two pegs driven between the stones of the wall.

"The keeper of the records," Mr. Oakes said, and sighed briefly before he smiled at Christopher in the candlelight. "We are like two friends," he added. "One showing the other his house."

"But—" Christopher began, and Mr. Oakes laughed.

"Let me show you my roses," he said.

Christopher followed him helplessly back into the hall, where Mr. Oakes blew out the candle and left it on a shelf by the door, and then out the front door to the tiny cleared patch before the house, which was surrounded by the stone wall that ran to the road. Although for a small distance before them the world was clear of trees, it was not very much lighter or more pleasant, with the forest only barely held back by the stone wall, edging as close to it as possible, pushing, as Christopher had felt since the day before, crowding up and embracing the little stone house in horrid possession.

"Here are my roses," Mr. Oakes said, his voice warm. He looked calculatingly beyond at the forest as he spoke, his eyes measuring the distance between the trees and his roses. "I planted them myself," he said. "I was the first one to clear away even this much of the forest. Because I wished to plant roses in the midst of this wilderness. Even so," he added, "I had to send Circe for roses from the midst of this beast around us, to set them here in my little clear spot." He leaned affectionately over the roses, which grew gloriously against the stone of the house, on a vine that rose triumphantly almost to the height of the door. Over him, over the roses, over the house, the trees leaned eagerly.

"They need to be tied up against stakes every spring," Mr. Oakes said. He stepped back a pace and measured with his hand above his head. "A stake—a small tree stripped of its branches will do, and Circe will get it and sharpen it—and the rose vine tied to it as it leans against the house."

Christopher nodded. "Someday the roses will cover the house, I imagine," he said.

"Do you think so?" Mr. Oakes turned eagerly to him. "My roses?"

"It *looks* like it," Christopher said awkwardly, his fingers touching the first stake, bright against the stones of the house.

Mr. Oakes shook his head, smiling. "Remember who planted them," he said.

They went inside again and through the hall into the kitchen, where Aunt Cissy and Phyllis stood against the wall as they entered. Again they sat at the stone table and Aunt Cissy served them, and again Mr. Oakes said nothing while they ate and Phyllis and Aunt Cissy looked down at their plates.

After the meal was over, Mr. Oakes bowed to Christopher before leaving the room, and while Phyllis and Aunt Cissy cleared the table of plates and cloth, Christopher sat on the bench with his cat on his knee. The women seemed to be unusually occupied. Aunt Cissy, at the stove, set down iron pots enough for a dozen meals, and Phyllis, sent to fetch a special utensil from an alcove in the corner of the kitchen, came back to report that it had been mislaid "since the last time" and could not be found, so that Aunt Cissy had to put down her cooking spoon and go herself to search.

Phyllis set a great pastry shell on the stone table, and she and Aunt Cissy filled it slowly and lovingly with spoonfuls from one or another pot on the stove, stopping to taste and estimate, questioning each other with their eyes.

"What *are* you making?" Christopher asked finally.

"A feast," Phyllis said, glancing at him quickly and then away.

Christopher's cat watched, purring, until Aunt Cissy disappeared into the kitchen alcove again and came back carrying the trussed carcass of what seemed to Christopher to be a wild pig. She and Phyllis set this on the spit before the great fireplace, and Phyllis sat beside it to turn the spit. Then Christopher's cat leaped down and ran over to the fireplace to sit beside Phyllis and taste the drops of fat that fell on the great hearth as the spit was turned.

"Who is coming to your feast?" Christopher asked, amused.

Phyllis looked around at him, and Aunt Cissy half turned from the stove. There was a silence in the kitchen, a silence of no movement and almost no breath, and then, before anyone could speak, the door opened and Mr. Oakes came in. He was carrying the knife from his bedroom, and with a shrug of resignation he held it out for Christopher to see. When Mr. Oakes had seated himself at the table, Aunt Cissy disappeared again into the alcove and brought back a grindstone, which she set before Mr. Oakes. Deliberately, with the slow caution of a pleasant action lovingly done, Mr. Oakes set about sharpening the knife. He held the bright blade against the moving stone, turning the edge little by little with infinite delicacy.

"You say you've come far?" he said over the sound of the knife, and for a minute his eyes left the grindstone to rest on Christopher.

"Quite a ways," Christopher said, watching the grindstone. "I don't know how far, exactly."

"And you were a scholar?"

"Yes," Christopher said. "A student."

Mr. Oakes looked up from the knife again, to the estimate marked on the wall.

"Christopher," he said softly, as though estimating the name.

When the knife was razor sharp, Mr. Oakes held it up to the light from the fire, studying the blade. Then he looked at Christopher and shook his head humorously. "As sharp as any weapon can be," he said.

Aunt Cissy spoke, unsolicited, for the first time. "Sun's down," she said.

Mr. Oakes nodded. He looked at Phyllis for a minute, and at Aunt Cissy. Then, with his sharpened knife in his hand, he walked over and put his free arm around Christopher's shoulder. "Will you remember about the roses?" he asked. "They *must* be tied up in the spring if they mean to grow at all."

For a minute his arm stayed warmly around Christopher's shoulders, and then, carrying his knife, he went over to the back door and waited while Aunt Cissy came to open it for him. As the door was opened, the trees showed for a minute, dark and greedy. Then Aunt Cissy closed the door behind Mr. Oakes. For a minute she leaned her back against it, watching Christopher, then, standing away from it, she opened it again. Christopher, staring, walked slowly over to the open door, as Aunt Cissy seemed to expect he would, and heard behind him Phyllis's voice from the hearth.

"He'll be down by the river," she said softly. "Go far around and come up behind him."

The door shut solidly behind Christopher and he leaned against it, looking with frightened eyes at the trees that reached for him on either side. Then as he pressed his back in terror against the door, he heard the voice calling from the direction of the river, so clear and ringing through the trees that he hardly knew it as Mr. Oakes's: "Who is he dares enter these my woods?"

Home

Ethel Sloane was whistling to herself as she got out of her car and splashed across the sidewalk to the doorway of the hardware store. She was wearing a new raincoat and solid boots, and one day of living in the country had made her weather-wise. "This rain can't last," she told the hardware clerk confidently. "This time of year it never lasts."

The clerk nodded tactfully. One day in the country had been enough for Ethel Sloane to become acquainted with most of the local people; she had been into the hardware store several times—"so many odd things you never expect you're going to need in an old house"—and into the post office to leave their new address, and into the grocery to make it clear that all the Sloane grocery business was going to come their way, and into the bank and into the gas station and into the little library and even as far as the door of the barbershop (". . . and you'll be seeing my husband Jim Sloane in a day or so!"). Ethel Sloane liked having bought the old Sanderson place, and she liked walking the single street of the village, and most of all she liked knowing that people knew who she was.

"They make you feel at home right away, as though you were born not half a mile from here," she explained to her husband, Jim.

Privately she thought that the storekeepers in the village might show a little more alacrity in remembering her name; she had probably brought more business to the little stores in the village than any of them had seen for a year past. They're not outgoing people, she told herself reassuringly. It takes a while for them to get over being suspicious; we've been here in the house for only two days.

"First, I want to get the name of a good plumber," she said to the clerk in the hardware store. Ethel Sloane was a great believer in getting information directly from the local people; the plumbers listed in the phone book might be competent enough, but the local people always knew who would suit; Ethel Sloane had no intention of antagonizing the villagers by hiring an unpopular plumber. "And closet hooks," she said. "My husband, Jim, turns out to be just as good a handyman as he is a writer." Always tell them your business, she thought, then they don't have to ask.

"I suppose the best one for plumbing would be Will Watson," the clerk said. "He does most of the plumbing around. You drive down the Sanderson road in this rain?"

"Of course." Ethel Sloane was surprised. "I had all kinds of things to do in the village."

"Creek's pretty high. They say that sometimes when the creek is high—"

"The bridge held our moving truck yesterday, so I guess it will hold my car today. That bridge ought to stand for a while yet." Briefly she wondered whether she might not say "for a spell" instead of "for a while," and then decided that sooner or later it would come naturally. "Anyway, who minds rain? We've got so much to do indoors." She was pleased with "indoors."

"Well," the clerk said, "of course, no one can stop you from driving on the old Sanderson road. If you want to. You'll find people around here mostly leave it alone in the rain, though. Myself, I think it's all just gossip, but then, I don't drive out that way much, anyway."

"It's a little muddy on a day like this," Ethel Sloane said firmly, "and maybe a little scary crossing the bridge when the creek is high, but you've got to expect that kind of thing when you live in the country."

"I wasn't talking about that," the clerk said. "Closet hooks? I wonder, do we have any closet hooks."

In the grocery Ethel Sloane bought mustard and soap and pickles and flour. "All the things I forgot to get yesterday," she explained, laughing.

"You took that road on a day like this?" the grocer asked.

"It's not that bad," she said, surprised again. "I don't mind the rain."

"We don't use that road in this weather," the grocer said. "You might say there's talk about that road."

"It certainly seems to have quite a local reputation," Ethel said, and laughed. "And it's nowhere near as bad as some of the other roads I've seen around here."

"Well, I told you," the grocer said, and shut his mouth.

I've offended him, Ethel thought, I've said I think their roads are bad; these people are so jealous of their countryside.

"I guess our road is pretty muddy," she said almost apologetically. "But I'm really a very careful driver."

"You stay careful," the grocer said. "No matter what you see."

"I'm always careful." Whistling, Ethel Sloane went out and got into her car and turned in the circle in front of the abandoned railway station. Nice little town, she was thinking, and they are beginning to like us already, all so worried about my safe driving. We're the kind of people, Jim and I, who fit in a place like this; we wouldn't belong in the suburbs or some kind of a colony; we're real people. Jim will write, she thought, and I'll get one of these country women to teach me how to make bread. Watson for plumbing.

She was oddly touched when the clerk from the hardware store and then the grocer stepped to their doorways to watch her drive by. They're worrying about me, she thought; they're afraid a city gal can't manage their bad, wicked roads, and I do bet it's hell in the winter, but I can manage; I'm country now.

Her way led out of the village and then off the highway onto a dirt road that meandered between fields and an occasional farmhouse, then crossed the creek—disturbingly high after all this rain—and turned onto the steep hill that led to the Sanderson house. Ethel Sloane could see the house from the bridge across the creek, although in summer the view would be hidden by trees. It's a lovely house, she thought with a little catch of pride; I'm so lucky; up there it stands, so proud and remote, waiting for me to come home.

*

On one side of the hill the Sanderson land had long ago been sold off, and the hillside was dotted with small cottages and a couple of ramshackle farms; the people on that side of the hill used the other, lower, road, and Ethel Sloane was surprised and a little uneasy to perceive that the tire marks on this road and across the bridge were all her own, coming down; no one else seemed to use this road at all. Private, anyway, she thought; maybe they've talked everyone else out of using it. She looked up to see the house as she crossed the bridge; my very own house, she thought, and then, well, *our* very own house, she thought, and then she saw that there were two figures standing silently in the rain by the side of the road.

Good heavens, she thought, standing there in this rain, and she stopped the car. "Can I give you a lift?" she called out, rolling down the window. Through the rain she could see that they seemed to be an old woman and a child, and the rain drove down on them. Staring, Ethel Sloane became aware that the child was sick with misery, wet and shivering and crying in the rain, and she said sharply, "Come and get in the car at once; you mustn't keep that child out in the rain another minute."

They stared at her, the old woman frowning, listening. Perhaps she is deaf, Ethel thought, and in her good raincoat and solid boots she climbed out of the car and went over to them. Not wanting for any reason in the world to touch either of them, she put her face close to the old woman's and said urgently, "Come, hurry. Get that child into the car, where it's dry. I'll take you wherever you want to go." Then, with real horror, she saw that the child was wrapped in a blanket, and under the blanket he was wearing thin pajamas; with a shiver of fury, Ethel saw that he was barefoot and standing in the mud. "Get in that car at once," she said, and hurried to open the back door. "Get in that car at once, do you hear me?"

Silently the old woman reached her hand down to the child and, his eyes wide and staring past Ethel Sloane, the child moved toward the car, with the old woman following. Ethel looked in disgust at the small bare feet going over the mud and rocks, and she said to the old woman, "You ought to be ashamed; that child is certainly going to be sick."

She waited until they had climbed into the backseat of the car, and then slammed the door and got into her seat again. She glanced up at the mirror, but they were sitting in the corner, where she could not see them, and she turned; the child was huddled against the old woman, and the old woman looked straight ahead, her face heavy with weariness.

"Where are you going?" Ethel asked, her voice rising. "Where shall I take you? That child," she said to the old woman, "has to be gotten indoors and into dry clothes as soon as possible. Where are you going? I'll see that you get there in a hurry."

The old woman opened her mouth, and in a voice of old age beyond consolation said, "We want to go to the Sanderson place."

"To the Sanderson place?" To us? Ethel thought, To see us? This pair? Then she realized that the Sanderson place, to the old local people, probably still included the land where the cottages had been built; they probably still call the whole thing the Sanderson place, she thought, and felt oddly feudal with pride. We're the lords of the manor, she thought, and her voice was more gentle when she asked, "Were you waiting out there for very long in the rain?"

"Yes," the old woman said, her voice remote and despairing. Their lives must be desolate, Ethel thought. Imagine being that old and that tired and standing in the rain for someone to come by.

"Well, we'll soon have you home," she said, and started the car. The wheels slipped and skidded in the mud, but found a purchase, and slowly Ethel felt the car begin to move up the hill. It was very muddy, and the rain was heavier, and the back of the car dragged as though under an intolerable weight. It's as though I had a load of iron, Ethel thought. Poor old lady, it's the weight of years.

"Is the child all right?" she asked, lifting her head; she could not turn to look at them.

"He wants to go home," the old woman said.

"I should think so. Tell him it won't be long. I'll take you right to your door." It's the least I can do, she thought, and maybe go inside with them and see that he's warm enough; those poor bare feet.

Driving up the hill was very difficult, and perhaps the road was a little worse than Ethel had believed; she found that she could not look around or even speak while she was navigating the sharp curves, with the rain driving against the windshield and the wheels slipping in the mud. Once she said, "Nearly at the top," and then had to be silent, holding the wheel tight. When the car gave a final lurch and topped the small last rise that led onto the flat driveway before the Sanderson house, Ethel said, "Made it," and laughed. "Now, which way should I go?"

They're frightened, she thought. I'm sure the child is frightened and I don't blame them; I was a little nervous myself. She said loudly, "We're at the top now, it's all right, we made it. Now where shall I take you?"

When there was still no answer, she turned; the backseat of the car was empty.

"But even if they *could* have gotten out of the car without my noticing," Ethel Sloane said for the tenth time that evening to her husband, "they couldn't have gotten out of sight. I looked and looked." She lifted her hands in an emphatic gesture. "I went all around the top of the hill in the rain looking in all directions and calling them."

"But the car seat was dry," her husband said.

"Well, you're not going to suggest that I imagined it, are you? Because I'm simply not the kind of *person* to dream up an old lady and a sick child. There has to be some *explanation*; I don't imagine things."

"Well . . ." Jim said, and hesitated.

"Are you sure you didn't see them? They didn't come to the door?"

"Listen . . ." Jim said, and hesitated again. "Look," he said.

"I have certainly *never* been the kind of person who goes around imagining that she sees old ladies and children. You know me better than that, Jim, you know I don't go around—"

"Well," Jim said. "Look," he said finally, "there *could* be something. A story I heard. I never told you because—"

"Because what?"

"Because you . . . well—" Jim said.

"Jim." Ethel Sloane set her lips. "I don't like this, Jim. What is there that you haven't told me? Is there really something you know and I don't?"

"It's just a story. I heard it when I came up to look at the house."

"Do you mean you've known something all this time and you've never told me?"

"It's just a story," Jim said helplessly. Then, looking away, he said, "Everyone knows it, but they don't say much, I mean, these things—"

"Jim," Ethel said, "tell me at once."

"It's just that there was a little Sanderson boy stolen or lost or something. They thought a crazy old woman took him. People kept talking about it, but they never knew anything for sure."

"What?" Ethel Sloane stood up and started for the door. "You mean there's a child been stolen and no one told me about it?"

"No," Jim said oddly. "I mean, it happened sixty years ago."

Ethel was still talking about it at breakfast the next morning. "And they've never been found," she told herself happily. "All the people around went searching, and they finally decided the two of them had drowned in the creek, because it was raining then just the way it is now." She glanced with satisfaction at the rain beating against the window of the breakfast room. "Oh, lovely," she said, and sighed, and stretched, and smiled. "Ghosts," she said. "I saw two honest-to-goodness ghosts. No wonder," she said, "no *wonder* the child looked so awful. Awful! Kidnapped, and then drowned. No *wonder*."

"Listen," Jim said, "if I were you, I'd forget about it. People around here don't like to talk much about it."

"They wouldn't tell me," Ethel said, and laughed again. "Our very own ghosts, and not a soul would tell me. I just won't be satisfied until I get every word of the story."

"That's why *I* never told you," Jim said miserably.

"Don't be silly. Yesterday everyone I spoke to mentioned my driving on that road, and I bet every one of them was dying to tell me the story. I can't wait to see their faces when they hear."

"No." Jim stared at her. "You simply *can't* go around . . . *boasting* about it."

"But of course I can! Now we really belong here. I've really seen the local ghosts. And I'm going in this morning and tell everybody, and find out all I can."

"I wish you wouldn't," Jim said.

"I know you wish I wouldn't, but I'm going to. If I listened to you, I'd wait and wait for a good time to mention it and maybe even come to believe I'd dreamed it or something, so I'm going into the village right after breakfast."

"Please, Ethel," Jim said. "Please listen to me. People might not take it the way you think."

"Two ghosts of our very own." Ethel laughed again. "My very own," she said. "I just can't wait to see their faces in the village."

Before she got into the car she opened the back door and looked again at the seat, dry and unmarked. Then, smiling to herself, she got into the driver's seat and, suddenly touched with sick cold, turned around to look. "Why," she said, half whispering, "you're not *still* here, you can't be! Why," she said, "I just looked."

"They were strangers in the house," the old woman said.

The skin on the back of Ethel's neck crawled as though some wet thing walked there; the child stared past her, and the old woman's eyes were flat and dead. "What do you want?" Ethel asked, still whispering.

"We got to go back."

"I'll take you." The rain came hard against the windows of the car, and Ethel Sloane, seeing her own hand tremble as she reached for the car key, told herself, don't be afraid, don't be afraid, they're not real. "I'll take you," she said, gripping the wheel tight and turning the car to face down the hill, "I'll take you," she said, almost babbling, "I'll take you right back, I promise, see if I don't, I promise I'll take you right back where you want to go."

"He wanted to go home," the old woman said. Her voice was very far away.

"I'll take you, I'll take you." The road was even more slippery than before, and Ethel Sloane told herself, drive carefully, don't be afraid, they're not real. "Right where I found you yesterday, the very spot, I'll take you back."

"They were strangers in the house."

Ethel realized that she was driving faster than she should; she felt the disgusting wet cold coming from the backseat pushing her, forcing her to hurry.

"I'll take you back," she said over and over to the old woman and the child.

"When the strangers are gone, we can go home," the old woman said.

Coming to the last turn before the bridge, the wheels slipped, and, pulling at the steering wheel and shouting, "I'll take you back, I'll take you back," Ethel Sloane could hear only the child's horrible laughter as the car turned and skidded toward the high waters of the creek. One wheel slipped and spun in the air, and then, wrenching at the car with all her strength, she pulled it back onto the road and stopped.

Crying, breathless, Ethel put her head down on the steering wheel, weak and exhausted. I was almost killed, she told herself, they almost took me with them. She did not need to look into the backseat of the car; the cold was gone, and she knew the seat was dry and empty.

The clerk in the hardware store looked up and, seeing Ethel Sloane, smiled politely and then, looking again, frowned. "You feeling poorly this morning, Mrs. Sloane?" he asked. "Rain bothering you?"

"I almost had an accident on the road," Ethel Sloane said.

"On the old Sanderson road?" The clerk's hands were very still on the counter. "An accident?"

Ethel Sloane opened her mouth and then shut it again. "Yes," she said at last. "The car skidded."

"We don't use that road much," the clerk said. Ethel started to speak, but stopped herself.

"It's got a bad name locally, that road," he said. "What were you needing this morning?"

Ethel thought, and finally said, "Clothespins, I guess I must need clothespins. About the Sanderson road—"

"Yes?" said the clerk, his back to her.

"Nothing," Ethel said.

"Clothespins," the clerk said, putting a box on the counter. "By the way, will you and the mister be coming to the PTA social tomorrow night?"

"We certainly will," said Ethel Sloane.

The Summer People

The Allisons' country cottage, seven miles from the nearest town, was set prettily on a hill; from three sides it looked down on soft trees and grass that seldom, even at midsummer, lay still and dry. On the fourth side was the lake, which touched against the wooden pier the Allisons had to keep repairing, and which looked equally well from the Allisons' front porch, their side porch or any spot on the wooden staircase leading from the porch down to the water. Although the Allisons loved their summer cottage, looked forward to arriving in the early summer and hated to leave in the fall, they had not troubled themselves to put in any improvements, regarding the cottage itself and the lake as improvement enough for the life left to them. The cottage had no heat, no running water except the precarious supply from the backyard pump, and no electricity. For seventeen summers, Janet Allison had cooked on a kerosene stove, heating all their water; Robert Allison had brought buckets full of water daily from the pump and read his paper by kerosene light in the evenings; and they had both, sanitary city people, become stolid and matter-of-fact about their backhouse. In the first two years they had gone through all the standard vaudeville and magazine jokes about backhouses and by now, when they no longer had frequent guests to impress, they had subsided to a comfortable security which made the backhouse, as well as the pump and the kerosene, an indefinable asset to their summer life.

In themselves, the Allisons were ordinary people. Mrs. Allison was fifty-eight years old and Mr. Allison sixty; they had seen their children outgrow the summer cottage and go on to families of their own and seashore resorts; their friends were either dead or settled in comfortable year-round houses, their nieces and nephews vague. In the winter they told one another they could stand their New York apartment while waiting for the summer; in the summer they told one another that the winter was well worthwhile, waiting to get to the country.

Since they were old enough not to be ashamed of regular habits, the Allisons invariably left their summer cottage the Tuesday after Labor Day, and were as invariably sorry when the months of September and early October turned out to be pleasant and almost insufferably barren in the city; each year they recognized that there was nothing to bring them back to New York, but it was not until this year that they overcame their traditional inertia enough to decide to stay in the cottage after Labor Day.

"There isn't really anything to take us back to the city," Mrs. Allison told her husband seriously, as though it were a new idea, and he told her, as though neither of them had ever considered it, "We might as well enjoy the country as long as possible."

Consequently, with much pleasure and a slight feeling of adventure, Mrs. Allison went into their village the day after Labor Day and told those natives with whom she had dealings, with a pretty air of breaking away from tradition, that she and her husband had decided to stay at least a month longer at their cottage.

"It isn't as though we had anything to take us back to the city," she said to Mr. Babcock, her grocer. "We might as well enjoy the country while we can."

"Nobody ever stayed at the lake past Labor Day before," Mr. Babcock said. He was putting Mrs. Allison's groceries into a large cardboard carton, and he stopped for a minute to look reflectively into a bag of cookies. "Nobody," he added.

"But the city!" Mrs. Allison always spoke of the city to Mr. Babcock as though it were Mr. Babcock's dream to go there. "It's so hot—you've really no idea. We're always sorry when we leave."

"Hate to leave," Mr. Babcock said. One of the most irritating native tricks Mrs. Allison had noticed was that of taking a trivial statement and rephrasing it downward, into an even more trite statement. "I'd hate to leave myself," Mr. Babcock said, after deliberation, and both he and Mrs. Allison smiled. "But I never heard of anyone ever staying out at the lake after Labor Day before."

"Well, we're going to give it a try," Mrs. Allison said, and Mr. Babcock replied gravely, "Never know till you try."

Physically, Mrs. Allison decided, as she always did when leaving the grocery after one of her inconclusive conversations with Mr. Babcock, physically, Mr. Babcock could model for a statue of Daniel Webster, but mentally . . . it was horrible to think into what old New England Yankee stock had degenerated. She said as much to Mr. Allison when she got into the car, and he said, "It's generations of inbreeding. That and the bad land."

Since this was their big trip into town, which they made only once every two weeks to buy things they could not have delivered, they spent all day at it, stopping to have a sandwich in the newspaper and soda shop, and leaving packages heaped in the back of the car. Although Mrs. Allison was able to order groceries delivered regularly, she was never able to form any accurate idea of Mr. Babcock's current stock by telephone, and her lists of odds and ends that might be procured was always supplemented, almost beyond their need, by the new and fresh local vegetables Mr. Babcock was selling temporarily, or the packaged candy which had just come in. This trip Mrs. Allison was tempted, too, by the set of glass baking dishes that had found themselves completely by chance in the hardware and clothing and general store, and which had seemingly been waiting there for no one but Mrs. Allison, since the country people, with their instinctive distrust of anything that did not look as permanent as trees and rocks and sky, had only recently begun to experiment in aluminum baking dishes instead of ironware, and had, apparently within the memory of local inhabitants, discarded stoneware in favor of iron.

Mrs. Allison had the glass baking dishes carefully wrapped, to endure the uncomfortable ride home over the rocky road that led up to the Allisons' cottage, and while Mr. Charley Walpole, who, with his younger brother Albert, ran the hardware-clothing-general store (the store itself was called Johnson's because it stood on the site of the old Johnson cabin, burned fifty years before Charley Walpole was born), laboriously unfolded newspapers to wrap around the dishes, Mrs. Allison said, informally, "Course, I *could* have waited and gotten those dishes in New York, but we're not going back so soon this year."

"Heard you was staying on," Mr. Charley Walpole said. His old fingers fumbled maddeningly with the thin sheets of newspaper, carefully trying to isolate only one sheet at a time, and he did not look up at Mrs. Allison as he went on, "Don't know about staying on up there to the lake. Not after Labor Day."

"Well, you know," Mrs. Allison said, quite as though he deserved an explanation, "it just seemed to us that we've been hurrying back to New York every year, and there just wasn't any need for it. You know what the city's like in the fall." And she smiled confidingly up at Mr. Charley Walpole.

Rhythmically he wound string around the package. He's giving me a piece long enough to save, Mrs. Allison thought, and she looked away quickly to avoid giving any sign of impatience. "I feel sort of like we belong here, more," she said. "Staying on after everyone else has left." To prove this, she smiled brightly across the store at a woman with a familiar face, who might have been the woman who sold berries to the Allisons one year, or the woman who occasionally helped in the grocery and was probably Mr. Babcock's aunt.

"Well," Mr. Charley Walpole said. He shoved the package a little across the counter, to show that it was finished and that for a sale well made, a package well wrapped, he was willing to accept pay. "Well," he said again. "Never been summer people before, at the lake after Labor Day."

Mrs. Allison gave him a five-dollar bill, and he made change methodically, giving great weight even to the pennies. "Never after Labor Day," he said, and nodded at Mrs. Allison, and went soberly along the store to deal with two women who were looking at cotton house dresses.

As Mrs. Allison passed on her way out she heard one of the women say acutely, "Why is one of them dresses one dollar and thirty-nine cents and this one here is only ninety-eight?"

"They're great people," Mrs. Allison told her husband as they went together down the sidewalk after meeting at the door of the hardware store. "They're so solid, and so reasonable, and so *honest.*"

"Makes you feel good, knowing there are still towns like this," Mr. Allison said.

"You know, in New York," Mrs. Allison said, "I might have paid a few cents less for these dishes, but there wouldn't have been anything sort of personal in the transaction."

"Staying on to the lake?" Mrs. Martin, in the newspaper and sandwich shop, asked the Allisons. "Heard you was staying on."

"Thought we'd take advantage of the lovely weather this year," Mr. Allison said.

Mrs. Martin was a comparative newcomer to the town; she had married into the newspaper and sandwich shop from a neighboring farm, and had stayed on after her husband's death. She served bottled soft drinks, and fried egg and onion sandwiches on thick bread, which she made on her own stove at the back of the store. Occasionally when Mrs. Martin served a sandwich it would carry with it the rich fragrance of the stew or the pork chops cooking alongside for Mrs. Martin's dinner.

"I don't guess anyone's ever stayed out there so long before," Mrs. Martin said. "Not after Labor Day, anyway."

"I guess Labor Day is when they usually leave," Mr. Hall, the Allisons' nearest neighbor, told them later, in front of Mr. Babcock's store, where the Allisons were getting into their car to go home. "Surprised you're staying on."

"It seemed a shame to go so soon," Mrs. Allison said. Mr. Hall lived three miles away; he supplied the Allisons with butter and eggs, and occasionally, from the top of their hill, the Allisons could see the lights in his house in the early evening before the Halls went to bed.

"They usually leave Labor Day," Mr. Hall said.

The ride home was long and rough; it was beginning to get dark, and Mr. Allison had to drive very carefully over the dirt road by the lake. Mrs. Allison lay back against the seat, pleasantly relaxed after a day of what seemed whirlwind shopping compared with their day-to-day existence; the new glass baking dishes lurked agreeably in her mind, and the half-bushel of red eating apples, and the package of colored thumbtacks with which she was going to put up new shelf edging in the kitchen. "Good to get home," she said softly as they came in sight of their cottage, silhouetted above them against the sky.

"Glad we decided to stay on," Mr. Allison agreed.

Mrs. Allison spent the next morning lovingly washing her baking dishes, although in his innocence Charley Walpole had neglected to notice the chip in the edge of one; she decided, wastefully, to use some of the red eating apples in a pie for dinner, and, while the pie was in the oven and Mr. Allison was down getting the mail, she sat out on the little lawn the Allisons had made at the top of the hill, and watched the changing lights on the lake, alternating gray and blue as clouds moved quickly across the sun.

Mr. Allison came back a little out of sorts; it always irritated him to walk the mile to the mailbox on the state road and come back with nothing, even though he assumed that the walk was good for his health. This morning there was nothing but a circular from a New York department store, and their New York paper, which arrived erratically by mail from one to four days later than it should, so that some days the Allisons might have three papers and frequently none. Mrs. Allison, although she shared with her husband the annoyance of not having mail when they so anticipated it, pored affectionately over the department store circular, and made a mental note to drop in at the store when she finally went back to New York, and check on the sale of wool blankets; it was hard to find good ones in pretty colors nowadays. She debated saving the circular to remind herself, but after thinking about getting up and getting into the cottage to put it away safely somewhere, she dropped it into the grass beside her chair and lay back, her eyes half closed.

"Looks like we might have some rain," Mr. Allison said, squinting at the sky.

"Good for the crops," Mrs. Allison said laconically, and they both laughed.

The kerosene man came the next morning while Mr. Allison was down getting the mail; they were getting low on kerosene and Mrs. Allison greeted the man warmly; he sold kerosene and ice, and, during the summer, hauled garbage away for the summer people. A garbage man was only necessary for improvident city folk; country people had no garbage.

"I'm glad to see you," Mrs. Allison told him. "We were getting pretty low."

The kerosene man, whose name Mrs. Allison had never learned, used a hose attachment to fill the twenty-gallon tank which supplied light and heat and cooking facilities for the Allisons; but today, instead of swinging down from his truck and unhooking the hose from where it coiled affectionately around the cab of the truck, the man stared uncomfortably at Mrs. Allison, his truck motor still going.

"Thought you folks'd be leaving," he said.

"We're staying on another month," Mrs. Allison said brightly. "The weather was so nice, and it seemed like—"

"That's what they told me," the man said. "Can't give you no oil, though."

"What do you mean?" Mrs. Allison raised her eyebrows. "We're just going to keep on with our regular—"

"After Labor Day," the man said. "I don't get so much oil myself after Labor Day."

Mrs. Allison reminded herself, as she had frequently to do when in disagreement with her neighbors, that city manners were no good with country people; you could not expect to overrule a country employee as you could a city worker, and Mrs. Allison smiled engagingly as she said, "But can't you get extra oil, at least while we stay?"

"You see," the man said. He tapped his finger exasperatingly against the car wheel as he spoke. "You see," he said slowly, "I order this oil. I order it down from maybe fifty, fifty-five miles away. I order back in June, how much I'll need for the summer. Then I order again . . . oh, about November. Round about now it's starting to get pretty short." As though the subject were closed, he stopped tapping his finger and tightened his hands on the wheel in preparation for departure.

"But can't you give us *some*?" Mrs. Allison said. "Isn't there anyone else?"

"Don't know as you could get oil anywheres else right now," the man said consideringly. "*I* can't give you none." Before Mrs. Allison could speak, the truck began to move; then it stopped for a minute and he looked at her through the back window of the cab. "Ice?" he called. "I could let you have some ice."

Mrs. Allison shook her head; they were not terribly low on ice, and she was angry. She ran a few steps to catch up with the truck, calling, "Will you try to get us some? Next week?"

"Don't see's I can," the man said. "After Labor Day, it's harder." The truck drove away, and Mrs. Allison, only comforted by the thought that she could probably get kerosene from Mr. Babcock, or, at worst, the Halls, watched it go with anger. "Next summer," she told herself. "Just let *him* try coming around next summer!"

There was no mail again, only the paper, which seemed to be coming doggedly on time, and Mr. Allison was openly cross when he returned. When Mrs. Allison told him about the kerosene man he was not particularly impressed.

"Probably keeping it all for a high price during the winter," he commented. "What's happened to Anne and Jerry, do you think?"

Anne and Jerry were their son and daughter, both married, one living in Chicago, one in the Far West; their dutiful weekly letters were late; so late, in fact, that Mr. Allison's annoyance at the lack of mail was able to settle on a legitimate grievance. "Ought to realize how we wait for their letters," he said. "Thoughtless, selfish children. Ought to know better."

"Well, dear," Mrs. Allison said placatingly. Anger at Anne and Jerry would not relieve her emotions toward the kerosene man. After a few minutes she said, "Wishing won't bring the mail, dear. I'm going to go call Mr. Babcock and tell him to send up some kerosene with my order."

"At least a postcard," Mr. Allison said as she left.

As with most of the cottage's inconveniences, the Allisons no longer noticed the phone particularly, but yielded to its eccentricities without conscious complaint. It was a wall phone, of a type still seen in only few communities; in order to get the operator,

Mrs. Allison had first to turn the sidecrank and ring once. Usually it took two or three tries to force the operator to answer, and Mrs. Allison, making any kind of telephone call, approached the phone with resignation and a sort of desperate patience. She had to crank the phone three times this morning before the operator answered, and then it was still longer before Mr. Babcock picked up the receiver at his phone in the corner of the grocery behind the meat table. He said "Store?" with the rising inflection that seemed to indicate suspicion of anyone who tried to communicate with him by means of this unreliable instrument.

"This is Mrs. Allison, Mr. Babcock. I thought I'd give you my order a day early because I wanted to be sure and get some—"

"What say, Mrs. Allison?"

Mrs. Allison raised her voice a little; she saw Mr. Allison, out on the lawn, turn in his chair and regard her sympathetically. "I said, Mr. Babcock, I thought I'd call in my order early so you could send me—"

"Mrs. Allison?" Mr. Babcock said. "You'll come and pick it up?"

"Pick it up?" In her surprise Mrs. Allison let her voice drop back to its normal tone and Mr. Babcock said loudly, "What's that, Mrs. Allison?"

"I thought I'd have you send it out as usual," Mrs. Allison said.

"Well, Mrs. Allison," Mr. Babcock said, and there was a pause while Mrs. Allison waited, staring past the phone over her husband's head out into the sky. "Mrs. Allison," Mr. Babcock went on finally, "I'll tell you, my boy's been working for me went back to school yesterday and now I got no one to deliver. I only got a boy delivering summers, you see."

"I thought you *always* delivered," Mrs. Allison said.

"Not after Labor Day, Mrs. Allison," Mr. Babcock said firmly. "You never been here after Labor Day before, so's you wouldn't know, of course."

"Well," Mrs. Allison said helplessly. Far inside her mind she was saying, over and over, can't use city manners on country folk, no use getting mad.

"Are you *sure*?" she asked finally. "Couldn't you just send out an order today, Mr. Babcock?"

"Matter of fact," Mr. Babcock said, "I guess I couldn't, Mrs. Allison. It wouldn't hardly pay, delivering, with no one else out at the lake."

"What about Mr. Hall?" Mrs. Allison asked suddenly, "the people who live about three miles away from us out here? Mr. Hall could bring it out when he comes."

"Hall?" Mr. Babcock said. "John Hall? They've gone to visit her folks upstate, Mrs. Allison."

"But they bring all our butter and eggs," Mrs. Allison said, appalled.

"Left yesterday," Mr. Babcock said. "Probably didn't think you folks would stay on up there."

"But I told Mr. Hall . . ." Mrs. Allison started to say, and then stopped. "I'll send Mr. Allison in after some groceries tomorrow," she said.

"You got all you need till then," Mr. Babcock said, satisfied; it was not a question, but a confirmation.

After she hung up, Mrs. Allison went slowly out to sit again in her chair next to her husband. "He won't deliver," she said. "You'll have to go in tomorrow. We've got just enough kerosene to last till you get back."

"He should have told us sooner," Mr. Allison said.

It was not possible to remain troubled long in the face of the day; the country had never seemed more inviting, and the lake moved quietly below them, among the trees, with the almost incredible softness of a summer picture. Mrs. Allison sighed deeply, in the pleasure of possessing for themselves that sight of the lake, with the distant green hills beyond, the gentleness of the small wind through the trees.

The weather continued fair; the next morning Mr. Allison, duly armed with a list of groceries, with "kerosene" in large letters at the top, went down the path to the garage, and Mrs. Allison began another pie in her new baking dishes. She had mixed the crust and was starting to pare the apples when Mr. Allison came rapidly up the path and flung open the screen door into the kitchen.

"Damn car won't start," he announced, with the end-of-the-tether voice of a man who depends on a car as he depends on his right arm.

"What's wrong with it?" Mrs. Allison demanded, stopping with the paring knife in one hand and an apple in the other. "It was all right on Tuesday."

"Well," Mr. Allison said between his teeth, "it's not all right on Friday."

"Can you fix it?" Mrs. Allison asked.

"No," Mr. Allison said, "I cannot. Got to call someone, I guess."

"Who?" Mrs. Allison asked.

"Man runs the filling station, I guess." Mr. Allison moved purposefully toward the phone. "He fixed it last summer one time."

A little apprehensive, Mrs. Allison went on paring apples absentmindedly, while she listened to Mr. Allison with the phone, ringing, waiting, finally giving the number to the operator, then waiting again and giving the number again, giving the number a third time, and then slamming down the receiver.

"No one there," he announced as he came into the kitchen.

"He's probably gone out for a minute," Mrs. Allison said nervously; she was not quite sure what made her so nervous, unless it was the probability of her husband's losing his temper completely. "He's there alone, I imagine, so if he goes out there's no one to answer the phone."

"That must be it," Mr. Allison said with heavy irony. He slumped into one of the kitchen chairs and watched Mrs. Allison paring apples. After a minute, Mrs. Allison said soothingly, "Why don't you go down and get the mail and then call him again?"

Mr. Allison debated and then said, "Guess I might as well." He rose heavily and when he got to the kitchen door he turned and said, "But if there's no mail—" and leaving an awful silence behind him, he went off down the path.

Mrs. Allison hurried with her pie. Twice she went to the window to glance at the sky to see if there were clouds coming up. The room seemed unexpectedly dark, and she herself felt in the state of tension that preceded a thunderstorm, but both times when she looked the sky was clear and serene, smiling indifferently down on the Allisons' summer cottage as well as on the rest of the world. When Mrs. Allison, her pie ready for the oven, went a third time to look outside, she saw her husband coming up the path; he seemed more cheerful, and when he saw her, he waved eagerly and held a letter in the air.

"From Jerry," he called as soon as he was close enough for her to hear him, "at last—a letter!" Mrs. Allison noticed with concern that he was no longer able to get up the gentle slope of the path without breathing heavily; but then he was in the doorway, holding out the letter. "I saved it till I got here," he said.

Mrs. Allison looked with an eagerness that surprised her on the familiar handwriting of her son; she could not imagine why the letter excited her so, except that it was the first they had received in so long; it would be a pleasant, dutiful letter, full of the doings of Alice and the children, reporting progress with his job, commenting on the recent weather in Chicago, closing with love from all; both Mr. and Mrs. Allison could, if they wished, recite a pattern letter from either of their children.

Mr. Allison slit the letter open with great deliberation, and then he spread it out on the kitchen table and they leaned down and read it together.

"*Dear Mother and Dad,*" it began, in Jerry's familiar, rather childish, handwriting, "*Am glad this goes to the lake as usual, we always thought you came back too soon and ought to stay up there as long as you could. Alice says that now that you're not as young as you used to be and have no demands on your time, fewer friends, etc., in the city, you ought to get what fun you can while you can. Since you two are both happy up there, it's a good idea for you to stay.*"

Uneasily Mrs. Allison glanced sideways at her husband; he was reading intently, and she reached out and picked up the empty envelope, not knowing exactly what she wanted from it. It was addressed quite as usual, in Jerry's handwriting, and was postmarked "Chicago." Of course it's postmarked Chicago, she thought quickly, why would they want to postmark it anywhere else? When she looked back down at the letter, her husband had turned the page, and she read on with him: "*—and of course if they get measles,*" *etc., now, they will be better off later. Alice is well, of course; me too. Been playing a lot of bridge lately with some people you don't know, named Carruthers. Nice young couple, about our age. Well, will close now as I guess it bores you to hear about things so far away. Tell Dad old Dickson, in our Chicago office, died. He used to ask about Dad a lot. Have a good time up at the lake, and don't bother about hurrying back. Love from all of us, Jerry."*

"Funny," Mr. Allison commented.

"It doesn't sound like Jerry," Mrs. Allison said in a small voice. "He never wrote anything like . . ." She stopped.

"Like what?" Mr. Allison demanded. "Never wrote anything like what?" Mrs. Allison turned the letter over, frowning. It was impossible to find any sentence, any word, even, that did not sound like Jerry's regular letters. Perhaps it was only that the letter was so late, or the unusual number of dirty fingerprints on the envelope.

"I don't *know*," she said impatiently.

"Going to try that phone call again," Mr. Allison said. Mrs. Allison read the letter twice more, trying to find a phrase that sounded wrong. Then Mr. Allison came back and said, very quietly, "Phone's dead."

"What?" Mrs. Allison said, dropping the letter.

"Phone's dead," Mr. Allison said.

The rest of the day went quickly; after a lunch of crackers and milk, the Allisons went to sit outside on the lawn, but their afternoon was cut short by the gradually increasing storm clouds that came up over the lake to the cottage, so that it was as dark as evening by four o'clock. The storm delayed, however, as though in loving anticipation of the moment it would break over the summer cottage, and there was an occasional flash of lightning, but no rain. In the evening Mr. and Mrs. Allison, sitting close together inside their cottage, turned on the battery radio they had brought with them from New York. There were no lamps lighted in the cottage, and the only light came from the lightning outside and the small square glow from the dial of the radio.

The slight framework of the cottage was not strong enough to withstand the city noises, the music and the voices, from the radio, and the Allisons could hear them far off echoing across the lake, the saxophones in the New York dance band wailing over the water, the flat voice of the girl vocalist going inexorably out into the clean country air. Even the announcer, speaking glowingly of the virtues of razor blades, was no more than an inhuman voice sounding out from the Allisons' cottage and echoing back, as though the lake and the hills and the trees were returning it unwanted.

During one pause between commercials, Mrs. Allison turned and smiled weakly at her husband. "I wonder if we're supposed to . . . *do* anything," she said.

"No," Mr. Allison said consideringly. "I don't think so. Just wait."

Mrs. Allison caught her breath quickly, and Mr. Allison said, under the trivial melody of the dance band beginning again, "The car had been tampered with, you know. Even I could see that."

Mrs. Allison hesitated a minute and then said very softly, "I suppose the phone wires were cut."

"I imagine so," Mr. Allison said.

After a while, the dance music stopped and they listened attentively to a news broadcast, the announcer's rich voice telling them breathlessly of a marriage in Hollywood, the latest baseball scores, the estimated rise in food prices during the coming week. He spoke to them, in the summer cottage, quite as though they still deserved to hear news of a world that no longer reached them except through the fallible batteries on the radio, which were already beginning to fade, almost as though they still belonged, however tenuously, to the rest of the world.

Mrs. Allison glanced out the window at the smooth surface of the lake, the black masses of the trees, and the waiting storm, and said conversationally, "I feel better about that letter of Jerry's."

"I knew when I saw the light down at the Hall place last night," Mr. Allison said.

The wind, coming up suddenly over the lake, swept around the summer cottage and slapped hard at the windows. Mr. and

Mrs. Allison involuntarily moved closer together, and with the first sudden crash of thunder, Mr. Allison reached out and took his wife's hand. And then, while the lightning flashed outside, and the radio faded and sputtered, the two old people huddled together in their summer cottage and waited.

ALSO AVAILABLE

THE BIRD'S NEST
Foreword by Kevin Wilson

COME ALONG WITH ME
*Classic Short Stories and an
Unfinished Novel*
Foreword by Laura Miller

HANGSAMAN
Foreword by Francine Prose

THE HAUNTING OF HILL HOUSE
Penguin Horror Series Editor:
Guillermo del Toro
Introduction by Laura Miller

LIFE AMONG THE SAVAGES

RAISING DEMONS

THE ROAD THROUGH THE WALL
Foreword by Ruth Franklin

THE SUNDIAL
Foreword by Victor LaValle

**WE HAVE ALWAYS LIVED IN
THE CASTLE**
Introduction by Jonathan Lethem